Praise for Jessica James' books

5 STARS for *Meant To Be*
"A captivating and mesmerizing read."

— READERS' FAVORITE, Cheryl E. Rodriguez

"Reminds me of *American Sniper* and *Lone Survivor*, but accompanied with a beautiful and epic romance that is completely unforgettable."

— LAUREN HOFF, United States Air Force

"This stunning story captures the reader's attention from the start. A moving account of two people who are drawn into an untenable conflict and find love, despite their opposing beliefs."

– RT BOOK REVIEWS / *Shades of Gray*

"Readers will find the attention to historical detail impeccable and the characters are strongly drawn."

– FOREWORD MAGAZINE/*Shades of Gray*

"Has the power to touch you deeply."

– MYSHELF/ *Noble Cause*

"[Emotions] seem to transcend the pages to settle in the very marrow of the reader's bones. Jessica James has produced a tremendous and wonderful saga about love, loyalty and honor for which she must lauded."

– KRISTEN PACE, BOOKPLEASURES

Other Books by Jessica James

Above and Beyond

Noble Cause
(An alternative ending to *Shades of Gray*)

Shades of Gray

The Gray Ghost of Civil War Virginia

Liberty and Destiny

JESSICA JAMES
HONOR COURAGE LOVE

www.jessicajamesbooks.com

For God and Country

WAR HEROES

Book 1

Meant To Be

A Novel of Honor and Duty

Jessica James

PATRIOT PRESS
Gettysburg, Pa.

We hope you enjoy this book from Patriot Press. Our goal is to provide high-quality, thought-provoking books that honor the spirit, courage, and devotion of American heroes, past and present.

www.patriotpressbooks.com

Dedication

To my loyal group of readers and Beta Readers, thank you for helping me craft this novel. And to our amazing troops all over the world, thank you for your courage, sacrifice, and service.

ISBN 978-1-941020-02-9
Library of Congress Control Number: 2014954018

Edited by Jody Roth
Interior Design: Patriot Press
Cover Design: Cathi Stevenson

June 2015

Proudly Printed in the United States of America

Books and Awards
Jessica James

Liberty and Destiny (2014)

Valley Forge Romance Writers Sheila Award Finalist

Above and Beyond (2013)

2014 John Esten Cooke Award for Southern Fiction
2014 Reader's Crown Award Finalist
2014 Next Generation Indie Award Finalist in Fiction/Religious
2013 USA "Best Books 2013" Finalist in Fiction/Religious

Noble Cause Awards (2011)

2012 Foreword Magazine Book of the Year (Bronze) in Romance
2011 John Esten Cooke Award for Southern Fiction
2011 USA "Best Books 2011" Finalist in Historical Fiction
2011 Next Generation Indie Award for Best Regional Fiction
2011 Next Generation Indie Finalist in Romance
2011 Next Generation Indie Finalist in Historical Fiction
2011 NABE Pinnacle Book Achievement Award

Shades of Gray Awards (2008)

2010 Stars and Flags Book Award in Historical Fiction
2009 HOLT Medallion Finalist for Best Southern Theme
2009 Nominated for the Michael Shaara Award
for Excellence in Civil War Fiction
2008 Indie Next Generation Award for Best Regional Fiction
2008 Indie Next Generation Finalist for Best Historical Fiction
2008 IPPY Award for Best Regional Fiction
2008 ForeWord Magazine Book of the Year Finalist in Romance

"The opposite for courage is not cowardice, it is conformity. Even a dead fish can go with the flow."

— Jim Hightower

PART I

THE BEACH

ONE

Ocean City, Md.
August 30th

L auren Cantrell inhaled the salty air and tucked her hands into her sweatshirt to warm them against the ocean breeze. The sun was barely a hint in the distance, just a ribbon of orange-laced clouds sandwiched between midnight blue water and a vast expanse of dark sky. Staring in silence at the colorful horizon, she heard the first sullen call of a seagull join the rhythmic, soothing sound of waves licking the shore.

She loved this time of day. With the beach all but empty, everything appeared still except for the constant, cadenced ebb and flow of the surf. She pictured the ocean as a living thing and this was its pulse and heartbeat. From the glittering sun on its surface to the thriving unseen dimensions below, the sea represented life in all its majesty and mystery.

Lauren closed her eyes and took another deep breath, allowing the sensation of peace and contentment to wash over her. Standing at the water's edge, she marveled at the ocean's infinite power, a living force that could welcome her with open arms—or eat her alive at will.

The sudden shock of cold water hitting her toes brought Lauren back from her reverie. As she leaned down to roll up her sweatpants, she spotted a white circular object in the sand and stepped excitedly into the receding water to retrieve it. Just as she bent down to grab the shell from the rush of an incoming wave, a gust of wind lifted her ball cap and sent it sailing down the beach. By the time she snatched the sand dollar out of the water and turned around, the hat was well out of reach, tumbling and bouncing down the beach like it had assumed a life of its own.

"Darn it. I just bought that yesterday." Lauren shoved the shell into her sweatshirt pocket and sprinted after the hat, but stopped when an approaching jogger scooped it up in mid-bounce without breaking his stride.

When he reached Lauren, he stopped. "This yours?"

"Yeah. Thanks. Sorry to interrupt your run." As Lauren took the hat and gazed up into the jogger's steel gray eyes, her heart gave a sudden lurch. It only lasted a moment, kind of like the flash from a lightning bolt, but it caught her off guard and left her incapable of speech. She stood spellbound, staring at him in awkward and uncomfortable silence.

"No problem, ma'am." The sound of his deep voice affected her almost as much as his captivating good looks. Lauren dropped her gaze to the hat she held in her hand, anxiously trying to pull her drifting thoughts together, and then focused her attention once again on the jogger.

His smile revealed straight white teeth, and his manners implied a military background. Yet his brown hair curled from beneath the ball cap he wore, and his face showed more than a day's worth of stubble. He continued looking down at her with the kind of careless confidence that comes from immense physical strength, and when she didn't say anything else, nodded politely and continued his jog.

Lauren sat down where she stood and put her head between her knees. *Geez! They don't make them like that where I live.* She raised her head and stared out into the ocean, mumbling out loud, "Way to make conversation with one of the most gorgeous men ever created, Lauren."

Wishing she had some reason to talk to him again, she looked to her left, but he must have gone from a jog to a sprint because he was now just a dot in the distance on the long stretch of beach.

Exasperated with herself, Lauren lowered her head again. Oh well. It wasn't like anything would have come of it anyway. She reminded herself she came here to relax, and that is what she intended to do. She needed this place. Tomorrow she would be on a plane back to that God forsaken land where she'd spent the last five years of her life. This was her chance to unwind and slow down. Just breathe.

It had been two weeks since she'd landed in the States—just enough time to get accustomed to the culture and lifestyle of America again, but not enough time to really relax. In fact, the first ten days had brought their own level of stress as she'd attended a seemingly endless barrage of meetings, conferences, and classified briefings. Now it was just her, the sun and the sand. She intended to use the last twenty-four hours to revitalize her senses and restore her soul. She didn't have the time or the inclination to be distracted by romantic notions.

Inhaling the salty fragrance of the ocean again, Lauren tried to settle her mind. With her forehead resting on her knees, she dug her hands into the sand and let it fall out slowly between her fingers. Even with her eyes closed, she knew the sun had fully breached the horizon. She could feel the light flooding over her, enveloping her with its warmth like a comforting hug.

Relax. Relax. Lauren continued to clear her mind and concentrate on soaking up the sensations, allowing the sounds and scents to wash over her, bringing back memories of carefree days and seemingly endless summers spent here. Even though she hadn't visited Ocean City for years, it still felt comfortable, familiar—almost like coming home.

No wonder. A stroll on the iconic Boardwalk the previous evening had taken her past many of the same businesses she remembered as a child. Hard to believe almost a decade had passed since last she'd strolled down those weathered boards, and now another generation of beach-goers was learning about this vibrant beach getaway in Maryland.

The relaxed and welcoming atmosphere was exactly why Lauren had chosen this place. When her boss had tacked two more days to her time in the States and told her to go anywhere she wanted to "think over" an important decision, she knew she had to come here. Experience had taught her decisions were easier to make when your toes were buried in the sand—even life and death ones.

With her palms straight down, Lauren inhaled slowly again and watched images flit through her mind like a movie. Not wanting to miss anything, she became absorbed in savoring each thought and storing each recollection. This place was special—more like a tradition than just a vacation place—with rich memories that could never be replaced. How many magnificent sun swept days had she spent here with friends and family—celebrating, relaxing, laughing…living? With her parents now gone, the people from her past seemed almost like figments of her imagination or characters from a dream. She didn't want to forget anything. She didn't want to move. Concentrating on breathing deep and slow, she tried to memorize everything about this moment in time—the feel of the sand, the warmth of the sun, the sound of the ocean. She wanted to be able to recall every detail over the next few months, no matter what happened or where she was.

When she felt a shadow pass over her, Lauren instinctively tensed as if sensing someone was near. But before she opened her eyes, she remembered where was. *Relax. It's just a cloud blocking the sun.*

"Are you okay?"

Realizing her first instinct had been correct, Lauren jerked her head up and squinted.

The owner of the voice stood directly beside the rising sun, making it difficult to see. After blinking a moment at the brightness, she recognized the jogger who had retrieved her hat.

"Sorry," he said. "Just checking to make sure you're okay."

Lauren stared into his mesmerizing eyes as she tried to calm her pounding heart. She couldn't believe she had let her guard down like that. There was no excuse for being careless, even on a quiet beach.

"I'm… just thinking. You know… about … stuff." She groaned inwardly at her inability to make a sensible statement or even put a cohesive sentence together.

The man, apparently on his way back from his jog, sprawled out on the sand beside her, still breathing heavily. "Oh, well, it gives me a reason to take a breather anyway."

A little startled by his boldness, Lauren glanced over at him and decided he was probably in his mid-30s—slightly older than she.

"You find something worth keeping this morning?"

Lauren cocked her head, unsure of his meaning as she dug her sunglasses out of her sweatshirt pocket so she could stop squinting.

"In the water." He nodded toward the shoreline. "Before you lost your hat."

"Oh, yeah." She patted the pocket. "A nice shell. Got it right here."

She didn't elaborate. Her mind was racing. So much for her situational awareness skills—being cognizant of one's surroundings at all times. Not only had she let down her guard in a big way, but she was sitting beside someone who apparently had not. He'd been aware of what she was doing on the beach before she even knew he existed.

A flicker of apprehension coursed through her, but the reason was more complex, or at least more confusing, than this stranger's attentiveness to his surroundings—and her lack of it. Lauren could not understand why her heart throbbed with so much force she could feel it in her throat, a circumstance she found both ridiculous and frightening—and therefore bewildering. Conversing with complete strangers as part of her job, even heads of state and military officers, had never been a problem. Yet making small talk with an incredibly attractive man on a social level was suddenly beyond her control.

The jogger didn't seem to notice—or care—about her discomfort. "You come here a lot?" He tilted his head and stared at her, waiting for a response.

Lauren shrugged to show outward calm, but the trickle of trepidation creeping up her spine began turning into a wave of anxiety. *Is this guy trying to make polite conversation or pick me up?* She was so unaccustomed to being in a civilized society, she didn't know if she should be thrilled or scared to death.

"Sometimes," is all she said.

The man smiled and held out his hand, ignoring her intentionally vague statement. "My friends call me Rad."

Lauren stared at the hand, then into his gray eyes—now more blue— and finally extended her hand. "Lauren."

Trying not to appear startled at the strength of his grip, Lauren studied him a moment once he'd released her hand. His smile appeared playful, yet she had the feeling he didn't really use it that often. He seemed like a very serious guy, trying to act casual. Her usually—suspicious nature began to ramp up as she continued to analyze him. This just didn't make sense. Why would such a good-looking guy be paying attention to *her?*

For a moment they both sat silently, engrossed in watching a sailboat float across the water toward the orange fan of color created by the sun. Once the craft had glided over the glassy-hued reflection and returned to the dark mass of water beside it, Rad picked up the conversation again.

"Now that we're no longer strangers, maybe you can tell me how long you're staying." He leaned back on his elbows and crossed his legs as if chatting with an old friend.

Lauren's heart thumped again. "I leave tomorrow morning. Just came for some quick R&R."

He sat back up and put his arms over his knees, sighing heavily. "Yeah, me too, actually."

Lauren felt a sense of relief, swiftly followed by a wave of disappointment. The dueling sentiments surprised her, but she didn't have time to question them.

"Since time is so short, maybe we can get together later this morning… you know, for coffee or something." He did not say the words tentatively as if testing the idea, but rather seemed to imply that such an arrangement was the only possible remedy to their predicament.

Flattered by the invitation, but still leery of his intent, Lauren almost laughed out loud. Good looking as he was, she had no intention of having a one-night-stand with the man—or ever seeing him again for that matter. She had responsibilities—big ones—and a job that pretty much prevented her from even considering the idea. Tomorrow she would be on a plane to the other side of the world, with no plans for returning to the United States in the near future. What would be the point of getting involved with someone?

Anyway, she worked with enough Alpha males and egotistical supervisors to have a good bit of mistrust—and maybe even a little disdain— for the entire species. Relationships made her uneasy, even short ones that might come with no strings attached.

Without thinking, Lauren's attention shifted down to his left hand where there was no sign of a ring. *Seriously, how could this guy not be married?* She came to the only logical conclusion she could think of. He didn't like relationships either—and picked up a new girl on the beach every morning during his jog.

Lauren tried to act casual when she finally answered, but his cool stare when she lifted her gaze unnerved her. "N-n-o," she stuttered. "Sorry. I have plans." She tilted her head down to look at him over the top of her sun glasses and felt like he had read every thought with his searching eyes.

"You're not a very trusting person, are you?"

"Should I be?"

He stood and brushed off his sweatpants. "I guess not. You'll probably live longer that way."

He bent down and shook her hand again. "Nice to meet you, Lauren. Maybe I'll see you around."

Lauren nodded and watched him jog away. She put her head back down into her knees and chastised herself. *What are you afraid of, Lauren? Maybe he was just trying to be nice. Not everyone is the enemy for heaven's sake.*

When she raised her head, she almost expected him to be standing beside her again and was disappointed when he was not. She lay back and stared at the sky, forcing herself to think of something else. But try as she might to delete the last hour from her mind, her thoughts kept drifting back to *him*.

He was a tall man. She liked that. Physically imposing, strong, masculine. She liked that too—almost as much as the way he grinned from one side of his mouth and the way his eyes seemed to sparkle. In fact, if she had a list of things she wanted in a man, she could pretty much look at that guy named Rad and check them off.

Lauren sat back up, put her chin on her knees, and stared out at the water. But she didn't have a "man list." She didn't have time for things like that. Not with where she was going and what she would be doing.

She laughed to herself. What did it matter, anyway? He was gone now. She turned her head and scanned the empty beach. Yep. Definitely gone. And once the beach got crowded, there was no way she'd run into him again. In another hour or two every vacant foot of the beach would be filled with umbrellas, chairs, blankets, and people.

Lauren stood and dusted the sand off her pants, her mind preoccupied with a single regret. If things were different, she would have acted differently. She wished she could have told him that.

TWO

Lauren grabbed a bagel and another cup of coffee from a small shop on the Boardwalk and headed back to her room. When she was almost there, she stopped a moment and stared at some Ocean City trinkets on display outside a shop. *Oh, why not?* After making a couple of purchases, she continued to the hotel.

The sun was up in all its blazing glory now, so sweat pants and a heavy sweatshirt were no longer necessary. After throwing on a pair of cutoff shorts and a sleeveless tee shirt, she turned on the news for some background noise, sat down on the couch, and ate her bagel.

Thumbing absently through a visitor's guide of the beach, Lauren noticed a full page ad that blared in huge letters: *Where Truth is Always Stranger than Fiction.* She smiled as she gazed at the images from the Ripley's Believe It Or Not Museum. She'd never made it there, despite all the times she'd visited here. It looked like fun, although seeing two-headed animals, bearded women and shrunken heads, was actually tame compared to what she encountered every day in her job.

"Hot and sunny today, folks." A local meteorologist giving the weather report grabbed Lauren's attention as she pushed the advertisement aside and finished her bagel. *Good.* She wasn't interested in sunbathing—

her olive-colored skin from some Middle Eastern ancestor gave her the appearance of a tan already—but the warm rays and smell of coconut oil and French fries would still be welcomed.

After tidying up her room a bit, Lauren wandered out to the balcony and sat down. The sun was now high and people were scattered all over the beach. Propping her feet up on the banister, she watched families help their children through the sand and contemplated her own childhood here. She had no siblings but remembered making plenty of friends while building castles on the ocean's edge. Sighing with the memories, she went back inside and spotted the small bottle she had just purchased. It reminded her to tackle the most important item on her list of things to do for the day—paint her toenails.

Pulling over a second chair on the balcony to prop up her feet, Lauren meticulously applied a coat of bright polish, and then sat back to view her work. The color wasn't exactly what she had in mind, but it was bright and shiny, and it did the job. By the time she raised her gaze again the beach was a sea of color and movement with children of all ages running to and fro between towels, chairs, and umbrellas. After making sure the polish was dry, she went inside and stuffed some money and other essentials into her pockets so she wouldn't have to come back to the room anytime soon.

Glancing in the mirror as she walked by made Lauren do a double take. Accustomed to being covered from head to toe, usually in a drab, nondescript color—her beach outfit caught her off guard. Exposing this much skin in her future destination would be cause enough for execution.

She moved closer to the mirror and assessed the person gazing back at her, trying to ignore the tired-looking eyes. With her dark hair pulled back in a single, short braid, and a few loose tendrils accentuating her high cheek bones, she likened the image to an American Indian rather than the foreign ancestry that was her true heritage.

In that part of the world, women weren't given the opportunities she had been given and were lucky to receive any education at all. She slid her feet into a pair of flip-flops and admired her toenails once again. *I wonder what the punishment would be for painted toenails?* She frowned and grabbed her sunglasses and ball cap before heading to the door. Funny how this one little ritual helped keep her sane. She considered herself more of a tomboy than the *girlie* type, but painted toenails somehow made her feel more powerful and less irrelevant in a culture where women were treated as second-class citizens.

Despite the activity on the beach, Lauren easily found an empty bench on the Boardwalk and propped her feet on the seawall. In between reading the paper she'd picked up in the lobby and sipping her coffee, she stared at the ocean, mesmerized by the gulls running toward the surf and racing out again. Close as the water came, their timing was always perfect. They never seemed to get their feet wet.

Hope my timing and instincts are that good in the next couple of weeks.

"Hey, stranger."

Lauren looked up to see Rad ambling toward her from the beach, wearing a pair of faded jeans and a snug white tee shirt. Clean shaven now, he advanced with a long, relaxed, deliberate stride that conveyed an underlying potency that made her heart pitch once again.

In her line of work, Lauren had learned to spot people who were capable of being physically dangerous—the way they carried themselves, their build, a certain look in their eyes that revealed a complete lack of fear. The man strolling toward her possessed all that and more. He exhibited a certain confidence or authority that could be felt from a distance and discerned in his eyes, yet he was an inconspicuous kind of guy who would not stand out in a crowd—if not for his blatant good looks.

When he reached her, Rad placed his tanned forearms on the seawall and leaned forward. "Fancy meeting you again." He smiled at her with a lopsided grin and pushed his ball cap up, revealing more clearly his piercing gray-blue eyes.

"Yeah, fancy that." Lauren folded the newspaper. The sight of his boyish smile somehow warmed her heart, yet she still felt somewhat uneasy. "Are you stalking me, or what?"

"Yeah, right." His smile disappeared as if disappointed by the response, but it reappeared in an instant. "Actually, I'm staying close to here with some of my buddies and was just walking around taking in the sights."

At that moment, two darkly tanned, bikini-clad women strolled past. Over their sunglasses, they stared openly at him.

"You're not the only one taking in the sights." Lauren nodded toward the admirers.

Rad gave the two spectators an indifferent glance before bringing his attention back to her. But in that brief moment, Lauren had the opportunity to study the powerful stance of his body. Although he talked with surprising gentleness, he seemed the type of man who could knock aside anyone who got in his way with no remorse or pity. His tight tee shirt revealed an athletic, fit physique, yet he didn't seem like the type of guy who spent countless hours in a weight room. Rather, his broad shoulders and sinewy forearms looked like those of a hard-working farm boy who had grown up throwing bales of hay.

"Hey, have you ever been to the Ripley Museum?"

Lauren stared at him curiously, as if he had some magical powers allowing him to see what she had seen. "No."

He hesitated, seeming to measure her for a moment. "Wanna go check it out?

"With *you?*"

"Why not?" He vaulted over the sea wall so effortlessly, Lauren blinked and shook her head. Although the wall only stood about two and a half feet high on her side, it was close to five feet on his.

Lauren's surprise altered into suspicion as she instinctively scanned the jam-packed beach and crowded Boardwalk. How had he found her so easily? It seemed improbable, if not impossible, that he'd just stumbled upon her. Yet when he sat down and looked into her eyes with a friendly, unassuming expression, her uneasiness faded, and she felt, once again, like an awkward schoolgirl.

"They say that truth—"

"Is stranger than fiction," Lauren finished for him. "Yes, I've seen the ad. No, I don't want to go." She tried to give the impression his invitation was a matter of supreme indifference to her, yet her pounding heart continued to disclose something completely different.

"You said you were here for some R&R. Why not kick up your heels and enjoy yourself?"

She regarded him with an incredulous gaze. "First of all, R&R means rest and relaxation—not, 'kick up your heels,' and secondly—"

With one swift movement, Rad stood, and gently but firmly, pulled her off the bench. "Oh come on. Don't go getting all technical on me. I have no plans, and yours seem vague, so why not?"

"But I don't even *know* you!"

Lauren peered around for help, but Rad merely stopped and cocked his head. "Yes you do. We met his morning, remember?" He checked his watch. "We've known each other more than two hours now." He chuckled and gave her such a charming smile she allowed him to lead her down the Boardwalk. She had pretty good instincts about people, and even though she remained suspicious about his actions, he didn't strike her as the dangerous, sinister type. What could he do to her in broad daylight with all these people around anyway?

"Why don't your buddies go with you?" Lauren walked fast, trying to keep up with his long strides.

"They've all been there." He paused and stepped aside for an elderly woman on a bike before resuming his brisk pace. "I'm the only one who's never been to this beach before."

"But seriously," Lauren tried to reason with him. "How do I know you even *have* any buddies? How do I know you're not—?"

"Tell you what. You can meet them tonight." He looked back at her playfully and winked. "They're having a little party on the beach."

Lauren reached out and pulled him to a stop. "Oh? And I'm going?"

He threw his hands up in the air as if exasperated, even though his eyes were laughing. "You just insinuated you wanted to meet them, right?" He put his hands on his hips. "Anyway, I told them you'd be there. I hope you're not going to stand me up in front of my buddies. Believe me, I'd never live it down."

Lauren shook her head and started walking again. Two hours ago she had never met this man, and now he was trying to make her feel guilty if she didn't go meet his friends. Should she be worried? Or excited? She glanced up at his carefree smile and tried to relax, yet still the questions kept on coming. Should she trust her instincts? Keep up her guard? Maybe things like this happened all the time in the United States now. Certainly things had changed since the last time she had touched down here.

But things weren't adding up. *There's no way a man this good-looking can be unmarried or unattached.*

Lauren decided the best course of action was to come right out and ask him. "Okay. So level with me."

"Sure." He didn't stop moving, and she wondered if he wanted to get her far enough from her hotel room that she wouldn't be likely to change her mind and go back.

"Not to get personal or anything, but I don't see a wedding ring, and I'm wondering—"

He didn't let her finish, glancing down at her with an unperturbed expression. "I don't see a ring on your finger either."

Lauren frowned. "That's different."

"How?" He came to a stop and crossed his arms as he stared at her with a penetrating gaze.

"B-b-because, I-I travel a lot."

He turned and began walking again. "So do I as a matter of fact. What else do you want to know?" Before she had time to answer he came to a halt again—so abruptly—she almost ran into him. "Hey, maybe we could be friends on Facebook or something."

"No. Actually, we couldn't." Lauren gave him a look of annoyance. "I'm not on Facebook."

"Yeah, me neither."

Lauren grabbed his arm before he could take off again. "Then why did you ask?"

He merely shrugged. "I dunno. It was just a thought. You know, since we both travel."

"Okay. So let me get this straight." She shook her head in exasperation. "You're not married. And you're not attached. And you're not on Facebook—"

"Same as you."

Lauren frowned since he made a good point, but kept right on with her questioning. "So maybe you're on the rebound—just need someone to talk to. And I'll be the first to tell you I'm not the most sociable—"

"Good one!" For the first time he actually laughed out loud. "But no, for the record, I'm not on the rebound."

When he noticed she wasn't laughing with him, he got serious and pulled her to the side of the Boardwalk, putting his hands on her shoulders. "Sorry if I'm being pushy and forward." He paused and took a deep breath. "Seriously. I'm not usually like this."

Lauren stared up at him and tried to read the sincerity in his eyes.

When she saw how distraught he seemed, she softened her tone. "Yeah, well, I know I'm not the most trusting person in the world."

He smiled with a cockeyed grin. "I've noticed that, Miss Lauren."

Lauren wasn't the type of person to rush headlong into anything, but neither was she the type to run away from something that alarmed her. She actually enjoyed the thrill of the unknown. And when the unknown came in the form of a tall, dark, handsome stranger, it seemed perfectly natural she should take a slight leap of faith.

What was the worst thing that could happen? Would it really matter if she discovered this infatuation was superficial? That he wasn't the type of guy she ever wanted to see again?

The opposite scenario—the one that could have far greater consequences—never entered her mind because love him or hate him, she'd be leaving in the morning.

The thought of getting on that plane and heading half way around the world almost made her shudder. *Why not throw reason to the wind and have a good time while I can? Heaven knows there will be no handsome, charming men to socialize with where I'm going.*

"Tell you what." His deep voice interrupted her thoughts. "If it helps any, we can lay some ground rules."

She looked up at him curiously and felt impaled by his steady gaze. "Like what?"

"Like, you don't have to feel obligated to tell me anything about yourself you don't want to."

Lauren's heart skipped a beat. "And vice versa, I suppose?"

He grinned out of the side of his mouth. "Of course."

She mulled it over a moment. "Okay. Deal. Except I do have one question I'd like you to answer."

He glanced at her suspiciously.

"It's just a yes or no answer—nothing too revealing."

"In that case, okay."

Lauren studied him, her brows creased. "You're not an escaped convict, right?"

Rad put his head back and laughed. "No." He held up his hands, palms out, to show his innocence. "No criminal record. Scout's honor."

His smile was so irresistible, Lauren had to chuckle too. "That makes me feel a little better."

"It's good to be cautious, I guess." Rad shook his head.

"Can't blame a girl for being careful." Lauren hoped her cheeks weren't as red as they felt.

"No. I don't."

His voice was soft, and the sincerity in his gaze made her heart throb in her throat again. Taking a deep breath to steady it, Lauren made her decision. With an attraction she could not account for and feelings she could not control, it seemed reasonable to ignore her usual suspicions and let down her guard. "I guess I should let loose and just go with it, right?"

"Yes, ma'am." He smiled and winked. "Let's just go with it."

THREE

L auren relaxed a little as she took in the old familiar sites of the Boardwalk that never failed to flood her with happy memories. It was such a friendly, happy atmosphere, she found it impossible to feel anything but a sense of comfort and contentment.

"Here we are."

Lauren glanced up at the big red sign of the Ripley museum when Rad interrupted her thoughts.

"Two, please." He handed the cashier his cash, but Lauren grabbed his arm. "I can pay for my own."

"No, it's my pleasure."

Lauren cocked her head as she gazed at him. Something about how he said the words made them sound sensuous and intimate, leaving her spellbound—but Rad didn't notice. He clasped her by the wrist and led her through the turnstiles. "Here we go. Off to the Odditorium!"

His high spirits and childlike enthusiasm were contagious. For the first time in five years, Lauren forgot about her duties, her problems, her responsibilities—and even her upcoming trip as she followed Rad up the stairs to the first landing of the museum.

After pausing to read about the different exhibits on the way, they both grew quiet and meditative as they made it to the first floor and studied pieces of the Berlin Wall in rapt silence. The huge 10-foot by 10-foot cement blocks lay stacked to the ceiling in all their enormous severity.

The sign board indicated the original wall, built to separate East and West Berlin in 1961, was eleven to thirteen feet high and stretched twenty-eight miles. More than one hundred thousand people attempted to escape over it, but only a few thousand were successful.

Colorful graffiti still adorned the blocks, and one section in particular caught their attention. Written in huge scrawling letters was the phrase, *Don't Go With The Flow.* This powerful message from the past made Lauren stop and catch her breath. She felt as if the words were speaking to her, like a voice from beyond.

"That's powerful." Rad's voice interrupted her thoughts.

Lauren nodded and laid her hand flat on the wall. "Imagine the courage it took to resist."

"And the desperation."

"Yeah." She took a deep breath and let it out slowly. "Freedom—or the lack of it—is a powerful motivator."

After staring at the wall in silence a few more moments, Rad's voice broke through her thoughts again. "Now that we've had a history lesson, let's go this way." His fingers took her arm with gentle authority and guided her past more exhibits, then through a door where they watched a projected image of Robert Ripley, the founder of the museum, greet them from behind a desk.

Lauren leaned closer, enthralled by the realistic display, her eyes roaming over every detail of the room. When she glanced over her shoulder, she found Rad gazing at her with a look of faint amusement.

"Having fun?"

He didn't give her a chance to answer, but took her hand again and led her toward a huge swirling kaleidoscope-like tunnel that made them both dizzy as they walked through. Laughing and amused, Lauren continued her exploration, stopping at different displays that caused her to groan, close her eyes, and shriek with amazement.

Rad, always a few steps ahead, would come back, grab her hand, and say, "Hurry up. Come see this." And then he would stand there and watch her reaction as she gazed upon the vampire killing kit or the bone flute skin mask covered with real human skin, and she would find it impossible not to return his captivating smile.

Lauren was particularly fascinated by the photograph of a man who had been shot by a firing squad and survived. He had nine documented bullet wounds, including one through his jaw. "Guess it wasn't his time to go," Rad said, staring at the photo.

"Guess not." Lauren had a smile on her face as she turned to the next exhibit, but it disappeared when she entered what was called the "torture room."

"What's wrong?" Rad must have noticed the change in mood as he came up beside her and read about the iron gibbet—a devise used to hang prisoners on the outside of castle walls until they succumbed to the elements.

"They would be left for months to be picked clean by birds to serve as a deterrent for other lawbreakers." He read the last sentence out loud and then glanced at her. "That would suck."

Lauren nodded as she continued to stare at the metal contraption. "I'm not afraid of dying, but I'd rather not do it slowly."

Her reaction seemed to amuse him. "I don't think you have to worry about dying slowly in a gibbet. Just sayin'."

Lauren forced a smile. "Yeah, guess you're right."

By the time they got to the optical illusion part of the museum, the torture room was long forgotten. They giggled like children as they tried to "touch the jewel" that could not be touched and laughed hysterically as they tried to read a sign, saying the words that were written rather than the color they were written in.

When they walked out of the museum into the bright sunlight, they were still laughing and in high spirits. Lauren turned toward the Board-walk, assuming they were going to hike back the way they came, but Rad grasped her hand and grinned. "No, this way."

Confused, but in a light-hearted mood, she followed as he led her into another storefront.

"You didn't think you were going to get away that easily, did you?" Rad smiled and winked as she realized they were about to enter the LaseRace room—another Ocean City attraction Lauren had never experienced.

"You paid for this too?"

"Yep."

"And it's something you thought I wanted to do?" She shot him a look of exasperation mixed with curiosity.

Rad chuckled. "Let's just say you seem like the competitive type, and I knew you'd be game."

Lauren smiled. Well, he had that part right. And from what she had read about it this morning, it might be fun.

She stood beside Rad, listening intently as the operator explained what would happen when they entered the room individually. The objec-tive was to race across the floor as quickly as possible, push a button on the opposite side, and then race back—all while trying to avoid the web of laser beams that crisscrossed the room.

"You go first." Rad pushed Lauren toward the door. "So I know what I have to do to beat you."

When the door closed behind Lauren, she had a moment of low-grade panic. The room was dark and full of haze. She didn't like enclosed places. But as soon as she stepped across a line on the floor, the lasers appeared, and she forgot her fears. She bolted over one beam, under another, over and under, until finally she saw the red button on the opposite wall. She lunged for it, gave it a push, and then scooted across the floor on her stomach, under the beams, until she got to the other side and slammed the last buzzer.

When the door opened, Rad was there looking at the results screen with a serious expression on his face. "Hmmm. That's better than most people do."

"You look scared."

"You didn't let me finish." He gave her a lighthearted grin. "That's better than *most* people. Too bad, it's not good enough to beat *me*."

Lauren smiled. "Go for it, buddy." She watched the screen and bubbled over with excitement when she saw the final results. Their times were only seconds apart. He was faster, but she had one fewer beam disruption.

The operator shrugged and shot Rad a sympathetic gaze. "Looks like a tie."

Lauren looped her arm in Rad's as they walked away. "That's no fair. I think she thought you were good looking and scored it a tie so she didn't hurt your feelings."

"Really? If anyone won, it was me," he responded. "I had the better time."

"But what's a good time if you hit the beams? Anyone can run across the room in record time." Lauren was so intent on the conversation she didn't notice where he was leading her. All of a sudden they were in a strange, dimly lit room with loud music and flashing lights on the floor that made her dizzy. When Rad walked away, she froze, afraid to move forward and afraid to move back. She knew where she was now because she had seen it in the tourist guide—The House of Mirrors. Just seeing the pictures and description in the booklet this morning had made her heart race. "Wait. Stop. Don't leave me!"

Rad glanced over his shoulder at the tone of her voice, as if to see if she were serious, but before he could react, Lauren lunged forward and grasped the solid strength of his arm. "I'm serious. Get me out of here."

He apparently thought she was joking. "Yes, that's the idea, but it's not going to be easy." He walked and hit a mirror then turned another direction and did the same thing.

Lauren closed her eyes tightly and hung onto him as if her life depended on it.

"If you open your eyes, you'd be able to help," he said, looking down at her. "And I could use it, obviously."

She just shook her head. "I'm really claustrophobic. Please. Get me out of here."

"It's okay. We'll get out. Just stick with me, kiddo."

Even though it was obvious Rad had no idea how to get out, he took charge with quiet composure, patting the hand that still clenched his arm with a confident and convincing touch that assured Lauren he was in control. She opened her eyes only once, but instantly shut them again, preferring the darkness and Rad's voice to the confusing lights and mirrors.

"Here we go," he'd say in a calm, soothing tone after finding his way through a doorway. "I think we're almost there."

After what seemed like hours, but was only about ten minutes, they arrived at a sign that said, *"You have found the maze exit. If you want a challenge, go back and find the entrance."*

"I'm up for a challenge, how about you?"

Lauren barely even heard Rad. She was already out on the Boardwalk, her face to the sun, heaving the sweet, salty air into her lungs.

"I'll take that as a *no*," he said as he came up behind her. "I'll take this as a *no* too." He rubbed the arm where she had been clinging to him with an iron-like grip. "I think I'm going to have a bruise."

"Good," she said. "Maybe it will serve as a reminder for future reference."

He studied her for a moment as if reflecting on her use of the word *future*. "I think I'll remember." He quickly changed the subject. "I've worked up an appetite. How about you?"

"Not exactly the top thing on my mind right now, but okay."

She started to move away, but he touched her arm and stopped her. "You really scared in there?" His voice was low and serious… and gentle.

Lauren frowned. "Let's just say, if I had the choice between being stuck in a confined space and instant death, pretty sure I'd take the latter."

"So no gibbets or prison cells for you." Rad smiled, obviously trying to make a joke, but Lauren's thoughts turned serious.

"Yeah, if I had any choice in the matter."

"Well, sorry about that." Rad put an arm over her shoulder and pulled her against him in a brotherly way. "Like the old saying goes, *what doesn't kill you—*"

"Yeah, yeah, I know—*makes you stronger,*" she finished for him.

"Yup. That's what they say." He let her go and strode ahead, apparently with food on his mind. "My buddies told me Thrasher's Fries are the best."

Lauren chuckled. "Oh, good. We're going for the health food menu."

Rad flashed a smile that sent her pulse racing again. Every fiber in her being warned Lauren to keep up her guard, but the charm and magnetism he radiated was becoming impossible to resist.

Once they got to the counter, Rad ordered a bucket of fries and two drinks. "Well, it's like this. Where I'm going there aren't any fries, so I'm binging today."

"Good idea." Lauren smiled and popped one in her mouth. "I like the way you think."

FOUR

R ad took the bucket of fries and Lauren the two drinks, and they searched for a place to sit on the crowded thoroughfare. "This seems like a good one for people watching." Rad nodded toward a bench facing the Boardwalk and leaned down to read the memorial plaque on the back before sitting down.

The look that crossed his face made Lauren pause to read the inscription too. *Like the mighty waves surging from the sea. Darling, so it goes, some things are meant to be.*

When Lauren's gaze met his, Rad smiled, but offered no comment. She sat down and handed him his soda.

"So you've been here before?" He leaned back and surveyed the Boardwalk while popping a French fry into his mouth.

"Many times." Lauren took a deep breath as she regarded the familiar landmarks surrounding her. "My grandmother owned a little house a few blocks back, so we came here every summer."

"You're an East Coast girl, then."

Lauren tried to decide how much she wanted to tell him. He was, after all, still a stranger. "Virginia," is all she said.

"What a coincidence. That's where I live now." Rad didn't elaborate

31

about where exactly, and she didn't ask. They continued with trivial conversation and laid back banter until the last fry was eaten. Then Rad patted his stomach. "I think we better walk this off. You up to it?"

Lauren smiled. "Sure. Why not?"

When she stood to throw away the trash, she realized Rad had not moved. "Why are you looking at me like that?"

"I'm surprised you agreed. I thought I'd have to argue with you first."

"I'm a fast learner." Lauren half-smiled and half-frowned as he stood. "Arguing with you gets me nowhere. You always win." She paused a moment and stared at him with her head cocked to the side. "Just so you know, that doesn't happen very often. I like to win too."

"Yeah, I noticed that in the laser room." Rad turned, but took only a few steps before he stopped and rubbed his hands together. "Speaking of winning, do you see what I see?"

Lauren followed his gaze and laughed. "I see what you see. Are you thinking what I'm thinking?"

"If you're thinking I'm thinking that I'm going to whoop your butt, then yeah."

"Bring it on." Lauren strode toward the bright lights of Marty's Arcade without pausing to see if he followed. But when she stepped inside to the clanging bells, buzzers, and flashing lights, memories came flooding back and almost overwhelmed her.

"You come here as a kid?"

She nodded, wondering once again how he was able to read her mind. "This place has been here forever."

Rad put his hand across her shoulder and gave it a quick brotherly squeeze of understanding, but then like a child in a candy store, started walking around looking at the different games.

"Where do you want to start?"

"I dunno." Lauren contemplated the wide array of choices, ranging from claw prize booths and pinball, to video games and skee ball lanes. "You see *Pac-Man* anywhere?"

Rad jerked his attention back to her, his eyes wide open in disbelief. "You haven't been to an arcade lately, have you?"

"Not exactly." Her gaze fell upon a game called *OuterSpace Galactic.* "Looks like they've updated things a little."

"Okay, honey, it appears you need a little schooling." Rad strolled over to a change machine and inserted bills.

"How about this one?" Lauren stood in front of one of the elaborate screens, reading the game rules.

Rad glanced over his shoulder at her and smiled. "Seriously? *Warland Defense?*"

"Sure, why not?" She read the last part of the panel out loud for him. "The goal of the game is simply to survive as long as possible in a land of violent oppressors." She nudged him with her elbow when he moved up beside her. "Sounds like fun, right?"

Rad shook his head. "You got some anger management issues I don't know about?"

"No. I just like shooting things up, I guess."

"Guess we have something in common then." Rad said the words lightly enough, but this time he didn't smile.

Lauren never pulled out her phone to see what time it was, but after playing *Warland* a few times they had moved onto another game and then another. She knew they must have been in the arcade for more than an hour, probably closer to two. Rad beat her—albeit barely—most of the time, so he didn't seem inclined to leave.

"I need to feel some sunlight and stretch my legs." Lauren finally pulled him away before he had time to put money in a new machine. "Let's go down to the inlet since we're so close."

Reluctant to leave, Rad followed, but kept glancing over his shoulder as they walked past the games he hadn't played yet. "Maybe we can come back later."

"Yeah, maybe." Lauren shook her head.

"Oh come on. I at least need a rematch on *Target Town*."

Lauren laughed. She had beat him two out of three times on that one, a first-person perspective gun game where you duck behind objects while reloading or changing weapons. Rad had beat her in the first match, but once she'd figured out when to use a pistol and when to switch to a machine gun or grenade launcher, he didn't stand a chance. "I whooped you fair and square."

"I'll never live it down if anyone finds out."

"Then you better not cross me, I guess." Lauren looked back over her shoulder at him and grinned. "Especially after I meet your friends."

"That's called blackmail."

"No. That's called an ace in the hole."

When they emerged onto the Boardwalk, they found it more crowded and harder to navigate than earlier, but Lauren could not have been happier. Walking in the brilliant sunlight with the sound of the waves hitting the shore and gulls calling to one another made her feel like she had somehow traveled back in time. She was a kid again, with no responsibilities and no worries.

When she glanced up at Rad, she found him studying her.

"Thinking about the old days?"

Caught off guard by both his words and the calm vibrancy of his voice, she pulled him to a stop. "How do you keep doing that?"

"Doing what?"

"Reading my mind."

He smiled. "I was just thinking about my younger years so thought you might be too." He started walking again. "I don't think anyone can read *your* mind."

"What's that supposed to mean?"

"It's a compliment, Lauren," is all he said.

The way he said her name sent a strange surge of emotion through Lauren's veins that almost made her tremble. The anxiety she had felt earlier was gone, but in its wake was a sea of confusion.

When they reached the benches overlooking the inlet, Lauren took a seat in the front row.

Rad sat down and stretched his long legs out in front of him. "That feels good."

"The sun? The breeze? Or sitting down?" Lauren talked casually, but she was acutely aware of his arm touching hers.

"All of the above." Rad gazed down at her with a sparkle of contentment in his eyes. "And the company's not too bad either."

Lauren smiled and looked away, afraid he would see her blushing and think she was a silly schoolgirl.

"So, your grandmother who had the house here. She still alive?"

His question brought Lauren back from her thoughts. "No. She died about five years ago."

"Oh, sorry about that."

"Unfortunately, the place where her house stood is now a parking lot for a hotel."

"That hurts. If it makes you feel better, they call it progress."

Lauren sighed heavily. "Yes, that's what they call it."

She leaned back and kicked her feet out in front of her too, staring at the dazzling landscape. "Doesn't it look like the sun has sprinkled the water with diamonds?"

"Yeah, now that you mention it."

"You know it's a biological fact that the percentage of salt in the sea is the same as in our bodies—in our blood, our sweat, and our tears."

"Interesting."

"I think I could die happy if I just had the sound of the ocean in my ears." As soon as she said the words, Lauren regretted them. Why was she blubbering on so much?

Rad didn't seem to take her statement too seriously. "Well hopefully that won't be anytime soon. You're having fun aren't you?"

Lauren nodded. "So far. Except for the Mirror Maze."

He laughed. "I'm sorry about that. You forgive me, don't you?"

"Yes, I forgive you." Lauren leaned into him slightly as she talked. "You had no way of knowing my weakness."

He studied her with a serious expression on his face. "We all have our weaknesses. No big deal." He stood and stretched. "You ready to move on?"

"Let's go."

As they made their way back down the Boardwalk, their gazes seemed to fall simultaneously upon the Ferris wheel ride rising up from behind the gates of the Jolly Roger Amusement Park.

"Speaking of childhood memories," Rad said, nodding toward the ride. "I haven't been on one of those in years."

"Me neither." Lauren linked her arm in his, somehow eager to take another trip down memory lane. "Let's do it."

She felt oddly comfortable with this man she'd just met, and delightfully carefree and happy for the first time in years. Her lighthearted and relaxed manner was partially due to the sunshine pouring down from overhead and the fresh scent of salty air, but it occurred to her the man beside her had a little bit to do with it too. He was the kindest, most genuine and persuasive person she had ever met—the kind of guy who could steal a woman's heart. Her thoughts drifted back to the odd twist of fate that had led their paths to cross, until the clanging, ringing, and buzzing sounds of more games tore her from her reverie.

"Keep walking and look straight ahead." Lauren held onto Rad's arm so he couldn't get away as they strolled through the entryway to the park.

"Aw, can't I play water pistols? Or balloon darts?" He strode with childlike impatience toward the booth. "Check out this huge stuffed bear I could win for you."

"Just what I need to get through airport security." Lauren pulled him back. "Maybe on the way out. We're riding the Ferris wheel, remember?"

"I think you're afraid I'll beat you." Rad glanced over his shoulder at the balloon darts they had passed.

"Like at *Target Town*?" Lauren smiled up at him. "In case you've forgotten, I beat you, quite convincingly I might add, two out of three times."

"Don't tell me you're going to use *that* against me all night." Rad's expression turned serious.

"Can I help it if you refused to take my advice about when to pull out the grenade launcher? I tried to help, but you just kept sawing away with a machine gun."

"I didn't want to use up my big stuff." Rad sounded offended. "You never know what's coming next."

"An armored robot-man in a video game requires the big stuff." Lauren laughed. "Even I know that."

"Well you still haven't promised you won't tell anybody." He came to a stop in front of the ride and stared at the top, the seriousness in his expression turning to a sparkle of amusement.

"Like I said, it's my ace in the hole."

After standing in line, it was finally their turn to climb into the seat. Lauren's heart pounded, partly from nerves, but mostly excitement. She was afraid of heights, and yet she loved being scared. She knew it was a strange combination, but thrill seeking was part of her DNA. Everything alarming and unnerving to most people seemed to energize and excite her. Everything except tight, enclosed spaces that is. Then it was pure girlie panic and terror.

Lauren felt her breath catch in her throat as the Ferris wheel began its ascent, and smiled with delight at what could be seen from the top. The bird's eye view of the park below them and the Boardwalk stretching out on each side was breathtaking. Before she could get a good look, the ride began its descent and picked up speed, causing her breath to whoosh out of her. The flashing lights and sound of the music blaring from below made Lauren half-dizzy, yet she felt like a teenager again. She wished it would never end.

They had only completed a few full revolutions when the ride slowed down. "I hope we don't have to stop at the top." Lauren gazed up at Rad with wide eyes, but saw only an amused smile playing on his lips.

Slower and slower they revolved until they reached the summit, and then the ride stopped with a sudden jerk. Instead of being sympathetic to her plea, Rad rocked the cart with childlike glee.

Lauren shrieked and grabbed him, telling him to stop. When he quit, she laid her head on his shoulder. "That's so-o-o scary. Don't do that."

Rad chuckled as the giant wheel descended again. "That's the oldest trick in the book," he said as he wrapped his arm protectively around her. "I can't believe it worked."

When they circled around and were at the top again, Lauren scooted over to the edge of the seat and leaned out for a better view.

"Wait a minute." He pulled her back in. "You weren't really scared when we were stopped at the top, were you?"

She shot him a mischievous grin. "I saw you talking to the operator before we got in and assumed you were going for the *oldest trick in the book*. I didn't want to hurt your feelings."

Rad put his head back and laughed. "Next time I'll think twice about spending the day with a woman who's smarter than I am. I think you are always two steps ahead."

"Part of my nature, I guess." Lauren looked away as her thoughts turned to her job for the first time all afternoon.

"It sure is a great view." Rad took a deep breath, inhaling the clean, salty air. "I haven't relaxed this much in years."

"Me neither," Lauren said as the Ferris wheel slowed to discharge passengers. "It's not going to be fun heading back to work."

"Yeah, let's not think about that." Rad helped her down the gangway, putting his hand on her back as he guided her through the maze of people milling around the park.

"It's a little crazy in here." Lauren stepped aside as some children with cones of sticky cotton candy scurried by. "Let's go out this way."

As she pointed Rad toward the back of the park where a pier jutted into the ocean, Lauren's phone vibrated in her pocket.

"Sorry, I need to take a call. Do you mind?"

Rad shook his head and motioned for her to go ahead while he continued toward the pier.

"Hey, what's up?" Lauren held her one ear closed so she could hear the voice on the other end of the line over the noise of the amusement park.

"You're all set." The voice sounded low and steady but conveyed a sense of concern. "The details aren't worked out, but as soon as you get confirmation it's him, they'll be ready to move. They've already activated an elite group to handle the mission."

"Wow." The breath rushed out of Lauren. She backed up to a bench behind her and mechanically sat down.

"You still there? You can still change your mind, you know. That's why I sent you there—to think about it."

"Are you kidding me?" She forced a laugh. "This is the best news I could get."

"Look, Lauren. No one will think any less of you if you decide to call it quits, but you need to do it now. Once we set this thing in motion, it will be too late."

"No way." She stood and paced as she talked. "This makes all the time spent living in that hell-hole worth it."

There was silence for a moment. "That's what I told them you'd say, but they wanted me to ask."

"Tell them I have my *Koran* to protect me," she said, trying to make a joke. The comment drew nothing but a long pause.

"I know you know what you're doing—but this is Non-Official Cover. We've bypassed standard operating procedures so there'll be no diplomatic protection."

Lauren understood completely. She would not be a coddled diplomat in the safety of an American Embassy. She would have no official ties to the United States government if caught.

"I know. I'm going to be on my own. No room for error. And no cavalry coming to rescue me."

"You got it."

"I prefer it that way. I don't want anyone risking their lives to save me if things go south."

Lauren waited, but heard nothing except static from the phone and silence on the other end. "You still there? Did you hear me?"

"Yes, I heard."

"I mean it, Hank. Promise me."

She heard him swallow loudly on the other end. "I'm not in the habit of making promises, but I can tell you I intend to respect your wishes."

"No extractions in Pakistan. No matter what. I know how fast things can get screwy. Put it in my file."

"You should never say never," he argued. "And anyway, no one's going to do an extraction. The United States is going to deny they even know who you are or that you ever existed."

"Okay, but put it in my file and make me feel better."

Again an awkward pause. "I penciled it in. It's there."

"Good. Thanks for that. So I'll be flying out of Dover, I hope."

"Yeah. A regular military transport to Bagram as part of one of the cooperating relief NGOs, which fits your profile. From there you'll go to Kabul. I haven't quite worked out the details on the final leg yet, but it'll be a quick skip back into Pakistan."

"Sounds good," is what she said. *A quick skip to hell,* is what she thought.

"This is probably the last time I'll talk to you... until it's over... so good luck."

"Yep. Don't worry. I'll be talking to you again before you know it. Get some Champagne, and we'll celebrate long distance."

"Deal. Be careful, Lauren."

"You mean, Aminah."

"Yeah, be careful Aminah. Do what you gotta do, but be careful."

"Roger that. See ya."

Click.

"Sorry about that." Lauren strolled up beside Rad who was leaning over the railing of the pier, staring down at the waves splashing against the pylons. "My travel agent wanted to go over my itinerary."

He glanced at her sideways. "Really? Looked a little more serious than that."

His manly intuition took Lauren by surprise, scattered her thoughts, and melted away her composure. "Yeah, well, um, I have a lot of layovers and ahh, stuff."

Rad studied her intently, his steady gaze piercing through her in silent concern. "You *could* just say it's none of my business."

Lauren found it somehow comforting he knew she was lying, yet also disconcerting that after all the years she had worked alone, someone knew her that well—cared to know her that well. Yet how could he, dammit? She had just met him. Her emotions were suddenly all knotted up and strained almost to a breaking point. Under his unyielding scrutiny, she could not think.

"There you go again."

She started to walk away, but he pulled her to a stop. "What do you mean?"

"Trying to read my mind."

"I'm not reading your mind, Lauren." He had a tight grasp on her wrist. "It doesn't take a rocket scientist to see the strain on your face. Look, you're practically shaking."

"It's adrenaline, that's all." Lauren pulled her hand away. She wished she could explain to him that everything she had been working for over the past five years was finally paying off. The end game was near, and she could hardly wait. But it was all so complicated, that even if she could divulge the information, she wouldn't know where to begin.

Lauren knew one thing. She didn't want to lie. Not to this man. Not with those sincerely concerned eyes staring down at her.

She masked her inner turmoil with deceptive calmness and told him the truth—a slice of it anyway. "The thing is, I have a really important meeting as soon as I get back. I get shaky thinking about it."

"Okay, just so it's not fear." His face appeared troubled and tense.

"No, it's not fear. Believe me, I'm not afraid." Lauren took a deep breath and stared out over his shoulder, irritated at herself. She had to conquer this involuntary reaction to that tender, worried look of his. What had happened to the level-headed, independent, young woman of yesterday?

Rad walked in silence for a moment as they headed around the outside of the park toward the Boardwalk, but there was an almost imperceptible note of anguish on his face. "I get the feeling you're not afraid of much of anything. That can be dangerous."

"You have a short memory," Lauren said. "Remember the Mirror Maze?"

That brought a smile to his face—but it was short-lived as he seemed to continue to dwell on the topic.

"I guess I should be flattered you're worried about me, but there's no need. I'm a big girl."

"I know." He slid his hand around her waist and pulled her into him protectively. "Even so, I kind of wish I could go with you."

No you don't. She gave him a solemn smile. *Believe me. You don't.*

FIVE

L auren noticed Rad was so deep in thought he didn't argue about not getting to try his hand at the games he'd wanted to play on the way into the amusement park. His brow was creased as he stared straight ahead, his jaw was set, and his expressive face now seemed somber.

She wondered what to say or do to get him to smile again when a booming voice with a strange accent broke the silence. "Stop. Let me tell your fortune."

They both turned around at the same time and stared at the turban-headed mechanical man inside an ornate fortune-telling booth. "Your fortune is mine for the telling and yours for the hearing."

Rad nudged her. "You game?"

Lauren didn't want to have anything to do with a fortune teller, but since Rad was almost smiling again, she consented and stepped closer.

"I can see your future." The fortune-teller wore a bright yellow silk shirt with a black vest and numerous jeweled necklaces. "Step closer and you shall see it too."

"Okay." Lauren pulled a bill out of her pocket and stuck it in the slot. "I'll give it a shot."

"Zoltar the Gypsy, at your service." The supposed fortune-teller inside the booth came alive, waving his jeweled hand back and forth over a crystal ball. "Today is your lucky day, my friend."

Rad stepped closer, smiling broadly now.

"Never forget that you can tell a wise person by what they *don't* say as much as by what they say. Sometimes it is wiser to say little rather than much."

They looked at each other with quizzical expressions.

"Give me your treasure," Zoltar continued. "I have much wisdom to share."

"What's that supposed to mean?"

"It means he wants another dollar. Let's go."

Before they turned around, a ticket popped out of the machine that said, "Your Fortune."

Lauren tried to grab it, but Rad had it in his hand and was reading out loud before she had time to react. "Okay, this is more like it. It says: *When you pull a card and receive a heart, you and your beloved will never part.*"

He held up the piece of paper for her to see. "Look, you got a heart." He showed her the artwork of an Ace of Hearts.

Lauren attempted to grab the ticket, but he deftly avoided her and began reading again. "Hold on. There's more." He cleared his throat. "'You are a strong believer in fate. You feel you have no control over your destiny.'"

He raised his gaze to hers. "True?"

Before she had time to answer, he continued, "Fortunately, you are destined to be very happy indeed."

"Wow," Lauren said, making one last attempt to snatch the paper from his grasp. "I feel better already."

"But wait, there's more. It says down here at the bottom you have a graceful walk and a determined step." Rad smiled reflectively. "I can vouch for that."

"Now you're just making things up." Lauren crossed her arms and stared at him.

"No, I'm not." He pointed to the paper. "It says, 'you always walk as though you know exactly where you're going.'" He nodded. "Um hmm. Right again. Now, let's see here."

The next words made Lauren's heart pick up its pace.

"'You will endure a great hardship in the near future, but everything will turn out for the best, and unending happiness will be yours.'"

Lauren wrinkled up her nose and pretended to be unaffected. "That's silly. You don't believe in that stuff, do you?"

"Seemed to be right on target until the end." He stared at her thoughtfully. "By great hardship, it's probably talking about a late flight or something."

"Geez. Hope *that* doesn't happen." Lauren pretended a long layover would be the worst thing in the world that could happen, even though she knew she faced hardships of far greater consequence. "Good to know everything will turn out in the end."

Amusement flickered in the eyes that met hers. "See? You do believe." He took her hand and started walking. "You got this little obstacle coming, this little hardship, and then, *bam*—unending happiness is all yours, baby." He squeezed her hand. "Zoltar has spoken."

Lauren laughed, partly because of his words and the optimistic way in which they were spoken, and partly because of the sensation of her hand in his. The contact had produced an unexpected jolt that was almost electric, but Rad just whistled as if he didn't have a care in the world—as if it was perfectly natural for him to be walking hand in hand with a girl he'd just met.

He nodded toward the far end of the Boardwalk. "Think we can make it all the way to the end?"

"If you're up to it." Lauren said the words jokingly as she ran her gaze over him. Frankly, he looked like he could walk to the Pacific Ocean with her on his back if the need arose.

"Let's give it a whirl."

Lauren tried to keep her mood light and imitate his carefree demeanor, but she didn't have much practice in the art of cheerfulness, especially over the past five years. She found her thoughts drifting to what tomorrow would bring and the endless and difficult tasks that needed to be accomplished once she landed. When Rad's protective hand tightened and pulled her closer, she knew he was reading her mind again and drawing her back to the present moment. She smiled up at him, thanking him wordlessly as a warm glow flowed through her.

The silent conversation they shared was not without its effect on Lauren. Something in this man's manner soothed and calmed her, and left her feeling blissfully happy and fully alive. She felt a strange, numbed comfort as she focused on the feel of her hand in his, a hand that was strong, firm, supportive and kind.

And then she focused on something else. With her fingers comfortably laced in his, Lauren discerned a rough callous on his hand—the type of callous caused by target practice.

A lot of target practice.

Like hours of target practice every day.

She should know. She had a blister on her hand from the last few days on the range.

Lauren pondered her discovery. Was he a police officer? Or an assassin? Those were the only two professions she could think of that would require long hours of range training and excellent marksmanship. Rad didn't seem inclined to talk about his career, and she didn't want to ask. It would only result in the obvious question of what she did for a living.

"So when you're not traveling, you still call Virginia home?"

Rad's voice interrupted her thoughts, and his question made Lauren pause to think. The last time she 'hadn't been traveling' was back when she was still in school. That seemed like a long time ago—days when getting to class and writing papers had been pretty much the limit of her responsibilities. She'd been out of the country almost continuously for close to five years now and didn't have anywhere here to call home.

She took so long to answer that Rad must have thought she didn't want to.

"I mean, you still have family in Virginia?"

"No." That one didn't require a lot of thought. "No family. I'm an only child and my parents both died."

"Oh, sorry. Didn't mean to get so personal."

"No. That's okay." Lauren took a deep breath and stared out over the water a moment, trying to decide how much more she wanted to say. This was not something she usually talked about, especially not with a stranger. Yet for some reason, she felt it necessary to share.

"They were on Flight 77." She paused and closed her eyes. It was hard to even say the words. "On 9/11."

She heard Rad murmur, "The Pentagon flight."

Lauren had tried to put that tragic time behind her, but it wasn't something she could ever forget. The incident was stamped on her conscience as distinctly as a dark tattoo etched on pale skin. It was the day she had gone from a carefree—somewhat wild—teenager, to a focused, motivated adult, intent on preventing anything like that from happening in the United States again. It was the impetus for who she was and everything she did. It both drove her and sustained her.

"I'm sorry," Rad said again, obviously distressed at himself for bringing it up. "I'm sure it hurts to talk about it."

"I don't usually tell anyone." Lauren blinked back the moisture building in her eyes. "It's hard to share, even after all these years."

Rad put his hand on her shoulder and gave it a firm, compassionate squeeze. "I'm honored you shared it with me."

Lauren caught the reflection of his thoughts in his eyes as he stared down at her and felt held fast by the intensity of the sympathetic and supportive look.

"How about you?" Lauren tried to change the subject. "You from a big family?"

"I got some brothers and sisters here and there. Parents in Texas."

"You're from Texas? I didn't detect an accent."

"My dad's military. We've lived all over." He chuckled. "Nowhere long enough to get an accent I guess."

"My dad was military too," Lauren said. "Navy. I guess that's why I love the ocean so much."

"Yeah, having a sailor for a dad will do that to you." He glanced over his shoulder at how far they had come. "You need a break yet?"

"No, I'm good." She gazed up at him with half a smile. "Unless you're having trouble keeping up or something and need to sit down."

That caused him to laugh loudly. "You're still trying to beat me, aren't you?" He rested his arm across her shoulders for a moment. "Don't get your hopes up. I think I've got enough in me to make it until the bitter end."

As they continued walking, Lauren observed other women noticing Rad, and she had to smile. She didn't blame them. He was a tall, rugged-looking man, and the way his tee shirt emphasized the breadth of his shoulders was enough to make even some of the grandmothers turn their heads.

Seemingly oblivious to the complimentary looks, Rad glanced up at the sun. "It's getting hot. Maybe I do need a break. How about some ice cream?"

"Good heavens." Lauren shook her head. "I'm going to have to go on a diet after today."

Rad put his hand out and squeezed one of her biceps. "You seem to be in pretty good shape to me. I don't think a little ice cream will hurt you one bit."

Lauren felt the color rising in her cheeks at the compliment and scolded herself for blushing like an enraptured teenager. No one knew how hard she worked to stay physically fit with no gym—and no one had ever noticed or cared. Not that they *could* notice with what she normally wore. She shook it off and pushed her way to the counter, pulling out a twenty dollar bill and slapping it down by the register. "My treat this time."

"Okay. Okay. Equal rights and all that. I get it." Rad held up his hands and laughed. "But don't go getting all feminist on me."

"No need to worry about that." Lauren squinted at him. "I just want to pay my fair share."

Rad ordered his ice cream and turned to face her. "Maybe you're paying your fair share simply by being here." He didn't give her time to analyze his words but took his ice cream and her free hand and pulled her back onto the walkway. "Let's go. We're not to the end yet."

They ambled along eating their ice cream without talking, sidestepping people and children, but keeping a steady pace. With the Boardwalk now teeming with people, it took some effort and concentration to walk without getting tangled up in a baby carriage or bike.

Lauren finally paused a moment to wipe some sticky ice cream off her hand with a napkin. "Where're you and your buddies staying anyway?"

"Down around 15th, about a block off the beach."

"Oh, one of those frat-house type of places."

"Yeah, right. I don't think my buddies would like the comparison."

"Well, how would I know? I just met you. Remember? And I still haven't met your so-called buddies."

"Guess you're right. Feels like I've known you forever."

Rad kept walking, licking his ice cream cone as if the words he'd said were nothing to him, but Lauren's heart picked up its pace again. It wasn't because she feared or felt threatened by him now—but because she felt the same way. How could that be? In the breadth of half a day she had told this man more about herself than she had shared with some people she had known for years. Why did she feel so safe and secure with him? And what was this startling and exhilarating sensation that overtook her when he gazed deep into her eyes or wrapped his fingers around hers?

She shook her head to clear her thoughts. Her life was complicated enough. She made up her mind right then and there not to add to the complexities and confusion by fretting over where this was going. They would both be leaving tomorrow and never see each other again. *Today is all that matters. Just go with it.*

When they were done, and they had removed the worst of the sticky ice cream off their fingers, Lauren sat down on a bench facing the ocean. "Okay. Now it's break time."

"If you say so." Rad took a seat beside her.

"You were just waiting for that, weren't you?" Lauren gazed up at him. "You wanted me to sit down first."

He held his hands in the air innocently and shrugged. "Hey, if you need a break, that's fine. It's not like this is a competition or anything."

Lauren could tell from the tone of his voice that a competition was exactly what it was, and his next statement confirmed it.

"But for the record, you did call it quits first."

She laughed loudly and with obvious amusement. "You are almost intolerable. You know that?"

"Pretty sure I've been called worse." He sat back and crossed his arms. "Almost intolerable. Geez. That's *almost* a compliment."

"I should have known you'd see it that way." Lauren shook her head.

Rad kicked his legs out in front of him. "So what's your favorite memory about your grandmother?"

Lauren took a deep breath as she thought about it. "Probably hunting seashells. We used to get up early every morning so we'd be the first ones on the beach."

"Hmm." Rad nodded. "Like this morning."

"Yeah."

"So what was the best thing you ever found?"

Lauren crossed her arms, closed her eyes, and leaned her head back. "My best find ever was actually this morning."

"Really?" Rad laughed. "Thank you."

"No-o, not you." Lauren elbowed him playfully. "I found a sand dollar." She paused for a moment as the memories came rushing back. "My grandmother always talked about sand dollars—the elusive treasure we could never find." She looked up at him. "It's like she put it there for me to find this morning. You know what I mean? It's so rare."

"That's pretty special. Worth losing your hat over."

Lauren smiled. "Thanks to you, I didn't lose it." She stared at the lacey-looking whitecaps dance and dissolve on the dark waves. "You ever hear the sand dollar legend?"

"Something your grandmother told you?"

"Well, there's actually a poem about it that's told at Christmas and Easter." Lauren had left the shell in her room, so couldn't show him, but she tried to describe it. "There are five slits on the shell that represent the wounds on Christ when on the cross, and then there's something that looks like an Easter lily with a star in the middle that represents the star of Bethlehem. On the back is the outline of a Poinsettia, the Christmas flower."

"That's pretty neat." Rad stared out at the water. "All in one little shell."

"Yeah. They also say that when the sand dollar is broken apart, the pieces resemble five doves spreading good will and peace."

"Then I guess you have a real good luck charm."

"Yep. A gift from the sea. Or heaven." Lauren sighed and propped her feet up on the sea wall. "I'm not sure which."

Rad's attention drifted instantly to her toes. "Nice pedicure."

Lauren smiled. "No pedicure. Just painted them this morning." She lifted her leg and pointed her toes, twisting her foot one way and then the other as she admired her work. "It's supposed to be a shade called Sensational Sunrise, but I think it looks more red than pink."

Rad's gaze moved slowly from her foot, up her leg, until his sparkling eyes were focused on hers. "Well, at least they got the sensational part right."

Lauren felt a whooshing in her ears, like an ocean wave had landed on her head. What kind of man noticed a woman's toenails? And complimented her on them? And was a perfect gentleman? And fun to talk to? And as comfortable to be around as a best friend?

She reached for the arm of the bench to steady herself. Was she awake? Was this for real?

Rad leaned forward and touched her little toe, which rested unnaturally under the one beside it. "What's up with this?"

"Oh, I broke the little toe and taped it to the next one as a splint." She tried to wiggle her toes, but those two didn't move. "I guess I didn't do a very good job and it healed that way."

"You didn't get it set by a doctor?" His brow creased with astonishment.

Lauren shrugged as if it wasn't something she'd ever thought about. "No. It was just a broken toe."

"Must have been a pretty bad break. How'd you do it?"

"Geez. You really want to know how I broke my toe?" Lauren could feel her cheeks turning red.

"Well… yeah. Why not?"

"I was a teenager and it's embarrassing."

"Then I definitely want to know."

Lauren took a deep breath and thought about it. "You have to promise not to laugh."

Rad didn't respond so Lauren bumped him with her shoulder. "Promise or I won't tell."

"All right. I promise."

"Well…" Lauren hesitated, not sure how to proceed. "Okay. So I was riding my horse in my bare feet and decided to jump a fence." She gazed up at Rad to make sure he was keeping his promise. He appeared to be picturing the scene rather than getting ready to laugh, so she continued. "The top rail was down so it wasn't that high, but my horse had second thoughts and veered to the left." She brought her foot up and pulled her toe out from the others as far as she could. "My little toe hit the fence post as we were going over and snapped back to about here." She pulled even harder, but her toe wouldn't move, so she pointed to where it had been flayed out from her other toes.

Rad cringed. "Too bad it didn't catch the stirrup, instead of your toe."

"Oh yeah, except, no saddle," Lauren said, sheepishly. "Bareback."

"Hmm. Barefoot and bareback. Great combination. Bet that hurt."

Lauren shrugged. "No more than getting stepped on by a twelve hundred pound horse in your bare feet." She pointed to a toe on her other foot that had been broken as well."

"There's a way to prevent that." Rad looked down at her in a brotherly way. "It's called *shoes*."

"Yeah, that's what my dad used to say." Lauren had been staring out over the water but turned to Rad. "You ride?"

"I did in Texas. Western though—no jumping fences." He shook his head. "And I used a saddle and wore boots."

"Okay, rub it in. You promised you wouldn't laugh."

"I'm not laughing," he said seriously. "I'm just picturing this little hellcat on horseback."

"To tell you the truth, the only reason I rode bareback was because I wasn't strong enough to lift a saddle onto a seventeen-hand horse."

Rad whistled. "Seventeen hands? How'd you get on?"

"Fence. Tree. Boulder. Bucket. Whatever was around at the time."

"You still crazy like that?" He gazed at her with a curious expression. "Or did you grow out of it?"

Lauren laughed. "I guess it depends what your definition of crazy is." She stopped laughing and studied him. "I don't imagine you've ever done anything that someone might think is crazy."

"You got me there," Rad said, frowning slightly. "You got me there."

SIX

"You ready to eat some real food?" Rad draped his arm over Lauren and gave her shoulder a squeeze after they had resumed their journey and strolled quite a while without speaking. She loved how he spoke when words were needed and shared her silence when they were not. Although she hadn't been on many dates, she found men usually tried to fill every minute of dead space with their voices rather than being content to enjoy a quiet moment.

"By real food, do you mean popcorn?"

Rad chuckled. "No, I was thinking more along the lines of a sandwich or something."

"Sounds good." Lauren scanned the signs in front of them. "But I can't leave here without some Fisher's popcorn."

"That's a deal. There's a place up ahead. Ever heard of it?"

Lauren studied the sign. "No, but looks good to me."

After they sat at a table overlooking the Boardwalk and ordered their food, Rad leaned forward in his chair and put his arms on the table. "Okay. I have a confession to make."

"Uh, oh."

"Yeah." He pulled his wallet out of his back pocket with a solemn expression on his face. "Remember when I told you I was completely unattached? That there were no females in my life?"

Lauren blinked as her heart did a flip. "Yes. I remember."

He pulled out a picture and laid it on the table. "I lied."

Is he really going to show me a picture of someone now? Just when I'm starting to like him? Seriously, God?

Her gaze drifted slowly down to the table, and then she smiled with relief.

"You have good taste. She's beautiful." She picked up the photo. "Purebred Shepherd?"

"Yep. That's my girl, Tara." He took the photo and put it back in his wallet. "I wanted to come clean in case anyone brings it up."

"Like who?"

"The guys you meet tonight. They like ribbing me about my Tara."

Lauren shook her head in exasperation as she took a sip of water. "Oh yeah. I almost forgot about *the guys*." She glanced up at Rad and noticed he was studying her with a strange, guilty expression. "Looks like you might have something else you want to share with me."

"Now that you mention it." He smiled and leaned back just as the waitress brought their food.

Lauren waited until she left, and then leaned forward. "Out with it."

"Okay, so I told the guys I would be bringing someone I ran into on the beach."

"So? What's wrong with that? It's the truth."

"Yes. I *told* the truth." He took a sip of his drink. "But I may have *insinuated* I knew you longer than that."

"Oh, you *may have* insinuated?" Lauren thought about that for a moment. "How strongly did you *maybe* insinuate?"

Rad had already begun to dig into his food as if his conscience was clear now that he had told her. "Pretty strongly, I reckon. They probably think we go way back."

"And by *way back*, what exactly do you mean?"

"You know, like forever." He shrugged. "I didn't give an exact time."

Lauren took a deep breath and rolled her eyes as she thought about it. *Does it really matter? I'll meet them, say goodbye, and then never see them again anyway.*

She shook her head and picked up her fork. "I guess I'll just have to go with it."

"Yep. I knew you'd understand, babe."

Lauren raised her gaze and expected to find Rad smiling at his joke, but he simply took another bite of his sandwich as if he had no idea he had just sent her head spinning again.

"Holy cow, I'm full." Rad leaned back in his chair.

"Let's walk on the beach a little instead of the Boardwalk. That's more of a workout."

"Lead the way."

Lauren didn't bother to argue. She knew it would be useless.

They both took off their flip-flops as they walked close enough to the breaking waves to let the foamy water surge across their toes.

Lauren finally broke the silence. "So, what's your favorite song?"

"You're going to try to analyze me by my song choice?"

"Just curious." She cocked her head as she regarded him. "Trying to get to know you better."

"Off the top of my head, I'll say 'Time in a Bottle.' Jim Croce."

"That's interesting. I would have taken you for a rock and roll guy."

"See? You are trying to analyze me."

Lauren tried to remember the words to the song and sang a few lines. "Yeah, that's a good one," she admitted. "If you're into sappy love songs."

Rad kicked some water on her. "Love song, yes. But it's really not that sappy."

They both paused a moment and watched a large kite as it spiraled toward the beach and then rose into the air again.

"Your turn. Favorite song."

"Don't know what this says about me, but I'll go with 'Somewhere Over The Rainbow.'"

"Seriously?"

"Can't help it." She gazed up at him, challenging him with her eyes to tease her.

"I get it—it's the 'dreams that you dare to dream,' part. Right?"

She threw her hands in the air. "Of course. Dreams coming true. What could be better than that?"

"So, I take it *The Wizard of Oz* is your favorite movie, too?"

"I've probably seen it a few hundred times, so yes."

"Hmmm. Definitely not sure what that says. That you like sparkly red shoes, maybe?"

"Now who's trying to analyze whom?" She laughed. "Anyway, what it says is I believe the power to achieve lies within us. Poor Dorothy spends the whole movie looking for the wizard when, all along, she had the power to get back home."

"Well, you gotta admit, the red shoes helped."

"Oh my gosh. Stop with the red shoes." She punched him good-naturedly in the arm. "Anyway, there's another theme in there too—"

"There's no place like home," he finished for her.

"Exactly." She nodded and stared out at the ocean. "And since Dorothy lived with an aunt and uncle, I think the message is that *home* is wherever you feel comfortable and loved."

"Yeah, I get that. I'm kind of at home right now."

Lauren raised her gaze to search his eyes for the meaning in his words, but he didn't give her time analyze them.

"Anyway, not to change the subject, but I bet you have a pair."

"Of what?"

"Red shoes. Heels."

"Geez." Lauren shook her head and gave up trying to get his mind off red shoes. "As a matter of fact, I wear them almost every day to work. They go perfectly with my short black skirt."

"Umm. That's what I figured." He remained silent for a moment. "I could tell you were a bank executive or something, a take-charge person."

Lauren suppressed the outburst of laughter that almost consumed her. "You nailed it. That's me."

They walked along in silence for a few moments, both perfectly comfortable in the quiet company of the other. Yet there was a subtle energy in the air neither one could deny, or on the other hand, outwardly admit.

"I hate to see it end," Rad finally said.

"See what end?"

"Today." He turned and glanced back at the sun lowering in the sky. "It feels like time is flying faster than usual."

Lauren remembered watching the sun come up, seemingly only a few hours ago. "Yeah, it does."

"Hey, there's Pops and Annie."

Lauren saw a man with salt and pepper hair helping a young woman put up a canopy. They were laughing, but it appeared things were not going smoothly.

"Hey, we'll give you a hand."

Rad grabbed one of the poles and Lauren grabbed another, and with all four lifting at once, the canopy maneuvered into place.

"Thanks for the help," the woman said shyly. "We would have been at each other's throats in another minute." She gazed at Lauren with big, brown eyes that were full of friendliness, and stepped forward with her hand out. "I'm Annie."

"Oh yeah, sorry," Rad said. "Lauren, this is Annie, and that's Pops." Pops gave her a nod as he continued pounding stakes into the sand. Even though his hair had some gray in it, he didn't appear any older than Rad. "They're the old, married couple of the crew."

"We're not old!" Annie rolled her eyes and shook her head. "I swear, sometimes I think he needs someone to knock some sense into him."

"Yes, I've thought the same thing." Lauren gazed over her shoulder and gave him a sly smile.

"That's just great." Rad threw his hands in the air. "Two women ganging up on me already, and the party hasn't even started." He turned back toward Pops. "Where is everyone anyway?"

"They're coming. Getting prettied up, I reckon."

Rad rolled his eyes. "That could take a while."

"Actually, that sounds like a good idea," Lauren said. "I need to change into a pair of jeans at least."

Annie talked while setting up chairs under the canopy. "Yes, the mosquitoes get bad at night, and it's supposed to cool down later."

Before Lauren had time to say anything else, a group of men came into view. A couple of them lugged coolers, others carried a lawn chair in each hand, and at least one carted a case of beer on his shoulder.

"Looks like the gang's arriving." Annie stood with her hands on her hips, eying the boisterous group, then turned her head toward Lauren. "I hope you aren't offended by foul language and bad jokes."

"She can take it." Rad came up behind her and put his arm around her waist possessively while leading her toward the men.

"Hey guys, this is Lauren."

Lauren noticed a slight pause as they all surveyed her, as if they were taken somewhat by surprise, but then they smiled and nodded. "Nice to meet you."

All but one, that is. He put his cooler down inside the canopy and then strode up to her, looked her straight in the eye and said, "What in the hell is a good-looking dame like you doing with *him*?"

Rad shook his head. "This is Wynn, Lauren. Do your best to ignore him."

Lauren laughed and held out her hand. "Nice to meet you, Wynn."

He winked at her to let her know he was kidding, and then went back to the cooler and grabbed two beers. "Ready for a cold one, Miss Lauren?"

"Sure." She watched Wynn twist the top and hand her the bottle. He wasn't quite as tall as Rad but was just as broad shouldered. His hair was dark, and even with at least a week's worth of facial hair, he was still incredibly handsome.

"Guess I have to get my own." Rad reached into the cooler, shaking his head.

"Yeah, I'm not waiting on you, bro. You're on your own."

"Where's your better half anyway?" Rad straightened and twisted the cap before taking a quick sip. "She leave you before the wedding?"

"No, she didn't leave me." Wynn shook his head. "She stopped to buy something on the Boardwalk. You know how women are."

Another one of the guys walked up and nudged Rad. "Wondered where you've been all day." He glanced over at Lauren and gave her a big smile. "It just wasn't the same without Rad around."

"Yeah, right." Rad slapped the man on the back. "You probably didn't even notice I was gone until just now."

"Someone say there's cold beer in here?" Another one of the men strolled up to the canopy.

Rad turned toward Lauren. "That's Bipp on the left and Reese looking for beer. And stumbling up the beach, that's Tork and Crockett."

Lauren tried to memorize the names and features. Bipp was a little shorter and huskier than the others but still athletic looking. Reese had a couple of tattoos on his arm and was as big as a bear. Tork and Crockett were shorter, but lithe and trim.

She couldn't help analyzing them because it wasn't hard to see they were all Alpha males. Probably all cops—maybe even specialized SWAT.

"Uh oh," Reese said as he lifted his gaze from the cooler. He locked eyes with Rad who stood right beside Lauren. "Trouble at your four o'clock."

Lauren automatically turned her head over her shoulder to the right, as did Rad, and saw two young women wearing very short shorts carrying a cooler between them, struggling to walk through the sand.

"You said you wanted to go change. Right?" He started to lead Lauren away.

"Hey, Rad!" The girls set the cooler down with a loud thud, and one of them ran over to Rad. "Where have you been all day?" She threw her arms around him, though he didn't exactly return the gesture.

"Jackie, I'd like you to meet a friend of mine. This is Lauren."

Jackie turned around slowly and studied Lauren as if noticing her for the first time. "Nice to meet you." Despite her words, there was no mistaking the animosity in her gaze as she perused Lauren from head to toe.

Lauren nodded and forced a smile. "Same here." She sensed a history between this girl and Rad, and a feeling almost like jealousy crept up her spine. She scolded herself instantly. So what if Jackie was an old girlfriend?

"And that's Jasmine." Rad nodded toward the other girl, who had taken a beer out of the cooler and was already chugging it down.

"We'll be right back." Rad took Lauren's arm and led her away. "Going to change clothes," he said over his shoulder to Annie.

When he took her hand this time, it was with a tight clasp that afforded no refusal.

"You seem to be in a hurry all of a sudden."

"Just want you to get into some warm jeans," he answered curtly.

Lauren could tell he was lying. "That's nice of you."

As if sensing her sarcasm, Rad relaxed his grip, and by the time they made their way through the sand to the Boardwalk, he was acting normally again. "Your hotel's right down there, right?"

"Yeah, about two blocks. I think I can make it." Lauren grinned playfully, glad he was back to his old happy-go-lucky self.

"You sure?"

"I'll meet you here in thirty minutes."

Rad studied her a moment as if testing the truth. "Okay. What time you got?" He looked at his watch.

Lauren rolled her eyes. "Really? We're going to synchronize our watches?" She glanced down at her phone. "See you at 1730."

"Okay. Don't be late."

Lauren turned but could still feel his gaze on her. She wondered what he would do if she didn't show up in thirty minutes. She began to hurry.

Back in her hotel room, she hopped in the shower to rinse off, and then threw on a pair of jeans and a tee shirt. After running the hair dryer over her hair, she pulled it back into a loose ponytail and left the ball cap behind. With time running out, she applied a little mascara and some lip gloss and still had a few minutes to walk the two blocks back to where she was supposed to meet Rad.

SEVEN

When Lauren was about a half a block away, she saw Rad pacing in front of a bench. When at last his gaze met hers, he quite openly studied her with eyes that were piercing in their intensity, but with an expression she could not read.

"Where have you been?" He smiled in a careless manner when she reached him, but his tone had revealed emotion.

"What do you mean?"

"You're late."

"Not according to my phone. You worried about me?

"Let's just say I was getting ready to knock down the door of every hotel room on the block."

Lauren chuckled even though Rad did not appear to be joking. "Yeah, right. You were probably getting ready to leave, and I was only a minute late."

She started to walk down to the beach, but he pulled her to a stop. "Don't underestimate what I would do to find you."

His voice sounded serious, and the strength he exuded felt overwhelming, but when Lauren met his gaze, his expression was again unreadable. Maybe he was feeling what she was feeling. And maybe he was as mixed up and confused about it as she was.

"Anyway," he said, smiling now, "you just said you were on time."

"Okay. Perhaps I was a few minutes late. You can't expect me to be under the scrutiny of your friends without cleaning up a little."

His eyes swept her up and down appreciatively. "You win. It was worth the wait. I see you're taking this meeting-my-friends-thing pretty seriously."

She glanced down at what she'd thrown on. "It's just blue jeans and a tee shirt for heaven's sake."

"Um-hmm. But you make it look good."

Lauren smiled at him appreciatively while her eyes soaked in the sight of him. *You don't look so bad yourself.* He wore a navy blue tee shirt that emphasized the breadth of his shoulders, along with an unbuttoned denim shirt that was so faded it was barely blue. It occurred to her she should have brought something with long sleeves as well, but he soon interrupted her thoughts.

"Let's go." He casually draped his arm over her shoulders and strolled toward the party that had now grown even larger. Apparently a few females who had been strolling down the beach had been given an impromptu invitation by some of the guys—and there were a number of new male faces as well.

"Hey, Lauren." Annie beckoned her when they got near the canopy.

Lauren noticed that during their absence another canopy had sprung up, along with more coolers and food. "This is Heather, Wynn's fiancée." She had to speak loudly over the music now blaring. "Heather, this is Lauren."

"Great to meet you." Lauren shook hands with the tan blonde who wore a camouflage ball cap and a Duck Dynasty tee shirt with cut-off shorts. Petite and slim, she gazed at Lauren with big, brown eyes that reflected welcome and acceptance.

"We don't know what she sees in Wynn, but apparently she's here to stay," Rad said as he opened the lid to the cooler.

"Geez Rad, that's not very nice." Lauren shook her head.

"Oh, that's tame for him." Heather's brown eyes twinkled. "He must be on his big-boy behavior with you around."

Rad spoke to Heather as he handed Lauren a beer. "Some things are just between us, Heather. No need to spread unfounded rumors."

Heather spilled over with contagious laughter, which drew Wynn and a few of the other men to the tent. "Wynn, I think Rad is worried we will tell stories about him. Why don't you share what he's really like?"

Wynn gazed at Heather a moment and then his eyes shifted over to Rad, appearing to ponder whose side to take—his fiancée's or his friend's. "You mean how he's a perfect gentleman at all times? Never late, organized, good manners, all that?"

That made the whole group laugh. Heather just shook her head and looked over at Annie, who shrugged as if to say, *they've got each other's back—even here.*

"Come on Lauren, there's someone I want to introduce you to over here." Rad turned with Lauren in tow, but Wynn touched her on the shoulder to stop her. "I can tell you one thing about him. He's got the biggest balls of anyone here."

"Good heavens, Wynn!" Heather shook her head. "Sorry. He can be blunt—and tactless."

Lauren smiled and trotted to catch up to Rad. "But it's true," she heard someone from behind her say with a mixture of respect and joviality in his voice. "That's the modern-day John F'ing Wayne right there."

Lauren usually hated parties, detested trying to make small talk, and despised having to pretend she was having a good time. The realization she was actually enjoying herself hit her with an unexpected jolt. Rad had kept close tabs on her at first, but now she was talking with Reese and Bipp about different places they had visited in Ocean City while he conversed with Pops.

Reese must have noticed Rad raising his drink and winking at her in the midst of a conversation. "What'd you do to him anyway? Cast a spell or something?"

Lauren cocked her head. "What do you mean?"

"He's like the most antisocial man I've ever met."

"Really?"

"I mean, don't get me wrong. He'd do anything for his friends—it's just hard to become one."

Lauren laughed at that. It hadn't seemed hard at all. One moment she was sitting on the beach. The next thing she knew she was attending a beach party and meeting his closest friends.

Her sudden outburst must have drawn Rad's attention. He strode over and stood behind Lauren with his hands on her shoulders. "What's going on over here?"

"Just talking to your girl." Reese cocked his head and stared at them. "So how long you two known each other anyway?"

When Lauren glanced up at Rad he shot her a "don't tell him" look, so she provided an answer without really answering. "Oh my goodness, it's been so long, I don't even know." She leaned back into him. "Do you remember how long we've known each other... *honey?*"

Rad smiled and wrapped both his arms around her. "All I know is, not long enough."

Without warning, Lauren heard a shutter click a few times and then noticed that the lens of the beach photographer's camera was aimed at her and Rad. Startled, she wriggled out of his arms and turned her back. "Tell him to delete anything he took." She hoped he would take her tone of voice seriously.

Before she walked away, she heard Rad talk to the man in a low voice as the photographer nodded his head.

Ocean City was well known for the "Scopes" photographers who roamed the beach seeking families and couples who would buy the pictures they shot. When she glanced over her shoulder, Rad was already heading back up to her while talking to Pops. The photographer was busy snapping photos of the other guys posing with their new girlfriends.

Lauren wanted to make sure Rad had watched the photographer delete the photos, but before she had time to ask, he grabbed her around the waist from behind, leaned down, and whispered in her ear—which made her completely lose her train of thought.

"Pops said we could use some more beer. You okay here for a couple of minutes?"

"Sure." She turned her head and stared up at him. "But hurry back."

Rad winked at her. "You can count on that."

Before he was even out of sight, she felt a tap on her shoulder from Reese. "I'm sure Rad would insist I keep your mind off his absence."

"Oh, that's very chivalrous of you." Lauren smiled up at the man who was even taller than Rad. He had wild, unruly hair, and a mouth that curled as if always on the verge of laughter.

"Yeah, who says chivalry is dead?" Reese nodded and belched at the same time. "Now, Rad, he's not like me at all."

Bipp and Wynn wandered up just then, each carrying a red cup that smelled of something stronger than beer. "You can say that again," Wynn said.

"No, Rad is not like me at all." Reese glared at Wynn for interrupting and continued. "He's more like the kind of guy who sets low personal standards, and then fails to achieve them."

That made every man there roar with laughter. Lauren wasn't sure if their amusement was caused by the fact that it obviously wasn't true, or because Reese didn't have the nerve to say it when Rad was present.

She stood silently observing the men until Wynn spoke. "Word has it Rad is pretty serious about you."

Lauren was in the middle of taking a sip of beer and almost choked. "Really? Why do you say that?"

"'Cause he wouldn't have introduced you to us if he wasn't."

She laughed, thinking now he was joking. "Oh, I see. So he needs your approval."

Wynn looked at her sheepishly. "Well, yeah. Sort of."

"Then I hope I passed your test."

Reese draped one arm over her shoulder and raised his cup in the other for emphasis. "Put it this way, if he lets you go, I'm available."

"Hey! What's going on?" Rad strolled down the beach with a thirty-pack in each hand. "Good grief, I leave you alone with my girl a few minutes and you make a move. Great friend you are."

All the men laughed, but Lauren noticed Jackie and Jasmine weren't sharing in the laughter. Rad had the sleeves of his shirt rolled up to his elbows, and both their gazes seemed locked on his tan, well-muscled forearms. Simultaneously, their attention shifted to Lauren, and the expression on their faces changed from smiling approval to glaring condemnation.

Lauren ignored them and helped Heather and Rad dump beers into the coolers.

"Hurry up, bro." Wynn slapped Rad on the back. "We're getting a volleyball game going."

Rad, who was leaning over a cooler, looked up at Lauren. "You in?"

"No way, but go ahead."

Rad hurriedly dried his hands on his shirt and took off after Wynn.

"Grab a chair, or here's a towel, if you want to sit closer." Heather pointed to a stack of towels under one of the tables.

"Wow, you girls have thought of everything."

"We're not really wives and girlfriends—we're mothers," Annie said. "As you can see, they are just a bunch of kids."

Lauren walked to the volleyball court with a towel and plopped down on the beach to watch. She knew how competitive Rad was and soon found out that every guy playing was equally as driven. They spiked, they cursed, they dove for balls, and bruised the other team with their power serves. The only problem was, there were two women on each team as well—none of whom seemed to care whether they won or lost.

Jackie and Jasmine, who had stripped down to bikinis, were on one team, and seemed more intent on trying to collide with the guys than actually recover a ball. The two pick-ups on the other team made an effort but had apparently never played before.

The sun, hanging low on the horizon, caught Lauren's eye, and her attention drifted from the game to the edge of the beach where dark waves laced with white foam lapped the sand.

"Sorry men, but I gotta take a leak." Everyone on the team, including Rad, groaned when Wynn made the announcement and ran off toward the Boardwalk. The two girls on the same team also decided to call it quits.

"Lauren, get in here and help us out." Rad waved at her. "We're down one point, and it's soon going to be too dark to see."

Lauren shook her head, but he came over and grabbed her by the arm. "Come on, we just lost three people. You can help us out."

"Me?" She looked around. "But what do I do?"

"Just stand here and if the ball comes your way hit it over."

Lauren walked reluctantly to the net and stood where Rad placed her. "So I just hit it when it comes to me?"

At that moment, one of the guys on the other team served a nice high ball over the net, right to her, expecting it to drop into the sand.

"Hit it, Lauren," they yelled, taunting her. "Just hit it."

Lauren jumped up and spiked the ball straight down between the front two players on the other side, too close to the net to be recoverable even if they had been ready.

"You mean like that?" She put her hands on her hips and blinked innocently.

"No fair! No fair!" Tork and a few of the other guys protested as they ran up to the net.

"No fair? You told me to hit it, right?" She turned and held her hand up as Rad walked by and slapped it with a loud high-five.

"We'll keep playing even though we're two-men down." He rubbed his hands together excitedly. "Our serve."

But Jackie and Jasmine had lost interest. "No, now you're even," Jackie said as they strolled away from the game, leaving the two teams with the same number of players.

"Even better." Rad smiled at Lauren. "Wanna serve?"

As he handed her the ball, he whispered, "Hit it to Tork. He's weak on serves."

Lauren didn't respond, other than with a slight nod of her head. When she got to the serving line, she held the ball as if she was going to bop it from underneath like a girl, but then she hesitated, shifting her weight back and forth for a minute. She hadn't played volleyball in years and wasn't sure she could hit it the way she used to. By this time, those who had their hands up in the air on the other side had started to lower them.

After another moment of deliberation, Lauren decided to go for the overhand power shot and hit the ball so hard, it slammed Tork in the chest before he even had time to lift his hands again.

"Tie game!" Rad ran over and gave Lauren another high-five just as Tork said, "What the hell?"

Lauren ran up to the net. "Sorry, Tork. I was afraid it wouldn't make it over, so I might have overcompensated."

"Game on, girl." Tork's eyes flashed with competitive fire. "Don't expect any special treatment when we serve."

When the ball came back for their team to serve, Rad flipped it to Lauren. "No pressure, but it's game point, and they're pissed."

Lauren frowned. "Thanks for reminding me, dude. Where do you want it to go?"

"Just hit it like the last one."

Nodding again as she lined up the shot, Lauren sent the ball sailing over the net. This time Tork was ready—at least enough to react. He put his hands up and made enough contact with the ball to keep it in the air. Bipp lunged in with a fist and sent it sailing back over the net.

Rad stepped up, and instead of hitting it back over, set it up for Lauren. She ran forward from the back row and spiked it over the heads of the front row who were trying to block the shot. It landed in the sand behind them without being touched.

Rad threw his hands in the air. "Game point!"

"We demand a re-match!"

Bipp and the rest of the team ran up to Rad, yelling and flailing their arms, acting like they had just lost the Super Bowl rather than an informal game of beach volleyball.

"You can't make substitutions in the middle of a game." Bipp planted himself in front of Rad with his arms crossed. "That's the rules."

"Funny, you didn't mention that rule when we were down three people and putting a girl in." Rad laughed. "Anyway, it's getting too dark to see." He took Lauren's hand. "And I need a drink."

Lauren waited until they were out of hearing range, and then leaned into him and said in a low, serious tone. "In case you're keeping score, I just saved your ass."

Rad's laughter broke out so loudly, everyone within hearing distance paused and looked over at the two of them.

Lauren didn't notice the disturbance the outburst had caused. Her attention, and her gaze, were locked on Rad and his captivating, magnetic eyes.

EIGHT

A full moon replaced the sun over the water so swiftly Lauren wondered if the day always melted away with so little notice. She had witnessed thousands of sunrises, but never paid much attention to the approach of night. It seemed like it had taken only moments for the last remnants of light to be pulled from the sky and the dark cloak of night to surround them. The rising moon took away some of the heavy darkness, making it light enough to see the frothy water licking the shore.

At some point after the volleyball game, wood had been gathered, and there was now a small bonfire on the beach. Some of the guys stood around it chatting quietly, while a number of women wrapped in blankets sat on lawn chairs near the blaze.

Lauren stood talking to Pops when his attention suddenly drifted to somewhere over her shoulder. She saw him nod, acknowledging some sort of message, but before she could turn around to see who was there, she felt a familiar arm wrap around her waist. "Hey, baby," Rad said in her ear. "The guys are getting together for a meeting further down the beach. You okay here?"

She nodded. "Sure. I'll talk to Heather."

"Good deal. I won't be long." He pulled off his shirt and put it over her shoulders. "Here, in case you're cold."

Lauren stood in the dark a moment with her eyes closed as she listened to him move away. His courtesy and consideration left her speechless, breathless. She put her arms into his oversized shirt and walked over to Heather who was sitting alone on a lawn chair beside the canopy.

"Mind if I sit?" Lauren nodded toward a blanket as she rolled up the sleeves of the shirt that completed covered her hands.

"No, not at all. You can grab the chair if you want. Annie ran back to the room to check on something."

Lauren sat down cross-legged on the blanket. "No, this is fine."

"It's nice to see him so happy," Heather said as if to herself.

Lauren followed Heather's gaze to Rad and watched as he tapped Tork on the shoulder at the campfire before melting away into the darkness.

"Is there some reason he shouldn't be?" She looked up curiously.

Heather appeared startled that she had spoken out loud. "Oh, no. Not really. I mean, he's had some tough times. He's over them now."

"Oh." Lauren continued to stare into the darkness as the sound of voices slowly faded away.

"I've probably made you curious now." Heather got up and grabbed a soda from the cooler. "I always talk too much."

"Kind of." Lauren shrugged. "I mean, I don't want to pry, but if he's a manic-depressive psychopath, I'd like to know."

Heather laughed as she sat back down. "Yep. I definitely said too much if you think that." She pulled the tab on her drink, took a sip, then leaned forward and talked in a soft voice. "Wynn said you two go way back, but I take it you don't know him that well."

Lauren smiled at Heather's female intuition but wasn't sure what to say. She didn't want to lie, yet she didn't want to completely destroy Rad's story. "I guess you could say we haven't seen each other for quite a while."

Heather sat back in her chair and took a deep breath. "Well, the short story is he was engaged to be married to a girl named Angie." She nodded toward the two girls who were still guzzling beer as they stood by the fire. "That girl on the left, Jackie, is Angie's cousin. Anyway, he came home from traveling about a month before the wedding to an empty apartment and a note."

"Oh." Lauren closed her eyes.

Heather looked down at her. "Yeah, he took it pretty hard. I think more because of the way it was done than who it was done by."

Lauren could tell from the tone of Heather's voice that her resentment for Angie was intense and personal. "Sounds like you didn't like her much."

"That's putting it mildly." Heather leaned back and stared out at the darkness. "Nobody did."

"Except Rad."

"Well, he was young and they had been together a pretty long time, so I guess it seemed like a logical step. Plus, she's manipulative and conniving, and he just got sucked up in it." She took a sip of her soda. "He knows now what a big mistake it was."

"How long ago was this?"

"Almost three years."

"And he hasn't been seeing anyone?"

"No." Heather was quiet a moment as if thinking about it. "I'm sure it had more to do with where he was in his career than just swearing off women all together. I mean, really the only women these guys meet are hanging out in bars." Her attention turned toward Jackie and her friend. "Or the ones that invite themselves to parties at the beach."

Lauren noticed Heather's hostile expression and followed her gaze. She got the feeling Heather didn't care too much for Angie's cousin or her friend either. She took a sip from the mini-bottle of water she had pulled out of the cooler. "So I take it Angie was cheating and left him for another guy."

Heather nodded forcefully. "Oh yes. She sure did." Then she got serious and spoke in a low voice. "She's married to a senator now and has a big house and a high-paying job at CNN." She stretched her legs out in front of her and shook the sand off her toes. "If you don't mind my saying so, she got the poor end of the bargain."

Lauren was silent for a moment, trying to picture the type of woman who would throw away the affection and generosity of a man like Rad for money and power. Then she decided to change the subject. "Wynn and Rad seem really close."

"Yeah, they are. Inseparable."

"So you've known Rad a long time too?"

"I started dating Wynn about four years ago. It didn't take me long to learn it was a package deal." Heather laughed. "Rad is part of the package."

Lauren smiled. She could feel that warmth and love from everyone here. It seemed like a very tight-knit group. If you loved one, you had to love them all.

"Same would be true of you if you stick with Rad."

Lauren glanced up at Heather with a questioning look, not understanding.

"Wynn and I are part of a package deal."

That made Lauren laugh. "Sounds good to me. Three for the price of one." She turned over on her side and propped her head on her hand. "So is this get-together celebrating something in particular or do you do this all the time?"

Heather hesitated, as if figuring out what exactly to say. "No, it's not exactly a celebration. The guys are leaving for… some training, so it's kind of a send-off."

"That's nice." Lauren lay back on the blanket and put her hands behind her head. "It seems like everyone gets along... like you're one big family."

Heather grinned. "Yes, some of them can get a little temperamental at times, but we're still pretty tight-knit." She pointed to some of the other women sitting around the fire. "I don't know if you met Molly, the redhead there in the middle. That's Tork's girlfriend. And the brunette on the end is Connie. That's Bipp's better half. They came late."

"Thanks. It's nice to know who goes with whom." Lauren stopped and blinked at her own words. Why did it matter to her who went with whom? She was leaving in the morning and would never see these people again. For the first time, she felt a tug of regret.

They were both silent for a moment, listening to the laughter and the low hum of voices around the campfire as they combined with the gentle pounding of the waves on the shoreline.

"How about you and Rad? Where'd you meet?" Heather grabbed a towel and threw it across her legs for warmth. "You two really seem to click."

Lauren swallowed hard. "Yeah, we do," is all she said.

"You seem so comfortable and at ease with each other." Heather paused and looked over at her. "Like you know what the other one is thinking."

"Well, he knows what I'm thinking, that's for sure." Lauren got up and grabbed a beer. "The other way around, not so much."

Heather chuckled. "Yeah, Wynn is the same way. Pisses me off sometimes."

"Maybe we knew each other in another life," Lauren said musingly.

"Sometimes it feels like that." Heather's gaze shifted out into the darkness where Wynn and Rad had disappeared. "It seems like I've known Wynn forever. I don't know what I'd do without him."

"So when's your wedding?"

"Next Spring. April… hopefully."

Lauren didn't have time to question Heather about what she meant by hopefully.

"Hey, girlfriends! What's going on?" Annie came up from behind them, carrying her flip flops in one hand and a small cooler in the other. "I see the guys deserted us."

"Yeah, they should be back soon." Heather patted the chair. "We saved your seat."

Lauren smiled. She worked almost exclusively with men and did not recall ever having any female acquaintances she would call *friends*. The women she did come in contact with were, for the most part, catty, spiteful, and shallow. Yet these two women were not like that at all. They appeared intelligent, sensible, and kind, and had accepted her as one of them—part of the family.

Annie sat down and opened the cooler. "How about a wine cooler, girls? I'm sick of beer." She gave one to Heather, but Lauren shook her head and held up her bottle. "Still working on this, but thanks anyway."

Lauren had lost count of how many beers she'd had. She hoped it was only two, but it may well have been three. In any event, it was more alcohol than she had consumed at one time in her entire life. Was it the alcohol causing this sensation of security and comfort? That made her wish she could feel like this forever?

Annie leaned back in her chair and propped her feet up on the cooler. "I had lots of emails, Heather. We should have at least a hundred pairs of shoes to pack when we get home."

"That's great. Biggest shipment yet." Heather smiled, and then looked down at Lauren. "I guess Rad told you about his shoe thing."

Lauren gazed up with a blank stare, making Heather bite her lip. "Or maybe he didn't."

Annie touched Heather's arm as if to say, *I'll handle this.* "Well you know how Rad is," she began. "He bought a couple of pairs of shoes for kids who didn't have any, and then his church back home heard about it, and now it's kind of taken off. This will make about five hundred shoes we've collected altogether."

Lauren sat silently with her eyes closed. *Yes, I know how Rad is. Generous. Thoughtful. Strong. Easy-going. Perfect. And I'm leaving in the morning.*

When she opened her eyes, Rad was walking up the beach in the moonlight between Wynn and Pops, his arms moving in conversation, all their faces showing deep concentration. When his gaze fell upon Lauren, he paused and studied her with an expression of solemn contemplation for a moment as if losing his train of thought. Then all three of them stopped and huddled as Rad picked up the conversation again. He spoke intently in hushed tones for a few more moments before all three headed toward the women. If ever there was a more complete specimen of vigorous, manly strength, she had never seen it.

Lauren had to struggle to suppress the panic building in her heart as she watched this larger-than-life man stroll toward her. She had no idea what time it was, but she knew it was late. Without thinking, she pulled his shirt more securely around her. Time was slipping away.

"You three being anti-social or what?" Pops came to a stop in front of Annie's chair. "Why don't you join the party by the fire?"

"We're just sitting here waiting for three knights in shining armor to come riding up," Heather said. "Figured we had a better chance over here."

"We're here, my lady." Wynn bowed deeply, and Rad grabbed Lauren's hand.

"My horse is lame, but I'll carry you to the fire if want."

Everyone laughed except Lauren.

"I don't think that will be necessary." She stood and followed him toward the now-raucous crowd.

"Something wrong?" he asked when they were halfway there. "You look upset."

"Really?" Lauren forced a smile. "Just missed you, I guess."

Rad put his arm around her waist. "That's what I like to hear."

NINE

The laughter emanating from around the fire was loud and contagious, and made Lauren wish to join the high-spirited group. But then again time was running out, and she selfishly—and unexpectedly—wanted to be alone with Rad.

As they approached the light from the flames, she gazed at the dark shadows that still sheltered and surrounded them. "Too bad it's so dark. We could go for a jog on the beach."

"That'd be fun." Rad nodded. "I'd even jog *slow*, so you could keep up."

Lauren turned her head toward him, knowing he was trying to stir up her competitive nature. "Really? You'd do that for me?"

By the time he answered, "Yup," she had taken off at a full run down the beach.

Lauren ran as fast as she could, headlong into the night, and thought for a moment Rad had not even taken up the chase. But suddenly from out of the darkness, almost in front of her, came two strong hands that wrapped around her waist like steel vices. She went down in the sand, half-laughing, half-screaming from the surprise of the capture. She had not even heard his footsteps.

"How did you do that?" She was still laughing as she found herself pinned on her back in the sand, looking up into his serious face.

Rad relaxed his grip slightly. "You're really beautiful when you laugh. You know that?" He leaned down still closer and studied her intently. "I get the feeling you don't do it very often."

Lauren's smile disappeared. "What are you? Some kind of super-athletic psychoanalyst or something?"

"Just an observation."

"Well stop observing—and get off me while you're at it."

Rad continued to stare deep into her eyes as if trying to read her thoughts, and for a moment she thought he was actually going to lean down and kiss her. He apparently thought better of it and helped her to her feet.

Lauren stood and brushed the sand off her jeans. "Okay, maybe jogging in the dark wasn't such a good idea." She shook out her hair and turned back toward the party, but Rad grabbed her hand and tugged her down the beach in the opposite direction. "Don't you hear it? Hurry up. They're playing our song."

"Our song?" She looked up at him. "I didn't know we had a song."

He led her closer to the source of the music that emanated from the balcony of a hotel room and pulled her into his arms for a slow dance just as the words from John Denver's "Sunshine on My Shoulders" reached her ears.

"I guess we do have a song," Lauren murmured as she put her arms around his neck and relaxed into him.

Lauren tried to concentrate on the words, but she couldn't stop her mind from racing. Who was this disarming, courteous man with his strong arms and his soft voice—a man with whom she felt no awkward strangeness, but only companionship and understanding. It was as though she had known him always—known him a lifetime ago and for an eternity.

When the song came to an end, Rad's embrace seemed to tighten.

"We should go back." Lauren didn't really want to return to the real world and end this dreamlike fantasy in which she was living. But neither did she want him to feel how fast her heart was racing against his.

"Yeah, I guess we should," he said without making a move to leave.

At last, with apparent effort he released her and turned back in the direction of the party. He did not speak, perhaps did not trust himself to do so, and neither did Lauren. Instead she walked slowly in silence, knowing each step took them closer to the party—and closer to the end of the night. When she saw the light of the fire up ahead and heard the sound of the party being carried on the breeze, she touched his hand. "Let's sit a minute."

Rad nodded and led her to a quiet, dark spot without saying a word. Sitting down, he patted the space in front of him. "Here," is all he said.

Lauren sat down between his legs, and leaned back into him. "This is cozy," she murmured. "Hope I don't fall asleep."

"Not sure what that would say about me." Rad sounded sullen as he wrapped his arms around her.

Lauren laughed. "It would say that you're comfortable."

"Just what every man dreams a woman will say about him. 'He was so comfortable that I fell asleep.'"

Lauren jabbed him lightly with her elbow. "All right. If it will hurt your male ego that much, I'll try to stay awake." She sighed as they both watched a ship's light twinkle on the horizon.

Once it disappeared from sight, Rad remained quiet and contemplative. Lauren leaned her head back and stared up at the stars.

"My grandmother and I used to bring a blanket down here and stare up at the night sky." She adjusted her position to get comfortable. "She'd tell me stories."

"Oh, yeah?" Rad leaned his head back for a better view of the sky, which was sprinkled here and there with stars. Clouds had begun to roll in and now covered the moon and bits and pieces of the night sky. "Like what?"

"Well, see all those stars?"

"Um-hmm."

"She would tell me they aren't really stars at all. They're eyes."

"Eyes?" Rad looked down at her.

"Angel eyes—loved ones who are gone, watching over us."

Rad laid his head back down and stared at the sky again. "Yeah, they do kind of look like twinkling eyes."

"She used to recite a poem to me… not sure I can remember it." Lauren tried to grasp the verse from the depths of her memory.

Shimmering stars gazing down,
Oh, tell me what you see.
Nocturnal eyes, gone from earth,
Still watching over me.

"Hmm. I'll have to remember that."

Encircled by darkness and his arms, Lauren enjoyed watching his face in the dim light as they continued to talk about inconsequential things that helped keep their minds off the passing time. When they ran out of things to say they just stared out toward the ocean, which they could not see, but could hear quite plainly. Lauren felt Rad pick up a handful of sand down by his leg. She turned her head slightly and watched him let it sift slowly out between his fingers. For once, she knew what he was thinking.

"Like sand through the hourglass," she said.

He chuckled. "Now who is reading whose mind?"

"A lucky guess, that's all."

"Because it's what you were thinking?"

She twisted her head and looked up at him. "Maybe." She took a deep breath and turned her head back toward the ocean. "It went by so fast. Too bad we didn't meet a day sooner."

"A *day?*" He practically choked the words.

Lauren understood what he meant. If they had met twenty-four hours earlier, these last few hours would have been just as hard. The time would have been just as short. She tried to think how much time would have been enough. A week? A month? A year? She sighed heavily. An eternity? And then she had a sinking feeling that he had come into her life not just a day—but a lifetime—too late.

She had faced many enemies, but none as elusive as this one—*time*.

"So when you're traveling, who takes care of Tara?" Lauren decided to change the subject—as much for her own benefit as his.

Rad's attention had been locked over the water, but he gazed down at her when he spoke. "My sister lives close by. I drop her off there when I'm deployed."

Lauren cocked her head and glanced at him, but he was either unaware of how much he had revealed or was aware and trusted her enough not to be disturbed.

Deployed?

Her thoughts turned back to the other guys she had met on the beach. They couldn't possibly be military. Many of them had beards. All had long hair—at least by military standards. No, they were probably some kind of domestic force that deployed to specialized emergencies.

After a few moments of complete silence, Lauren cleared her throat. "Can I ask you a question, Rad?"

"Sure." His voice sounded strangely soothing.

"Do you find this as strange as I do?"

"What?"

Lauren grunted in exasperation. "You know. Us."

"What about us?"

"Well... twenty-four hours ago—make that *less* than twenty-four hours ago—I didn't even know you existed."

"Yeah, kind of strange isn't it."

"Strange?" Lauren nearly choked. "It's more than strange. I don't do this."

Rad wrapped his arms around her and pulled her closer as he inhaled deeply. "I'm not exactly the type to do this either." He paused a moment. "But I've loved every minute of it."

He grew quiet then but shifted his weight in such a way Lauren knew he had something else to say. And finally he did.

"So can I ask you something now?"

Lauren shrugged. "Sure."

"How can I get in touch with you after tonight?"

She exhaled loudly. "You mean like a phone number or something?"

"Yeah, that would work."

Lauren bit her lip, trying to figure how to tell him she couldn't possibly give out her number.

"You still don't trust me, do you?"

She bent her head back and looked up at him. "Even if I didn't trust you, which I'm not saying I don't—it wouldn't necessarily mean I don't *like* you."

"Yeah, I get the feeling you don't trust much of anybody."

She was going to say, "You have good instincts," but he interrupted her.

"I'd give you my number, but we can't have phones with us during training so it wouldn't do much good."

"Well, it's not that I'm against giving you my number, exactly." Lauren inhaled deeply. "It's just that I don't get very good service where I'm going. And I don't even carry my phone half the time, and if I do the battery is generally dead."

"Hmm," is all Rad said, as if he didn't believe her.

Lauren closed her eyes, not knowing what else to say. The phone she had was for business, and as far as she knew, her direct superior was the only one who had the number.

"A business phone would work. I could leave a message."

"I'll think about it, Rad."

She felt him draw a deep breath, like a condemned person hearing that execution, though inevitable, had been postponed.

"Okay, well, think fast. Time's flying."

As if by magic, the moon suddenly burst out from behind a cloud, casting a brilliant beam of light over the ocean that reflected off the water like a pathway to heaven.

"It's the most beautiful thing I've ever seen," Lauren said excitedly, afraid to take her eyes off the mystical sight in case the moon would become covered again.

"Yes. It is."

The deep, sensuous tone of his voice made Lauren look up, and she found herself staring straight into his unwavering eyes.

"I'm talking about the moon," she said after a moment's hesitation.

"I'm not."

All was quiet for a breathless moment as both seemed to wait to see what the other would do. Then a voice interrupted the silence.

"Rad! Rad! You out here somewhere?"

"I'm right here." He sounded disappointed as he stood and pulled Lauren to her feet.

As they moved unhurriedly in the darkness toward the low hum of voices, Rad seemed somehow taller and more solid to Lauren, making her wish he would reach out and hold her one last time. She had the feeling he wanted to do just that—or at least say something—but if he did, he never had the opportunity.

"There they are." Someone from around the campfire had spotted them and pointed them out as they walked up the beach.

"Rad, get up here," Wynn shouted above the sound of the music. "We need you to settle something."

Both Rad and Lauren blinked at the brightness of the low flames of the fire as they approached the group standing around it. The size of the party had diminished to just a handful of men, so Lauren knew it must be late.

"Pops and Reese are having a discussion about horses," Wynn said. "They agreed to let you settle it."

"If you had the choice, would you want a Quarter horse or an Arabian?" Pops walked toward Rad and handed him a beer. "I say Quarter horse is the better breed. Reese likes Arabians."

Lauren answered for him. "Seriously? How about a Thoroughbred, or better yet, a Hanoverian?"

"You got to be kidding me," Reese said. "What are *they* good for?"

Lauren shook her head. "Who wants a weeny little Arabian or fifteen-hand Quarter horse between their legs when they can have the power of a Hanoverian?"

Rad twisted off the cap of a beer and spoke casually. "See guys, it's like I'm always tellin' ya." He took a long, slow sip before speaking again. "Size matters."

Lauren was the first to burst out laughing, but the others soon joined in before starting to gather their things to head back to their rooms.

"We're calling it a night. You two kids have fun." Wynn slapped Rad on the back, and the two had a quiet conversation while Lauren said goodbye to Reese and Pops.

"You guys have something to write with by any chance?"

After going through their pockets, Pops came up with a pen, and Reese had a book of matches. Glancing over her shoulder at Rad and Wynn still talking, Lauren ripped the cover off the matches and scribbled something down. "Thanks, guys," she said. "Very nice meeting you."

"Hope to see you again." Pops shook her hand.

Lauren smiled. "Please thank Annie for her hospitality. I had a great time."

"Will do. Ya'll have a good night."

As Lauren watched the two fade away into the darkness, she heard Rad's voice behind her still talking to Wynn.

"Yeah. We'll douse the fire before we head up."

She finished folding the matchbook cover into a tiny sliver just as Wynn reached her. "Nice to meet you, Lauren."

When she turned around, he surprised her by giving her a hug. "That guy's a keeper. Just sayin'," he whispered before letting her go and waving one last time.

Lauren gurgled with amusement that Rad's friend would provide such an endorsement. She wondered if Rad had put him up to it.

"I wish you would do that more often." Rad stood by the fire, kicking sand onto the dying embers.

Confused by his serious tone, Lauren stopped smiling. "Do what?"

"Laugh, dummy."

"Give me some time. I'm getting better." She bent down and picked up a discarded cup someone had forgotten. "There was a time when I didn't do it at all."

"Really?" Rad looked over at her. "When?"

Lauren walked to a trash can to get rid of the cup but turned her head toward him.

"Before you."

TEN

Rad and Lauren stood by the fire that was little more than a smoking pile of warm embers now. Nothing but inky blackness surrounded them, and nothing but the sound of waves reached their ears. It was as if they were in their own world of darkness and shadows.

Lauren gazed up at the sky, which was now completely devoid of starlight or moonshine. "Wow. It's really dark."

"It's always darkest right before the dawn."

"You had to say that, didn't you?" Lauren hesitated a moment. "I've been afraid to check the time, but I know I need to get going."

Rad glanced at his watch. "It's 0530."

Lauren inhaled a sharp breath of anguish, and without thinking, put her hands to her face in dismay and disbelief.

"Hey, there'll be none of that." Rad spoke with quiet authority as he moved toward her. "I want to see that smile." He seemed big as a mountain and just as solid as he pulled her hands away and wrapped his arms around her.

Lauren laid her cheek against his heart and reveled in his comforting embrace. She forced a smile and tried to sound cheerful. "The last twenty-four hours reminds me of that song from the show Aida."

"Something about being given paradise—but only for a day?"

Lauren looked up at him curiously "I didn't really expect you to know it."

He laughed. "Then why did you say it?"

"I don't know." Lauren continued to shake her head and stare at him. "But I definitely didn't peg you as a fan of tragic love stories."

"Not just tragic ones." He tried to defend himself. "Anyway, we're just saying goodbye—not being buried alive in a tomb like Aida."

The comment made Lauren smile and laugh, and then almost cry because she was laughing again even though it felt like her insides were being ripped to shreds.

She bent down to pick up the container of water Wynn had left and dumped it on the remaining embers, watching the smoke rise in the air. Then she walked to the trash can to throw it away while Rad mounded sand up where the fire had been.

He motioned for her when he was done. "Guess we'd better head back toward your hotel."

She nodded as she came up beside him. "Thanks for today, Rad. It was nice to forget the rest of the world for a little while."

He threw his arm over her shoulder and squeezed her close to him. "I'd be glad to do it again sometime."

Lauren just smiled and nodded as he slid his hand down and laced his fingers with hers. There was no talking now as each of them became lost in their own thoughts. At last Lauren looked up, and seeing where they were, turned toward the Boardwalk. She nodded toward the hotel. "That's it."

Rad stared grimly at the building, but made no comment other than to give her hand a reassuring squeeze.

When they stopped in front of the entrance, Lauren longed for a way to control her heart because it felt like it was going to pound itself right out of her chest. Not knowing what to say or do next, she stood there awkwardly until Rad pulled her gently toward him, his steady gaze searching hers in silent expectation.

"I'm an old-fashioned girl," she said half-jokingly. "I don't kiss on the first date."

"I kind of figured that." He did not release his hold, but the expression in his eyes was soothing in its assurance and power of restraint. "The average date is about two and a half or three hours tops."

"Yeah?" She studied him questioningly and found his expression so intense and galvanizing, it sent a tremor through her.

"And we've spent twenty-some hours together."

"So?" She still didn't know where he was going with his reasoning.

"So the way I figure it, we're well past our sixth or seventh date."

Lauren smiled. "Oh, I see your point." It took only another second for her to decide that this was one of those times when the present moment was worth anything that might catch up to her in the future. She had never intended to feel this attraction, but it was too late to stop it now. "In that case, I guess you have some making up to do."

Without giving her a chance to change her mind, Rad put a strong arm around her waist and pulled her even tighter, enfolding her securely into the circle of his arms. She could feel the heat of his body course through the entire length of hers as he lowered his lips, first in a soft, searching, gentle kiss, and then with more passion and need.

Lauren was shocked by her own response to his embrace. She had planned to resist anything more than a goodnight kiss, but his masterful touch melted her resolve. She clung to him, feeling the tight cord of muscles in his back and the strength of his powerful arms surrounding her. Every inch of him was solid and strong, like a mountain made of granite, yet his kiss was tender and loving, leaving her breathless and trembling and confused.

At last she pulled away. "Damn. This is all your fault."

Rad blinked and eyed her curiously, swiping a stray strand of hair from her face. "What's all my fault?"

"You made me have a good time today." She stared into his eyes and then looked away, not wanting to risk getting lost in his gaze. "And now I have to leave."

He smiled. "Do you regret it?"

"Only the leaving part," she said, dejectedly.

"Well, I'll take the credit for making you have a good time, but you'll have to take the blame for leaving."

"I don't have much choice in the matter."

"There's always a choice." He pulled her back against him, his touch firm and persuasive.

Lauren laid her head against his chest. "Why did you have to be so stubborn and obstinate and not take no for an answer?"

"Honey, if I had taken no for an answer, you would be sound asleep in your bed right now and wouldn't have half the memories to take with you."

She half-nodded in agreement and then gazed up at him. "Actually, I'd probably be up and packed." She glanced toward the hotel. "I really gotta go."

"Well, wait a second." He dug through his pocket. "I hope you don't mind. I got you something for our anniversary."

Lauren cocked her head. "Our anniversary?"

Rad nodded to something over her shoulder, so she turned around and saw the faint glow of the sunrise. "Don't tell me you forgot our anniversary. I met you exactly twenty-four hours ago."

Lauren turned back with a smile on her face and noticed he was holding a small red object in his hand. "It's not much, but I hope it will keep you from forgetting."

She took the small Scopes key chain and stared through the hole at the tiny piece of her life frozen in time. In the image, snapped by the photographer on the beach, Rad was standing behind her with his arms wrapped around her waist.

"Hope you're not mad."

"I thought you had it deleted." She didn't stop looking at the photo of the two of them together. She had never seen a picture of herself smiling like that. *Ever.*

She tore her gaze away from the image. "I don't like my picture being on file."

"I made sure they deleted it—after they made this. Took care of it myself when I went to get beer."

Lauren stared at it again and sighed.

"You're smiling." He nodded toward the key chain. "Something I hope to see a lot more of."

Thinking of how slim the chances were of that becoming a reality brought a frown to Lauren's face. "Yeah. Well, thanks. That's really nice."

Remembering her own gift, she pulled it out of her pocket. "Here. Funny. I got you something for our anniversary too."

"You did?" He spoke with childlike enthusiasm as she handed him the tiny bottle she had purchased the previous morning. "What is it?"

"It's a little bottle. It's got Ocean City sand in it, and I filled it clear up to the top with today's beach air." Lauren looked down, suddenly shy. "So, I guess you could say it's time in a bottle."

She thought she saw his hand tremble, which was in stark contrast to his unwavering eyes as he gazed at her. "I'll never forget this day as long as I live, Lauren."

Normally he had a calm, quiet unassuming manner and eyes that concealed rather than revealed. But Lauren had no trouble reading the yearning and devotion in them now.

His attention finally dropped back down to the bottle again. "Looks like there's a piece of paper in there too." He shook it and turned the bottle, holding it up to the dim light. "With a number." Then his eyes met hers as his mind grasped what it was.

"Yeah. It's my number. You won."

Lauren had not intended to give him her number, but when Wynn had kept Rad busy, and she'd been able to find something to write on, she'd chalked it up to fate. Why else would she have bought that bottle this morning and then stuck it in her jeans when she'd changed clothes? It just seemed like it was meant to be.

Rad's lips curled into a half-cocked grin as he took her back into his arms. "Yes, I definitely won," he whispered in her ear.

"I can't promise you'll reach me with that." She pulled away. "It's a sat phone, but still, like I said, I—"

"Yeah, I got it." His smile was contagious. "It'll be a week or two until I get settled in and can use it, just so you know."

Lauren nodded and took a deep breath, knowing she had to be the one to turn and walk away.

"Oh, I almost forgot." She started to take off his shirt. As well-worn and comfortable as it was, she knew it must be one of his favorites.

"No. Keep it." He stopped her. "You can give it back next time I see you."

How generous and thoughtful he is, went through her mind as she gazed up at him. And how comforting it would be to have him in her life, strong and in control—and always there.

Lauren found herself blinking back tears when she thought about where she was going and what she faced. "Okay. If you say so," she said, even though it did not seem possible to her that she would ever be coming back. *Why does he have to make this so hard?*

Rad pulled her into his arms again and kissed her slowly, sensually, as if he had all the time in the world and wanted to remember every detail. And then he stopped, but held her even tighter, seemingly to emphasize to her what she would be missing when she eventually turned and walked away. The feel of his embrace, the comfort and security it provided, was almost unbearable in its intimacy. Lauren's emotions whirled and skidded as she tried to resist the feelings that coursed through her.

But the tangible bond between them was too compelling to try to fight it. Lauren remained riveted to the spot, enjoying the feel of his heartbeat throbbing against hers with a similar erratic tempo. She knew her feelings for him had nothing to do with reason because she was incapable of logical thought. How could she think reasonably and rationally when all she wanted to do was feel like this forever? Who would have guessed that this raw emotion coursing through her—both exhilarating and terrifying in its intensity—would leave her breathless and wanting more?

As emotions continued to roll over her in one euphoric wave after another, Lauren remained silent and still, breathing in the scent of him and trying to memorize the feel of him. That's when it hit her that she, Lauren Cantrell, was standing on the Boardwalk with her arms wrapped passionately around the neck of a man she had just met this morning. No, actually yesterday morning, she told herself, as if that made all the difference in the world. And then she decided it didn't really matter when she had met him—because she knew she would never forget him.

Lauren took a deep breath and then reluctantly pulled away. "I gotta go. Goodbye, Rad." She turned to leave, then hesitated and turned back around as she remembered the fortune-teller's prediction.

"Miss me already?" he teased.

She smiled. "Yes, and I want you to know...to understand." She stopped and bit her lip. "That no matter what happens in the future, I had a really good time today."

He put her face in his hands. "So did I."

She looked down. "That's all."

"See ya, Lauren," he said as she started to walk away. "And don't forget."

She turned her head around and eyed him quizzically. "Forget what?"

"There's no place like home."

"While all secrecy requires deception, not all secrets are meant to deceive."

— Sissela Bok

PART II

FOR GOD AND COUNTRY

ELEVEN

R ad tried to get comfortable in the cargo hold of the C-130. He'd popped two Ambiens for the long plane ride even though he knew his body should be able to rest without them. But even with so little sleep and the pills, his mind raced with images of the previous day and night. He wanted it to stop—but he didn't want to forget a thing—so he just closed his eyes and tried to memorize every detail.

"You thinking about what's-her-name at the beach—Lauren?"

Rad opened his eyes and looked over at Wynn, who was staring at him with a serious expression."

"Why?"

"'Cause you're smiling like a damn love-sick schoolboy, that's why."

He shrugged. "Maybe."

Wynn moved closer and talked in a whispered voice, trying not to disturb the others who were attempting to relax and rest. "How long have you known her anyway? I never heard you talk about her before."

Rad glanced at his watch. "Hmm, thirty-some hours now."

"You got to be fucking kidding me." Wynn's voice grew loud, which caused a few grumbles around the plane, so he whispered again. "You two seemed like old friends."

Rad leaned back and closed his eyes again. "I know. Kind of crazy, but it felt like we were."

"You get her number?"

Rad smiled and nodded but didn't bother to open his eyes.

"Da-a-a-mn, man," Wynn said. "You're good."

"Good… or lucky, I guess." Rad never had any trouble attracting women, which was why he was known by the guys as the "babe magnet" when they went to bars. He found this natural magnetism to be an annoyance and a curse. His buddies called him the luckiest sonofabitch alive.

But Lauren stood out in stark contrast to the women who usually accosted him. Rad wondered if she thought he was crazy, or worse yet, a stalker. Heck, he probably would have if he were in her shoes. He'd never acted like that with a woman, and he wasn't sure why he'd been so bold—or trusting for that matter—with her.

One thing for sure. She wasn't like most women he'd met. She was distant and reserved, yet at the same time, down-to-earth and real. For some reason he found her detached and distrustful personality intriguing. He had felt an instant chemistry the moment he'd laid eyes on her, but had no idea if the feeling was mutual. Much as she thought he could read her mind, he'd found her extremely difficult to assess.

Rad continued to replay the events of the day in his mind like a mini-motion picture. He had not taken his eyes off her from the first moment he'd noticed the long-legged, slender form standing at the water's edge. The lone figure had appeared as just a dark shadow when he was still some distance away, but as he'd drawn closer, the graceful frame and athletic stance had come into focus.

The hat had been a godsend, giving him a reason to stop and talk. He remembered how his heart had skipped a beat when she'd first raised her gaze. Her eyes, though dark and mysterious, were touched with a peculiar velvety softness that made it hard to look away. Everything about her told of intelligence and resourcefulness and resolve. He couldn't explain what had induced him to go find her again, but it turned out to be one of the best decisions he'd ever made.

Every minute of the twenty-something hours they'd spent together held memories he didn't want to forget. He could still picture her in vivid detail, from the tips of her painted toenails to her dark eyes with their secretive expression. And then there was her walk—effortless and graceful, like Zoltar the fortune-teller had said—as if she knew exactly where she was going.

But the characteristic that attracted him the most and he most readily recalled was her laugh. Although quiet and meditative most of the time, he'd discovered that when she laughed, she did so loudly, and with a sound that was joyful and contagious.

Rad shifted his weight to get comfortable, still thinking about the wide array of memories that resulted from his short amount of time in Ocean City. It didn't seem possible that so much fun and laughter could have been experienced in a mere one-day span. And it was likewise inconceivable that he, Michael Radcliff, could have clicked so easily and effortlessly with a woman he'd just met.

Closing his eyes again, Rad pictured Lauren sitting on the bench with her feet propped up on the sea wall. Funny, but she had been the first woman he'd ever met who hadn't asked what he did for a living. Depending on the situation, he usually made up some innocuous occupation, but in this case there had been no need. Of course, she was also the first woman he'd ever met who could turn so instinctively to her four o'clock and could beat him with so little effort at *Target Town*. He assumed that being the daughter of a Navy veteran explained her familiarity with military terms and maybe even her quick reaction times. But there were other things, little things, he'd noticed that weren't so easily explained.

Like the way they both had tried to take the seat in the restaurant that allowed a visual of the entrance. She had conceded the chair to Rad without a word, but then casually positioned herself so she had at least a partial view as well. And when he had questioned her about why she so often glanced over her shoulder on the Boardwalk, she had just smiled and said she liked to see what was going on behind her.

Her reaction when he'd walked up on her while she sat on the beach with her head in her arms was no less guarded and unexpected. Even with her eyes closed, she had seemed to sense his approach. Every muscle in her body had tensed, and one hand had even gone to her hip in a seemingly reflexive move that suggested familiarity with having a weapon there. He could almost see her chastise herself for her instinctive reaction and deliberately try to relax. And when he had spoken to her, she had appeared more displeased at herself for allowing him to surprise her than startled at his presence.

But that was part of what attracted her to him. She was different. Friendly yet cautious. Easy-going yet alert. She seemed to study everything and everyone as if taking notes and putting them into a folder for a later date. She'd remembered the name of every person she'd met at the party and came across as friendly and amicable. Yet there was always a hint of wariness and watchfulness in her eyes.

Rad sighed and tried to force his mind back to the present. His time with Lauren had been magical, but now he had to focus on the mission at hand. While life went on as usual for Americans at beach resorts like Ocean City, he and his brothers were heading to the other side of the planet to help prevent what had happened to Lauren's parents from ever happening on American soil again.

The job he had to do wasn't easy or glamorous, but it was a necessary evil in a world of increasing fanatical ideologies. The thought made Rad wonder what Lauren would think of his career choice. Would she be appalled if she knew his typical workday could involve blasting into a quiet house in the middle of the night in a country whose language and culture were foreign to him? And would she be shocked to know that he often had no way of knowing if that house contained a family of four sleeping on the floor—or fifty armed insurgents opening fire? How do you even explain a job like that?

And how do you explain to someone that even if you're not actively deployed to the other side of the world, the majority of your days and weeks and months are spent training in some remote area of the United States?

Most people would probably think being surrounded by death and constantly in training would make someone lose touch with the softer side of humanity, but Rad found the opposite to be true. Living on the edge and constantly making life-or-death decisions made him and his comrades more acutely attuned to the fragility and preciousness of life. It also made them more aware of the important things in life—the things that mattered.

For a moment Rad's thoughts drifted to something he had never thought about before—a normal life. Although he'd never been in better mental or physical condition, he couldn't stay on the tip of the spear forever. In time his reactions would slow, and he would need to settle down. Seemed simple enough, but it couldn't be more complicated.

Protecting people was his calling in life. It wasn't something he could just walk away from and forget. He knew when he signed up for this gig that, in devoting himself to protecting the American dream for others, he would never be able to fully enjoy it for himself. That was just part of the job.

Like the sign displayed at the U.S. Naval Academy said:

Non sibi sed patrie. Not for self, but for country.

But now there was Lauren.

"Well, just be careful."

Wynn's voice interrupted his thoughts. Rad opened his eyes and lifted his head. "Whadyamean?"

"When you fall that hard for someone you're bound to hit hard at the bottom."

Rad lay back down. "No matter how hard I hit, it'll be worth it."

"Well, you got one thing going for you."

"What's that?" Rad didn't bother to open his eyes this time.

"Heather and Annie liked her."

Rad lifted his head again. "They did?"

"Yeah. They apparently talked a good bit."

"I hope not too much."

"You know you're safe with those two."

"Yeah, I know."

Wynn groaned as he eased himself into a more comfortable position. "So what does she do for a living?"

"Not sure, actually."

Wynn turned toward him, as if not believing he'd heard correctly. "You never asked her?"

"It never came up." Rad opened one eye and focused it on Wynn. "I didn't exactly tell her what I do, so I didn't think it was right to ask what she does."

Rad closed his eye and thought about it. When it came right down to it, he didn't know that much about her, and in the short time they'd been together, she hadn't done much to clear up the mystery.

"So she could be someone famous for all you know." Wynn sat up on one elbow and talked in an excited whisper. "You know, like an author or a movie star trying to hang out with the regular folks for the weekend."

Rad smiled. "Yeah, I guess so. If you want to consider *us* regular folks."

"Heather said she travels a lot."

"Yeah, I did get that much out of her. Sorry to ruin your fantasy, but I get the feeling she works in a bank or maybe an embassy or something overseas. Probably sits at a desk all day."

His mind wandered again. *And wears red heels and short black skirts.*

"Oh." Wynn sounded disappointed. "How's that gonna work if you're on opposite sides of the world all the time?"

"I haven't quite figured that one out yet." Rad lifted his head and shot him a piercing glance. "Get some shut-eye, would ya?"

TWELVE

Wynn laid his head back down and tried to rest like the others. Rad was right. He needed to get some shut-eye while he could. It would be a long trip, followed by more training and lots of nights with little sleep. They would be overworked and under constant threat—and no doubt loving every minute of it.

He turned and gazed over at Rad. It appeared he had finally drifted off. At least the goofy smile had disappeared. It worried Wynn just a little that his friend had fallen so hard so fast, especially considering the fact that he was the most level-headed, and frankly, detached and unemotional, member of the group. The thought made Wynn grin. On second thought, that's how he had fallen for Heather—hard and fast. Maybe it wasn't such a bad thing after all.

Wynn felt his eyelids get heavy as he glanced around the plane. None of the men surrounding him knew what their mission was going to be, but they all knew it was something big. They'd been training at a compound for two weeks before the short break to Ocean City, and now they were heading to Afghanistan to train some more. And then they would wait for permission to execute the operation they had already worked so hard to undertake—a go-ahead that may or may not ever come.

As he listened to the increasingly loud snoring of those who had drifted off, Wynn wished he could do the same. It wasn't the grunts and snorts of those surrounding him that kept him awake. They were as familiar and comforting to him as a child hearing his mother sing a lullaby. Rather, it was thoughts of the brief time he'd gotten to spend with Heather. The goodbyes seemed to get harder with each deployment, and he wasn't even married yet.

Wynn could hardly fathom what it would be like once she officially became his wife. Although he didn't let on to the guys how excited he was, Heather wasn't the only one counting down the days. He'd known she was "the one" the first time he'd set eyes on her at a party. The fact that she was with someone else at the time and he didn't even know her name had not deterred him. With Rad's help and prodding he'd tracked down her contact information and worked up the nerve to ask her out. He'd never really expected her to consent, but she had, and they'd been together ever since.

Well, together ever since in a military way. It took a special type of woman to accept the separation this way of life required. Frequent training phases followed by long deployments meant she was a single woman much of the time. But Heather was intelligent, practical, and independent. Much as she loved being pampered when he was home, she was perfectly capable of taking care of herself when he was not. Their time away from each other seemed only to make their connection stronger. She was his friend, his lover, and his soul mate—and would soon be officially joining his military family.

Wynn glanced around the plane at the men sleeping or resting in various and odd positions throughout the plane. Yep, this was the family she'd be joining, and it would be hard to ask for a better one.

These were the men to whom he entrusted his life on a regular basis, and who always had his back. They were more than teammates. They were brothers. Especially Rad. The two of them had hooked up early in their military careers and somehow ended up going through most of their training together. No one knew Rad as well Wynn—and vice versa. They'd been through the most grueling and demanding times together, seen each other's best and worst sides, and through it all, remained friends.

Wynn lifted his head, and seeing Rad appeared to have fallen asleep, tried to relax again by closing his eyes. Rad was one of a kind. Easy-going and laid back as he was when not on duty, he was a fighting force to be reckoned with when in the battle zone.

But then again, so were all the men here. They were the cream of the crop, the type of men who were willing to lay down their lives for the country they loved. This group would never ask, *How many will we be facing?* But rather, *Where are they?*

The sound of extra-loud snoring and snorting reached Wynn's ears, and his gaze shifted over to Bipp, whose nighttime wheezing was legendary.

Bipp was their explosives guy. Shorter and stockier than most of the other men on the team, he was a consummate professional. No matter how dangerous the situation, he approached each mission with an icy resolve, his expression, his composure, his demeanor, always calm and unruffled.

In this aspect, he resembled pretty much all the men on the team, Wynn thought to himself. No matter how strongly each one of them felt about what they were doing, they always appeared completely devoid of emotion. The more things heated up around these guys, the more they calmed down and focused.

Facing one's fears and not backing down was a character trait present in every single warrior Wynn had ever met. If there was danger around, they were actually grateful for the opportunity to go into harm's way. They did it for the man next to them, the men who had come before them, and perhaps most of all—for the men who had never come back from dangerous missions in dirty hellholes no one would ever hear about.

Wynn took a deep breath and let it out slowly. There was no group he'd rather be with than this one. All were good men, fighting men… men you were proud to go into battle with. His eyes flitted over the sleeping bodies in the plane. There was Reese, who was currently lying in the fetal position. Everyone called him the strong, silent type—mostly minus the silent. Burly, bearlike, and with an armful of tattoos, he was their sniper, and there was no one better at the job. He sometimes smoked two packs of cigarettes a day but could still run a six-minute mile and make it seem easy.

Beside him lay Pops, a guy everyone looked up to. Always calm, cool, and aloof, he was a gentleman, religious, and devoted to his wife. As an expert in communications, he was an absolute wizard at setting up the most sophisticated equipment in the most uncivilized and isolated places. At the age of thirty-five, he was a veteran of special operations and was one of the most respected and decorated guys in the group.

On the opposite end of the age and experience scale was Wink. At only twenty-four he was the baby of the team. Young, blond, and ripped, he was even more of a "babe magnet" at bars than Rad. But his proficiency did not lie in picking up women alone. He was a weapons expert and was absolutely indispensable to the team. He liked to play with toys, but in his case, the toys included pistols, sub-machine guns, sniper rifles, grenade launchers, and mortar systems.

Tork, who just got engaged to Molly, managed air support. He was a Texas cowboy who loved horses, the outdoors, and hunting anything that moved. Rough on the outside, he was what you would call a true brawler type—prone to smashing chairs or faces rather than turn the other cheek. Tall and lean, naturally muscular, he could drink a twelve-pack a night with no noticeable effect.

And then there was Crockett, a blue-eyed, blond-haired guy from Alabama—a strapping Southern boy of twenty-five. He spent every second off duty in the gym, improving and refining his tough exterior. Yet you could see in his eyes that he had a soft heart. That's what made him such a good medic and so essential to the team.

As his gaze fell upon each man, Wynn realized how indispensable each one was. All had a job to do and could do it without being told. They were all men with courage and character and a burning desire to win at all cost—the type of men who would rather die than quit.

Images of their last deployment replayed in Wynn's mind as he felt his body slowly relax. They never knew what to expect when called to duty, and that time six months ago had been no exception...

Just after being dropped deep in the Afghanistan mountains—eight of them with a couple of CIA spooks—they'd received word that a large convoy of Taliban was heading their way through the mountain pass... a convoy estimated at one hundred trucks with at least ten men in each one.

The team hadn't even had time to set up their outpost yet, but within minutes of hearing the news, Pops was in one corner of a small building using his pack as a low desk for his laptop while Crockett ran a second antenna wire through a small window. Wink was taking inventory of grenades, mines, and ammo clips piled on the cement floor. Everyone knew it was going to be a long night and probably an even longer day.

Wynn shifted his position to get more comfortable as the images of that night kept coming.

When Rad had returned from a meeting with the tribal leaders in the village that night, every member of the team immediately stopped what he was doing. Rad's expression told them the odds weren't good, but his calm, cool composure gave everyone confidence that the task was not insurmountable. "Okay guys, we've got a SNAFU," he said in a quiet, even voice as soon as the door closed behind him.

The news was not unexpected. In military terms that meant: Situation Normal: All Fucked Up.

"We need to do some quick terrain analysis." Rad sat down and started making a list "First, we need to find some high ground with a good view to direct air strikes. Pops, get command on the line and tell them we'll be in the shit tomorrow, if not tonight. Tork, get us some aircraft. Reese, you figure out a timeline. We need a solid plan in about sixty minutes."

That was all that was said, but in another five minutes every inch of floor was covered with maps, and half of the men were on their hands and knees studying them. Tork juggled between the radio, his laptop, and a cipher book, and within a few minutes announced that two F-18 fighter planes were inbound for reconnaissance.

The men lifted their heads from the maps to listen to the report, but then went right back to their work, pointing out positions they might occupy, and more importantly trying to figure out how to get there. The general buzz in the room was again interrupted by Tork. "The F-18s spotted eight trucks heading right for us. Are they cleared to engage?"

The room fell silent as each man appeared to be visualizing the valleys and roads and picturing what the pilots were seeing. They didn't want to endanger any civilians, but according to headquarters a force like this, moving in this direction and at this time of night, could only be Taliban. If this was an advance for the expected one hundred trucks, they had to slow them down to gain time. All eyes turned to Rad, who nodded. "Smoke 'em."

Tork keyed his hand mic. "Cleared hot," he told the pilots. The men then resumed their deliberations as if nothing of importance had occurred. But they all knew this was only the beginning of a long twenty-four hours that would likely require much more than just air power.

A thousand men are coming against our dozen. Wynn remembered thinking.

Not good odds. Not good odds at all.

The team finally decided on the high ground they would aim for at first light. The location seemed perfect on the map, but the landscape in that part of the region was a cluster of folded and furrowed ridges and hills, the type that creates a maze of passages, many of which culminated in dead ends. Wynn worried about what it would actually be like when they got there. Until they arrived on site, they couldn't really be sure.

As soon as dawn began to glow on the horizon, the team moved out in two Toyota pickup trucks to find cover and establish their observation post. They had no body armor or helmets—the same as the few locals that had come along to help—but they had a pretty substantial pile of weaponry and ammo.

Wynn had seen the concern on the faces of the men in the truck when the road began to turn and climb. This was not what they had visualized from the map. They continued advancing up the spine-jarring road, moving slowly because the shoulder was narrow and dropped off sharply into fall-you-die type of terrain. At last the road leveled out and the vehicles came to a stop.

Wynn's dread turned to excitement as he jumped out of the truck and took in the sight of the narrow valley below. The only road through the mountains lay just on the other side. The enemy convoy would have to travel across this valley floor to reach them. It was a perfect kill zone.

Rad turned around and shot Wynn a wide grin. "Pretty sure this is the nicest freaking view I've ever seen."

"Hot damn." Wink jumped out of the truck and began to pick out spots to hit the convoy with heavy machine guns and RPGs if they made it across the valley. Everyone knew that whatever vehicles survived the air strikes would try to make it up the narrow, steep road that climbed up toward them. The team planned to hit the lead vehicles, clog the route and keep the rest corralled in the valley where the pilots could pound them.

The enemy would be in the open with no way to escape except for the way they came.

Explosions began to echo in the distance and a few plumes of black smoke rose into the blue sky as aircraft pummeled the approaching convoy. Minutes later, the first of a long line of trucks spilled into the valley below as if trying to outrun the bombs falling from the sky.

After about an hour of watching the progress and listening to the explosions, Tork radioed the pilots and asked how many were left.

The answer had not been one to inspire optimism. Instead of a number, the pilot had simply radioed back in a low, calm voice. "Lots."

Wynn glanced over at Rad who gave him a grim smile and a wink. Wynn knew he wasn't just feigning a calmness he didn't feel. Rad was a warrior. His character, his leadership skills, and his calm demeanor in combat had earned him the respect of everyone he'd ever worked with. Nothing ever fazed him.

Despite multiple airstrikes raining down from dozens of aircraft, the enemy column continued forward relentlessly. It became an agonizing waiting game for those on the team who were not directing aircraft. They could do little more than scan the ridges, listen to the cross talk from the radios—and hope for the best.

Tork, on the other hand was very busy. Perched on top of gear in the bed of one truck, he took the lead in directing aircraft coming in from all over the country. As word went out that a lone team was in contact with the enemy, flights were diverted from other missions to lend a hand.

Late in the morning, one of the pilots apparently noticed that the dust clouds from the convoy appeared to be converging on a pair of trucks sitting on a ridge just outside the nearest town. "I think I see two friendly victors," the pilot radioed.

"Affirmative. That's us," Tork had responded calmly.

For a moment there was silence, then the pilot radioed back. "You mean that's all you've got against what's heading your way?"

Wynn, now half asleep, smiled to himself. That had been when things had gone from bad to worse. Not long after, the jet pilots came over the radio requesting permission to do strafing runs.

Wynn looked at Rad and stated the obvious. "Hey, dude. Sounds like they're out of fucking bombs."

Wynn remembered clearly how Rad had gazed out over the valley, his face striped with dirt and sweat, his uniform powdered with Afghan dust. He leaned back against the truck bed and sighed heavily, his piercing gray eyes standing out in stark contrast to his dirt-caked face. "Yep. Looks like we might be in trouble. Time to cowboy up."

The next minute Rad was on his feet, calmly barking out orders and setting up defensive positions as if he ran into this type of problem all the time. No matter how intense the fighting or how chaotic the field of battle, he could be relied upon to be a steadying presence, a voice of reason, a guiding presence that exuded confidence.

Even now, Wynn could feel the indescribable rush of survival and victory that had enveloped them all by the end of that day when they'd left that mountaintop intact and alive.

With his eyes heavy and his thoughts drifting, Wynn wondered why that particular battle had stuck in his mind. Truth was, there were a dozen other missions just as big and perhaps more dangerous. The fight never happened how you assumed it would, or when or where you supposed it should. That was the soldier's first challenge really, to be ready for the un-expected—especially when there was no reason to think it would appear.

The only reason a warrior is alive is to fight, and the only reason a warrior fights is to win.

This group of men was born for this. They were warriors.

Wynn's head swayed with the movement of the plane as he finally drifted off to sleep.

THIRTEEN

Washington, D.C.

The black limousine pulled up to the curb and a tall, distinguished-looking man with silver hair stepped out, his brightly polished shoes reflecting the light from the street lamps. It was Monday night—and late at that—but you would never know it by the size of the crowd inside the restaurant on M Street. This was where all of D.C.'s big hitters came to eat, drink booze, and schmooze. The day of the week meant little to those making their rounds inside.

Senator Gerald Powers nodded to his driver and proceeded into the restaurant with a graceful, confident stride. As far as Washington wealth and clout went, he was at or near the very top of the totem pole. After making a fortune on Wall Street that was more than a reasonable man would ever need, his attention had shifted to politics. As a senator he'd accrued the two things that were even more important than money in this town—influence and power. The Senator dominated the headlines with his likable, easy-going personality, and was mostly respected by both political parties, a rarity that made him somewhat of a celebrity.

When Powers entered the restaurant, there was a flurry of activity as both the general manager and hostess rushed forward to greet him. The Senator, who had just turned fifty-eight, was a handsome man and in relatively good shape considering how much he liked to eat, drink, and socialize. Deemed to be quite an athlete in his college years, he now kept his slightly-pudgy abdominal area well-disguised under expensive, tailor-made suits.

Powers leaned down to kiss the hostess on the cheek before taking the hand of the general manager.

"Senator Powers," the man said, "how good it is to see you again. Your table is ready."

"Wonderful. Wonderful." Powers strode through the restaurant like a king, stopping to pat men on the back or shake hands as he made his way toward the quiet, secluded table in the back. People were drawn to him. He possessed the type of magnetism that captivates and enthralls no matter how much you wanted to dislike him. With little actual effort, he attracted lobbyists, other politicians, constituents—and the opposite sex—drawing them in with his charming, amiable manner.

The Senator was almost to his table when a woman wearing high-heeled shoes, a black pencil skirt, and a blue silk shirt came walking toward him from the bar area with a large smile on her face. She held a glass of wine in one hand and an expensive leather purse in the other. Her blonde hair was pulled back in a bun, but a few strands had come loose, framing her face in a way that added to her allure.

A hush fell over the restaurant as every man in the place stopped what he was doing and watched the woman move across the room. Her looks alone were enough to cause the pause, but the fact that she was a well-known reporter on CNN *and* the wife of Senator Gerald Powers, helped create the image of a superstar. She seemed to know she was in the spotlight, and it didn't take a psychic to see she enjoyed every minute of it.

Senator Powers extended his hands and gave her a quick peck on the cheek she offered him before he turned to make sure she knew everyone at the table where he had paused. Then he reflexively put his hand on her back and guided her to their table.

Pulling out the chair for her, he noticed her half empty glass of wine. "Am I late?"

"No. I had a hard day and started early."

He pulled out his own chair and sat down. "You do that a lot lately, don't you?"

Before she could answer, a waiter showed up at the table with the senator's usual glass of expensive scotch. He thanked the man graciously and then raised his glass while his wife followed suit. "To you and your continued success."

"And to a successful campaign," she said as she clinked her glass against his.

Powers rolled his eyes and took a big gulp at the mention of the upcoming election. One third of the senate was up for vote, including himself. It wasn't something he was all that worried about, but finding donors and constantly trying to keep up with the Republican money machine did create added pressure to his already busy schedule.

After the waiter had taken their order and the two of them were alone, Senator Powers leaned in toward his wife. "Let's get business out of the way. Why did you want to have dinner with me tonight?"

Angela Powers fluttered her eyelashes provocatively. "Do I have to have a reason to have dinner with a handsome, wealthy and powerful man... who, by the way, happens to be my dear husband?"

The senator gave a grunt as he took another sip of his drink. He knew his wife—perhaps a little too well. She was good at acting, or more to the point, pretending to be something she wasn't. After less than three years of marriage, it was clear one of the things she pretended to be was in love with him. Sure, she loved his money and his power. And of course, she loved the lifestyle he provided. But no, she most definitely did not love *him*.

Angela responded by giving him a sad, pouty look that meant she was trying to get her way. "I don't know what *that* was supposed to mean," she said, referring to his grunt. "We've both been working long hours, and I never get to see you."

"Then you didn't want to see me just to find out what happened at the Intelligence Committee meeting today?"

Angela was in the middle of taking a sip of wine. She raised her eyebrows. "Oh? The committee met today?"

Powers sat back and laughed. He knew it bothered her to no end that she was married to the chairman of the Intelligence Committee and could never get him to reveal anything. But he didn't become a wealthy and powerful man by not being able to keep secrets. It came easy to him. Besides, how hard would it be to track down a leak when the chairman of the committee was married to a news anchor? He had set those rules before they wed, and she had agreed to them—even though she spared no effort to let him know she didn't *like* them. Powers knew, deep down inside, she had never thought for an instant he'd follow through once they were husband and wife.

"Good one, Mrs. Powers." He leaned forward at her stony silence. "Did your boss at CNN send you, or did you hear something and want to find out on your own accord?"

Her eyes grew stormy, and she set her drink down hard enough that wine almost splashed over the edge. "I don't know what you are talking about."

Powers leaned back in his chair, completely composed as he watched his wife pretend to be offended. "Be careful Angie. You don't want anyone looking over here and speculating that we don't have the fairytale marriage they think we do."

She forced a smile then and took another large sip of wine, obviously trying to look and act casual and in control. Her public image and the lie of their marriage obviously meant everything to her. "I don't understand why you have to be so mean."

Looking at her pouting face, Powers wondered why he had ever fallen for this charade. On second thought, he did. He had been blown away the first time he'd met her at a party in Georgetown and asked her to marry him six months later. He could hardly be blamed. She'd gone home with him after their first date, never bothering to inform him she was engaged to someone else at the time.

"Let's stop the game, Angie. You married me for my money, my power, and the information I can provide." He picked up his glass and studied the amber liquid for a moment. "Though I haven't figured out in what order yet."

"I resent that, Gerry," she said, trying to smile while talking through gritted teeth.

He leaned forward. "You may resent it, Mrs. Powers, but it's the truth. I was a fool to think a beautiful thirty-year-old had fallen in love with a man who was fifty-something." He paused a moment. "Especially considering the man you were engaged to at the time."

"That's not fair," she hissed. Then, without missing a beat, she leaned back and smiled when the waiter arrived at the table with their food. "Thank you, dear," she said, in a smooth, even tone as she lifted her empty wine glass. "Could I get another one of these when you get a chance?"

The waiter bowed. "Certainly, Mrs. Powers. And another for you, sir?"

Powers just nodded, keeping his eyes on his wife. "Keep them coming, Casey."

As soon as he departed, Angela started up the conversation again, but now that her act had been uncovered, she apparently decided honesty was the best policy. "I suppose I did know the committee met today." She toyed with her napkin with long manicured nails, choosing her words carefully. "But only because I could tell something was afoot in the Senate." She tilted her head and batted her long lashes. "Something big."

Their drinks arrived, but neither spoke, except to mechanically accept them with a nod of the head.

"Even if 'something big' was afoot, I wouldn't be able to talk about it, as you well know and understand."

"But I'm your wife."

"You're a reporter."

"I'm still your wife."

"And I'm still a Senator sworn to secrecy," he said, leaning forward. "I took an oath to defend the Constitution of the United States—"

"The Constitution?" She didn't let him finish. "Seriously? And *that's* more important than my career and reputation?"

Powers sat back in his chair and picked up his glass, studying it for a moment, as if it would somehow help him out of the mess he had gotten himself into.

"I may do a lot of things that aren't above board," he said, "but I'm not going to forsake the security of the United States by revealing foreign policy."

"Then something *is* going down."

"I didn't say any such thing."

"But why are you being so secretive?"

The Senator took a big gulp of his drink, set it down, and then rubbed his temples. "You can say whatever you want about how I conduct my business affairs, but I do love my country."

"Yeah." Her voice dripped with disdain. "More than you love me."

He shrugged without answering. A year ago he would have tried to deny the obvious, but now it seemed useless. Besides, honor and duty to country weren't principles she would ever understand.

Angela picked up her wine, took a few sips and looked away. "Duty to country," she said under her breath as if she'd read his mind. "I never thought you'd end up being just like my ex."

"It's an honor to be compared," Power quipped. "Now eat your food before it gets cold."

The two ate their meals in silence, with no bantering, no teasing or flirting like before. But the peaceful interlude was apparently just the quiet before the storm. After only a few minutes, Angela put down her fork and patted her lips delicately with her napkin. "I know about the special operations team training for a deployment that involves a High Value Target."

Powers washed down some food with a leisurely drink of water. "Good, then you already have an informant and don't need any classified information from me."

Angela's face turned red with suppressed rage. "That is hardly enough information to do a story, Gerry. I need information on who the HVT is, where the team is going, and why."

"Ask your source." Powers felt something like jealousy overtake him. How would she know about an upcoming action of that importance unless she talked to someone in special operations—like her ex-fiancée for instance?

"My source told me everything she knows." Angela wore her pouty, woe-is-me look again, and Powers relaxed.

Of course her informant wasn't Michael Radcliff. It was probably some low-level aide over on the Hill who had heard bits and pieces of what was going on. He laughed to himself. He doubted Radcliff would give Angela the time of day, let alone be a source of highly-sensitive information.

"Are you going to finish?" Powers nodded toward her plate. "I have an appointment in half an hour."

Angela pushed her plate away and crossed her arms on the table. "For some reason, I've lost my appetite."

He leaned over the table and gently pinched her cheek. "Sorry about that, baby. But you know the rules."

"I seem to remember someone telling me once that rules were meant to be broken." Angela cocked her head. "Oh, yes, I remember now. That someone was *you*."

"That had to do with business—not national security," Powers said sternly. "There's a big difference."

"National security is *my* business. It's my beat. It's what I do."

"Let's be honest, darling." He swiped his napkin across his lips and stood. "What you do is tell half-truths to the American public in such a way that it makes them a whole lie." He walked over and kissed her on the cheek as she pursed her lips and looked away. "I'll take care of the bill on my way out. Don't bother waiting up for me."

FOURTEEN

Lauren stood on the dirt road and stared out at the vista before her. What she saw was a stark and barren land that made her feel like she had taken a step back in time. Situated in Pakistan, but lying along the Afghanistan border, it was a desolate place—an ancient landscape made up of harsh terrain and inhospitable inhabitants who had witnessed nothing but bloodshed and violence for centuries.

The region was inhabited and known for its well-armed warriors—descendants and veterans of countless conflicts, who continued to carry on the same ancient customs and traditions as their ancestors. Having endured war and famine for generations, they survived with few resources in a daily struggle for their very existence.

The tribes themselves were bound by a strict code of honor that had lasted through the ages, but this land was now a safe haven for Islamic militants and criminals who had fled Afghanistan. Drug mafias had also moved in, and sectarian violence flourished as Sunni groups attempted to establish a Taliban-style government. The long tradition of war, pillage, and slaughter continued.

Although Lauren had been in Pakistan for almost five years, she had only resided in this mountain town for about a year. The nearest settlement to her was a smugglers' town called Landi Kotal, about five miles from the Afghanistan border. Beyond that town lay a viewpoint that looked out across tank traps of closely packed cement pyramids—the unnatural remnants of former wars.

Lauren adjusted her *dupatta*, a loose scarf worn around her head and shoulders to cover her hair, and glanced down at the nondescript *shalwar kameez* she wore. The pajama-like pants and tunic were a far cry from the shorts and tee shirt she had grown accustomed to wearing in the States. Still, the outfit was comfortable, if not fashionable, so she could not complain.

Since it was not unusual for a woman to walk for miles to fetch fuel, she did not feel out of place strolling around in this mountain hamlet with an armload of wood. The main street she walked on was lined with traditional Pakistan homes—compounds really, composed of a central courtyard and a couple of small buildings surrounded by an exterior wall. The place where she resided now was further up the winding road, somewhat isolated, except for the large terraced property directly across the dirt street.

Lauren raised her eyes and gazed at the ruggedly majestic mountains that rose around her. The scenery in that direction was breathtaking—yet so was the scent of the brown stagnant puddles of sewage at her feet. She moved to the other side of the road as she continued the long walk back to her residence, longing to fill her lungs with fresh, salty air.

In the daytime, the heat here was intense and unrelenting. At night the electricity often went out. It was evening now, and stove fires and kerosene lanterns illuminated her surroundings in a soft glow of light.

The journey to this remote village had been dangerous and grueling. Most NGOs, including the Red Cross, had already pulled out of this region due to the lawlessness and chaos—but Lauren was determined to stay. She couldn't leave. Not yet. She had worked too hard and suffered too much to throw up her hands now. Even though she didn't yet possess the hard evidence needed, she knew she was on the right track. The man she had been sent to find was here. She could feel it.

As she thought about her career, Lauren bent down and picked up a piece of wood someone had apparently dropped. This was certainly not the profession she'd dreamed about since she was a little girl. September 11, 2001, had changed all that. That single day, now a measure of time, had led her to be at this place at this moment—hopefully to keep anyone else from going through what she had.

Even though more than a dozen years had passed, she could still remember every detail of that Tuesday morning with perfect clarity. The sky was a brilliant blue as she'd walked to school—perfect weather for the flight her parents were about to take to visit friends in California.

But then bits and pieces of news reports began to circulate in the hallways at school about a plane crashing into the World Trade Center building in New York City, soon followed by another. Lauren remembered seeing teachers huddling together, talking in low whispers, some even wiping away tears.

It wasn't until hours later that she'd learned the full impact of the attack, and even then she could not accept that her parent's plane had hit the Pentagon. It was impossible, surreal... unbearable. From that moment forward, she had two distinct lives.

The one before 9-11. And the one after.

Lauren took a deep breath as she walked, more from the weight of her memories than the slope of the incline she traversed. She was proud she'd been able to keep her father's memory alive by attending the U.S. Naval Academy, but her goal to follow in his footsteps as a Navy language specialist had changed drastically.

With her Middle Eastern appearance and fluent language skills, she'd been taken under the wing of an influential military officer after graduation who'd given her the opportunity to trade a normal life in the military for a dangerous life of risk.

Strings had been pulled to place her in a clandestine service program where she'd been provided with additional training in tradecraft, deep reconnaissance, radio and satellite communications, and even survival and evasion techniques.

Her first official job had been working in the Defense Attaché Office in the U.S. Embassy in Islamabad as an interpreter for military personnel. With a new identity as a Pakistani national and a high level security clearance, she interpreted conversations for U.S. dignitaries and Navy officials as they negotiated critical deals with foreign powers.

That position had put her in direct contact with foreign officials in all positions and ranks as she attended parties, meetings, and conferences. Young and ambitious, not to mention relentlessly tenacious, she had gone out of her way to assimilate into the Pakistani culture. Using the name, Aminah Umar, she soon found herself mingling with high level officials and their wives both officially and socially. That led to a new position with the International Society for Women's Health, an organization that gave her more freedom to travel into the smaller villages and towns of Pakistan.

Because of her work with the charity, Lauren's reputation grew, leading to her acceptance by the Pakistani government as a candidate for the position of Lady Health Visitor. After attending health services training, she was now authorized to provide immunizations and offer family planning assistance to Pakistani women.

In a country where only a small percentage of women were permitted to work outside the home, this occupation provided the perfect cover for Lauren, whose main objective was to track down a man named Ahmed Arif.

Ahmed had been indicted in absentia in July of 2010 in New York for his role in a plan to attack targets in the United States. The plot, uncovered in 2009, was against New York City's subway system, but there was reason to believe he had been heavily involved in the planning of 9-11 as well. Having been under the direction of senior al-Qaida leadership in Pakistan, counter terrorism officials now feared that Ahmed had slipped out of the United States and made his way back to this country.

The charges against him included conspiracy to use weapons of mass destruction, providing material support to a foreign terrorist organization, receiving military-type training from a foreign terrorist organization, and attempt to commit an act of terrorism. Despite a large reward offered for his capture, Ahmed remained elusive, his exact whereabouts unknown.

And that's where Lauren came in. America's capabilities in using high-tech resources were of little use in the new war on terrorism. Since al-Qaida and other networks had learned the power of spy satellites and drones, they had gone low tech, using hand-delivered messages rather than communicating with phones or radios. This made eyes on the ground indispensable despite the obvious risk involved.

A break had finally come for the United States when a prisoner had leaked the name of a courier possibly attached to Ahmed during an intense interrogation. From that small tidbit of information, data had been compiled, surveillance initiated, and intelligence gathered. After more than three years, the pieces pointed toward this village, and under Lauren's vigilant watch for the past year, she felt she now knew the exact compound where he lived.

Lauren smiled grimly. All the United States wanted from her now was one hundred percent proof. Only then would they make their move.

Gazing up at the compound that loomed in front of her, Lauren opened the gate and grimaced when it whined and groaned beneath her hand. An adobe-colored building with a sagging roof and grime-covered windows appeared before her as she stepped through. "There's no place like home," she murmured to herself as she climbed up the steps of the dilapidated building. The sour stench of human filth assaulted her and again made her long for a deep breath of ocean air.

Lauren put the wood she had gathered on the porch and paused for a moment as she took in her surroundings. During the day she visited women at their homes, but in the evenings she could expect visits from others who needed health advice or first aid. This building where she lived was known throughout the region as the "health house," affording her a valuable cover as well as a sense of satisfaction. In a country where direct interaction between women and men was, for the most part forbidden, a female health care worker fulfilled a definite need.

With her mind wandering, Lauren thought about all the twists of fate that had brought her here. She had a feeling her neighbor, Ahmed, ironically had something to do with it. When the town leaders had been asked to suggest a location for the lady health worker assigned to them, this empty house on the edge of town had been Lauren's top choice. In the first place it sat higher than the other compounds, affording her a good view of the streets below. But more importantly was its close location to where she suspected the terrorist resided—directly across the street.

Apparently Ahmed had given his blessing to having her as a neighbor, probably assuming such an establishment—often teeming with civilians—would spare him from random drone attacks. Lauren had resided here for a year now, and although she had never actually *seen* him, she still believed Ahmed lived in the house across the street. She had no intention of leaving until she could prove it.

Lauren had no illusions about the deadly business in which she was engaged. It was hard to have any illusions as soon as one's feet touched the ground in this godforsaken country. Despite the fact that only a week earlier she had been a little tipsy playing volleyball on the beach, she was now focused on her agenda. It was a bit like being handed a free ticket to a wild and exciting adventure.

No, she decided, as she opened the creaking door and entered the musty-smelling building. Actually it was more like being given the chance to try to survive in one of the most dangerous and threatening places on earth.

Lauren's thoughts drifted back to the final twenty-four hours she'd spent in the United States and found it hard to grasp that it hadn't all been a dream. In the space of a little more than a week, she felt like she had somehow been transported in a time machine to a world two thousand years older than the one she'd left behind. She longed to return to the laughter, the light-heartedness, and the family-like comradery she'd experienced during her short trip.

As Lauren dumped some tepid water into a bowl and splashed the grime from her face, it occurred to her that she'd spent almost five years in this country, never thinking twice about the loneliness of her life or the pressures of her job. But that was before she had been wrapped in the warmth of strong arms, lying content by the ocean. That was before *him*.

In the middle of her daydream, Lauren realized just thinking about that day had brought a smile to her face. How strange. Here she stood, a woman on her own involved in a highly classified mission, living in a high-danger shithole of an environment, and she was grinning.

And here she was at the ripe old age of thirty, thinking about something she had never done before—*enjoyed* the vulnerability and the security of being held in a man's arms. The experience had shattered all previous conceptions and hit her even harder since she hadn't been expecting it, or even looking for it.

Lauren tried to change her thoughts to something else, to rouse herself from the numbness that weighed her down. She put her hand to her heart and wondered how it had changed so. She could feel it throbbing in there, yet there was also an undeniable void that made each pulsing beat almost painful.

She had always been independent and alone. Enjoyed it that way. But now she was powerless to resist this attraction to someone she didn't know if she would ever see again.

A year ago—heck, a month ago—Lauren would have laughed at anyone who believed in love at first sight. But what else would you call it? She had been entranced with Rad from the first moment their eyes met—and not just because of his blatant good looks. Something had sparked between them, something tangible and vibrant and real. Just thinking of him and the time they had shared caused a sensation of peace and contentment to wash over her.

Maybe it was time for a change. Maybe she was ready to give up her independence and rely on someone else. *Trust* someone else. And maybe Rad was what she needed. He was strength and comfort and calm… the key that could unlock her heart and soul.

But with these thoughts came a feeling of foreboding, a sense of apprehension so strong it almost made her shiver. It was as if an icy hand had wrapped its fingers around her heart in warning. She knew instinctively the message the warning conveyed.

She had met him too late.

Three days later, Lauren sat in the steamy top floor of her building taking notes on the compound across the street. With her clothes wet with sweat and beads of perspiration dripping down her face, she tried to imagine the feel of an ocean breeze. *The more you sweat in peace, the less you bleed in war* was one of her father's favorite expressions. Today, more than any other day, that sweat was worth it. She'd not realized what day it was until recording the date on the top of the journal, but the surge of emotion the realization caused was no less intense than that of previous years.

seat. Let's get started. We have a lot to cover."

The lights went out and a projector in the middle of the room came to life. "Gentlemen, I'm going to tell you everything I know, which isn't much, but I'm happy to announce we now have positive confirmation our HVT is holed up in a compound in Pakistan."

The men looked at each other as each repeated the word, "*Pakistan?*"

Although drone overflights of Pakistan had become routine, actual ground incursions were almost unheard of and practically impossible to get approved in Washington.

Reese cleared his throat. "So we're going to be working with PakMil?" It was obvious from his tone he did not think favorably of the Pakistani military.

"Absolutely not." McDunna lowered his voice as if telling a secret. "Too many radical fundamentalists are entrenched in their government."

"We're going in without Pakistan knowing?" Pops appeared incredulous.

McDunna nodded. "We think we can conduct the bulk of the operation without being noticed. Of course at some point the Pakistanis will find out. We're counting on you getting out of there before that happens. The White House will have to take care of smoothing over the aftermath."

"So the plan is to go in and grab this guy?"

"Grab him if he's unarmed—which is highly unlikely." McDunna paused and gazed around the room, knowing he didn't have to explain to these men what to do if he were armed. "This is going to be a surgical raid with a small team to minimize collateral damage. We want to pose as little risk as possible to non-combatants in the compound or to Pakistani civilians in the neighborhood."

Rad absently scratched his beard as he listened. Even though this was going to be a historic raid because of its location and target, it was, overall, pretty routine. They would be dropped into the middle of a hostile environment where they were guaranteed to draw heavy enemy fire. *Just another day at work.*

"We all know this is a big gamble." McDunna paced in front of the room with his hands in his pockets. "A lot of people in Washington and Pakistan are going to be upset they were left out of the decision-making process, but it's time to do something decisive. We need to make our own luck, and we need to do it quickly."

An image appeared on the projection screen of a man walking toward a pickup truck, followed by more shots from different angles as he got in.

"Radcliff, you'll be leading this junket so take a good look."

An aide tossed a file that contained the same hard copy photos in front of Rad so he could study the images more closely.

Because this was a "most-wanted" top-tier terrorist, Rad knew this was going to be one of the most important missions of his life—his country depended on it. But that didn't account for the sudden funny feeling he had in his gut as he flipped through the file. Whether it was instinct or impulse he looked up and asked, "Who took these shots? Are we sure we can trust him?" He threw the file back on the table and leaned back on two legs of his chair with his hands behind his head. "Frankly, I don't trust those Pakistani bastards."

McDunna rummaged through a folder of files. "It's not a Paki. It's an American." He pulled a file out and flipped through it. "She's been working in Pakistan for about five years now."

"*She?*" Again Rad felt a strange sensation, this time working its way up his spine in such a way that it was almost like a chill. "Can I assume this person is going to be pulled out before we go in?"

"No."

"I'm not sure I'm comfortable with that." Rad leaned forward and put his arms on the table. "I mean, I don't need any NGOs getting in the way of our takedown." Even though he was inwardly agitated, his relaxed posture spoke of confidence and conviction.

"Well, she's staying," the officer said. "And technically, she's not an NGO."

"What's that supposed to mean?"

McDunna sighed and slid the folder toward Rad. "You didn't see this. Take a quick look."

Rad took the folder and ran his eyes over the first page. It was a simple resume with no name attached: *Graduate of the U.S. Naval Academy (Arabic Studies, major/Political Science, minor).*

Fluent in Farsi, Urdu, Turkish, Kurdish, and Arabic.

Knowledge of Pashto, Dari, Persian, Hindi.

Extracurricular: High Power Rifle Team, Fencing and Pistol Shooting.

Rad blinked as he tried to read faster, knowing he would only be permitted to have the file for a few moments.

Interpreter for Defense Attaché Office in the U.S. Embassy in Islamabad

Turning to the last page in the folder caused the odd feeling in his gut to become a quiver of pure anguish. As the calm, low-toned voice of McDunna went on in front of him, realization of what he was staring at became a black abyss yawning before him.

Side by side were two low-quality, photocopied pictures, both so dark as to be barely distinguishable. The first was a standard military headshot, and the second was a woman wearing a headscarf, revealing only her eyes.

His gaze fell to the names beneath each photo, though he knew they were the same person. LAUREN CANTRELL and AMINAH UMAR.

Rad laid the file down as calmly as he could and shoved it back toward McDunna, hoping no one would notice his hand had begun to tremble. He continued to stare at the closed file as he talked because he didn't know where else to look. "So we're going to leave her in there after we invade a sovereign country and take out an HVT they've been protecting." It wasn't a question. It was a statement of fact he was trying to wrap his brain around. His voice remained calm despite the pounding and ringing in his ears.

McDunna shrugged. "She's getting her orders from somewhere upstairs, and the fact is the powers that be in Washington want eyes on the ground to confirm the location of the target and the overall dynamics that night."

"Screw Washington!" Rad uncharacteristically exploded, pounding the desk with his fist and causing his team members to look at him curiously, and then at each other with questioning eyes.

"Calm down," McDunna said. "Believe me, I'm with you. But the White House has been stalling us on this operation for months as it is. It's an election year and they can't afford to have anything go wrong."

"*They* can't afford it? How about my guys?"

Rad was tired of having to fight with one hand tied behind his back due to politics and limited rules of engagement. Protecting the lives of innocent civilians was one thing, but here the lines of "innocent civilian" and "guerrilla fighter" were indistinguishable.

Even though they were going into Pakistan, this was an al-Qaida stronghold, a village used to ferry men and supplies across the border, both of which were used to kill American soldiers. There likely wasn't an adult in the village—make that a person over ten years old—who wasn't a potential threat.

If America continued to respond in small increments instead of shocking the enemy with adequate fire power, they could soon be outnumbered. If that happened, the military would have to rely on bigger guns and larger bombs, causing even more damage and casualties. Rad believed in the creed that battles fought quickly and with all-out force saved lives in the long run. Kill one to save many. The administration, on the other hand, ran the war in such a way that protected the insurgents and required troops to defend the choices they made even in the midst of performing their duties.

He brought his thoughts back to the conversation at hand. "What about the informant? What's the plan for her?"

"She's been there more than year. She's basically a part of the landscape."

"So she won't be implicated?"

"Not if everything goes as planned."

McDunna clicked through a couple of images until an aerial view of the compound came up on the screen. "This is the compound," he said. "It's located at the very edge of the village and sits up away from everything, except this building." He pointed to a dilapidated three-story building along a dirt road with his laser. "Our informant lives and works here as the lady health visitor for the town."

"So there'll be civilians there?" one of the men asked.

"Not at the hour you'll be moving. In any event, it's a convenient location. That's how she got the shots." He nodded toward the photos lying in front of Rad.

"The building's close enough to have collateral damage if things go to shit," Rad said to no one in particular. "She's comfortable with that?"

"From what I understand, it's all part of the plan, so I assume so," McDunna said.

"It's not a plan, it's a freaking fantasy," Rad mumbled under his breath.

Either McDunna didn't hear him or chose to ignore him. "We have some urgency here because the spooks think Ahmed is up to something. We need to get this thing done within the week."

"What about close air support?" Tork asked.

"There'll be no CAS. You guys need to get in there, get the job done, and get out. Washington is counting on things not going to shit."

Rad shook his head, but remained silent. He wasn't concerned about his own safety or even that of his men. It was the welfare of the informant that worried him.

McDunna clicked back to the photo of the terrorist. "Here's what we know. Langley's been eavesdropping on telephone calls and pouring over satellite images of the compound now that positive ID has been made. That information, combined with HUMINT has given us a pretty good 'pattern of life' picture."

Rad leaned his chair back on two legs again, trying to appear relaxed as he stared at the face of the terrorist target on the projection screen. The photos were clear, many of them quite close. He suddenly remembered his phone call to Lauren, and out of curiosity, leaned forward to study the stamp at the top of the page on the handout. His chair hit the floor with a loud thunk, and his jaw tensed when he saw the date.

She'd had been taking those pictures while talking to him calmly on the phone. A Tier One, violent, American-hating terrorist, and she had bluffed her way right through, telling him she was shooting a pod of fucking dolphins.

Rad squeezed the pencil in his hand so hard it snapped in half with a loud crack, but the hum of a helicopter coming in for a landing drowned out the sound.

"That must be our informant now. This is a highly classified mission that requires absolute precision and accuracy so the head shed took the extra steps of bringing her in for a briefing. Obviously I don't need to remind you of the necessity of secrecy."

Rad stared absently out the window as a light wave of dust floated in from the chopper landing. "Isn't that dangerous?"

McDunna didn't seem worried. "She's apparently got a good cover story, and she'll be in and out in an hour or two. Hopefully she won't be missed."

"Yeah. Hopefully," Rad said under his breath.

One side of him wished it wouldn't be her, while the other side hoped to God it would. He felt like his heart was preparing for take-off when the trim, athletic figure of Lauren Cantrell came into his view. With a military escort by her side, she nodded her head in conversation while stuffing what appeared to be traditional Pakistani clothes into a bag. She was now dressed in a brown tee shirt, desert fatigues, and combat boots—with a SIG-Sauer 9 mm holstered at her side. Just watching her walk was entrancing. She was beyond a doubt the sexiest, most tantalizingly attractive woman he had ever laid eyes on.

SIXTEEN

There were fifteen men in the room—most of them with at least two weeks of scraggly facial hair—so Rad did not expect Lauren to notice him right away. She wasn't smiling when she walked in but moved with a poised, confident stride to the front where she shook hands with McDunna. In another moment the memory stick she handed him was attached to the computer and new images of the compound appeared on the screen.

"Gentleman, these are the latest pictures we have of the compound and surrounding area from the ground level," McDunna said, not bothering to introduce her. "You've already seen the aerials from the drones and have trained in a similar compound, but there may be something new here. Feel free to ask questions."

Lauren nodded and was all business as she took the laser McDunna handed her and ran it across the screen, pointing out different aspects of the buildings, the height of the walls, approximate number of steps from the street to the gate, and entry points of possible concern.

Since Lauren remained oblivious to his presence, Rad had the opportunity to stare at her in wistful silence. Although she appeared calm and self-assured, the tragedy of her past and the weight of her responsibilities were etched clearly on her face.

His gaze remained riveted, even though he knew he should look away. She wore her hair pulled back and wound in a bun, just the way he had pictured it when he thought of her. Only in his mind she had always been wearing a short skirt and heels, and was addressing a conference table full of well-dressed men at a board meeting—not giving intel to dirty, unshaven soldiers in a special ops briefing.

Rad slid his gaze over to Bipp and Reese and Pops, but they were busy taking notes and didn't seem to recognize her. Who in their right mind would expect a woman they had played beach volleyball with a few weeks ago to be *here?* Anyway, she wasn't quite the same person. She was professional, methodical, and businesslike—her eyes even more alert and her mannerisms more deliberate. Even her voice was different from the soft, affable one at the beach. It sounded clipped, clean, and disciplined now.

"How many guards?" one of the men asked.

"I've documented activity with times and dates, so that should be in your briefing packet," Lauren answered. "But the area of heaviest activity is here." She drew a circle with the pointer. "And here." She pointed to a second building that sat off to the side.

She continued her briefing, giving the approximate number of men, women, and children, and focusing for a few moments on details about an elderly man who likely lived on the third floor with the target. The man was Ahmed's father and was considered equally as dangerous.

"What about the inside of the house? Any intel on layout?"

"Good question." Lauren clicked back through the photos. "I visited the house yesterday on the pretense of a health check. I did get past the gate, but they were not very accommodating at the house. I can tell you the stairs are located on the right, immediately past a small entry foyer. That's all I could see."

She walked up in broad daylight and tried to make entry into the house? It bothered Rad she didn't seem to think the conditions she worked under were unreasonable or dangerous, or that the raid from her end would be a difficult challenge. Yet she resided in one of the most lawless places on earth and would be within a stone's throw of a barrage of automatic weapon fire, rocket-propelled grenades, and most likely, sniper fire from the rooftops. Danger would be everywhere.

"Weapons?" another asked.

"All I've seen are your standard AKs, but no doubt they have a mother-load of RPGs stored somewhere in there."

Some of the men laughed at her frankness, but she didn't crack a smile. As she glanced around the room seeking any other questions, Rad saw her gaze fall on Pops, then slide over and rest for a moment on Bipp. In another moment her searching eyes were locked on his, but it lasted only a moment. Calm resolve shielded any sign of surprise. Obviously an expert at hiding emotions and thoughts, she looked away, showing no outward sign of recognition.

"Any other questions?"

"Yeah," Rad said in a loud voice. "What's stopping you from getting out before we go in?"

Lauren opened her mouth to speak, but McDunna stood and took the question. "I told you Radcliff, the White House wants eyes on the ground."

"Come on. The White House doesn't know anything about fighting," Rad argued. "We've got the intelligence we need. The mission is not going to be successful if we end up having to do a high-risk extraction of an informant after the fact."

Lauren blinked repeatedly as if fending off some sort of unseen attack. But after giving Rad a defiant glance, she recovered, squaring her shoulders and presenting an image of strength that compelled admiration. Turning her head away, she calmly scanned the rest of the room.

"Any other questions?"

"We've got to think about weather conditions and the illumination cycle, among other things that are completely out of our control," McDunna said. "Do we have a definite timeframe?"

"The timeframe is the sooner the better." Lauren sounded authoritative and convincing. "You probably have more intel from different sources than I do, but the fact that Ahmed left the compound for the first time in a year means he's probably up to something."

"Then our window of opportunity to launch is short." McDunna walked over to a calendar and flipped through the pages. "The illumination cycle will start increasing next week. We won't have optimal conditions again for a month."

"The longer it's delayed, the greater concern for mission leak," Lauren added.

Wynn's voice then rang out from the back of the room. "To Rad's point, your building appears close enough to take some collateral damage or even become a hideout for squirters trying to escape the target compound."

Lauren never let him finish. "I have contingencies in place for my own wellbeing. Anyone else?"

Rad listened half-heartedly to the steady stream of questions while tapping what remained of his pencil on the table. Lauren avoided looking in his direction completely. When he turned to glance over his shoulder at the other men, he saw they were whispering among themselves—all except Wynn. He was leaning against the back wall with a cup of coffee in his hand, staring at Rad with a look of condemnation and disbelief.

Rad shrugged and turned back around.

"No more questions?" McDunna's voice broke through the silence. "I don't need to tell you guys how dangerous this one is. You'll be walking into a hornet's nest, past all the sleeping hornets to get to the queen. In the process, you're probably going to be giving the nest a good kick and will be surrounded and swarmed with angry hornets by the time you try to get out."

Rad gazed around at his men. "Yes, sir. We're good with that." His eyes shifted back to Lauren, who had let her guard down. She now studied him with an absorbed expression of questioning concern radiating from her eyes.

"Thanks for taking the time." McDunna shook Lauren's hand and walked her toward the door. "I know it will be a long day for you."

"No problem," Lauren said. "Looking forward to the ultimate outcome."

McDunna checked his watch. "The helicopter is about twenty minutes out. I'll have someone escort you down to the LZ."

"I'll do it." Rad jumped out of his chair and stepped forward. "Just thought of another question."

McDunna appeared a little confused, but nodded his head, and turned to Lauren. "This is Michael Radcliff. He'll be leading the mission."

Lauren nodded curtly, and then turned and walked toward the landing zone, not waiting to see whether he followed or not.

SEVENTEEN

L auren was barely outside the door when she heard footsteps fall in beside her.

"Good to see you again, Lauren."

His voice sounded just the way she remembered it—calm and almost jovial, as if they were taking a stroll along the beach. Yet she could feel the barely-controlled power that coiled within him as he walked.

"Really?" She didn't even bother to look over at him. "I'd hate to see how you treated someone you *weren't* glad to see."

"It's my job." His tone instantly changed to sharp and severe.

"So your job is to make the person giving a briefing look like she's incapable of doing *her* job?"

"My job is to make sure everyone comes out of this mission alive."

"What a coincidence." Lauren hated it when her voice got high and shrill like this, but she couldn't help it. "That's my job too."

"Now that you're finally letting me in on *that* little secret, any other ones you want to share?"

She heard anger in his tone now but forced a laugh. "Seriously, Rad. You can't think I was going to spill classified secrets to a total stranger. If you'll recall, I tried to dissuade you."

They were now down in a slight swale and behind a small fortification that hid them from view for a few minutes. Lauren didn't hold back as she began to walk and talk faster. "But did you take the hint, Michael Radcliff? No-o-o. You persisted. Remember? Tracking me down and teasing me with that damn irresistible schoolboy grin of yours." She pulled him to a stop and pointed her finger into his chest. "And anyway, I don't remember *you* sharing with *me* that you were heading to the biggest shithole on the planet for your so-called *training*."

She crossed her arms and turned her back on him, so didn't get to see that her words made him crack a smile—if only temporary.

"Maybe you're right." He grabbed her arm and spun her around. "But this is *crazy*. You can't be serious about this."

"What's crazy is that I've been working in this God-forsaken hellhole for five years, and now I have someone waltzing in here with the unmitigated gall to question my ability."

"I never questioned your ability." Rad sounded a little more apologetic now. "But you led me to believe you were a bank executive. Remember?"

"And you led me to believe you were a SWAT cop—not on a military hunt and kill team."

"I did?" He cocked his head as he stared at her. "Anyway, it's not a hunt and kill team. We locate. And then we eliminate."

"Even better." Lauren clapped her hands together. "Looks like I've done half of your job for you."

She turned and strode toward the landing zone again, her footsteps making a soft sound in the packed down dirt. She knew he was beside her because she could see puffs of dust rising from beneath his heavy boots as she stared at the ground. "Are you going to tell your CO?"

"Tell him what?"

Lauren rolled her eyes and stepped in front of him so he had to come to a stop. "About us."

Rad glanced at her, and then focused his attention over her head. "I'll tell him I know you. I'm not going to tell him I'm madly in love with you."

Lauren kind of laughed, not taking him seriously. "Yeah, that might be something you'd want to share with me first."

Rad took a deep breath and gazed down at her with a look that was disarming and alarming in its intensity. "I think I just did."

She blinked when she saw the expression on his face. "But I just met you."

"Can't help it." He brushed past her as if he wanted to end the conversation.

She trotted to catch up and grabbed his arm. "But you *have* to help it! I mean we're practically strangers."

He paused and studied her with disappointed eyes. "No, we're not."

"But we've been together, all told, the length of one summer day." Lauren tried to defend her point of view because she knew this couldn't work. She never dreamed he felt the same way about her as she felt about him. His admission had just complicated everything and made her responsibilities that much more complex.

Rad blinked as if warding off a physical blow while his expression changed to one of mingled pain and disappointment. "I guess I don't base the depth of my feelings on the number of counted hours spent with someone."

Lauren exhaled and shook her head. "It's too dangerous."

"I can handle it if you can."

She scrutinized him long and hard. "So you can promise me your mind will be on the mission and your men—not me—no matter what."

"I'm a professional," he said bluntly. "I do this for a living."

When she did not respond other than to give him a doubtful look, he threw his hands in the air. "You know what, Lauren? This whole issue could be resolved if you just stayed here like a good little girl—or better yet, got on a plane for the United States—and let *me* take care of the nasty stuff."

"Why you arrogant, self-righteous son-of-a—!"

"Whoa, girl." He cut her off, his eyes twinkling mischievously.

"I've been tracking down this terrorist bastard for five years, and you have the audacity to tell *me* to stay here where it's safe?"

Before she had time to say anything else, he glanced down at his watch.

"You got somewhere you need to be?" she asked, sarcastically.

"No. Just checking the date." Again he smiled a teasing grin. "To officially record our first fight."

Lauren shook her head in disgust and yet he made her smile. In the middle of a war zone, with danger and peril all around them, she knew he was attempting to lighten the mood.

He reached out and touched her arm. "I've got an idea. Dig out your red shoes, click your heels together three times, and go back home."

"You are freaking unbelievable." She turned away, but he moved to stand in front of her.

"Okay. Sorry." His voice was composed, low and even. There was an intensity and a calmness about him that made her feel safe—and made her wish they were both anywhere but here.

"I can promise you one thing. If he's where's he's supposed to be, we'll get him."

He spoke convincingly enough, but his grim face and concerned expression betrayed a sensitivity and compassion that threatened to undo her.

"He's there. You can count on it."

"I know my guys. He won't be planning any more attacks after this mission."

They were both silent a moment, and Lauren assumed he was thinking about what she was thinking about—all the obstacles that would have to be faced to accomplish this mission, and the complications that made it so dangerous. But when he spoke again, she realized that was not what he was silently contemplating at all.

"I wish you would be reasonable." He leaned down toward her, his gray-blue eyes filled with infinite longing and hope, and conveying a vague, yet discernible uneasiness.

"What does *that* mean?"

"Go *home.*"

"Damn you, Rad." Lauren shook her head. "These are my enemies as much as yours."

The look he shot her was piercing in its intensity. "Soldiers can afford enemies. *Spies* cannot."

The way he said the words, combined with the steely appearance of his eyes, told Lauren what she had already known. His reluctance to let her finish the job wasn't because he didn't think she could handle it, but because he felt it his duty to protect and shield her. His spirit and his character were forged for the fight. His innermost essence compelled him to shield and defend. He was a warrior, but he had a heart. A big one.

As Lauren gazed at him in silence she noticed that, despite his calm exterior, he appeared to be controlling his emotions with a mighty effort. His lean, square jaw was set determinedly, yet his brown, rugged face still betrayed anguish and torment.

"The risks are high, Lauren." His voice was low with barely-controlled emotion.

"I know that." She looked at him without blinking. "But so are the stakes."

His cheeks seemed to grow a little paler. "Then I have a question to ask you."

"Yeah? What?"

"You do understand the consequences if something should go wrong. If they suspect you in any way." His voice was calm, but his expression was not.

She regarded him defiantly, then shifted her attention to the distant mountain over his shoulder. "I understand what will happen if you and your men move blindly in a sovereign country."

He exhaled in exasperation and shook his head. "Why does it have to be like this?"

"Because you and I don't go with the flow I guess." She looked up to see if he thought her comment was funny, but he didn't even crack a smile. "Anyway, it'll be over soon," she murmured.

"And you'll get out of there?" She noticed he kept his hands in his pockets now as if to restrain himself, to keep from touching her.

"My orders are to stay and see this thing through."

"And then?"

She cocked her head and gazed up at him. "And then they'll pull me out."

"Do you know when exactly?"

She shrugged. "Not exactly. My guess is soon."

"What the hell does that mean?"

This was the first time she had seen Rad really agitated. "It means there will be increased security in the area when this goes down so I'll have to lay low a little while. If I make a move they might suspect me—and uncivilized countries like this don't treat spies very well."

Lauren expected a response from Rad, but he remained silent. When she looked up, the expression on his face made words unnecessary. He gazed straight ahead with a dull stare as if seeing imaginary rather than real scenes. It appeared he was visualizing what such countries did to spies and it had not helped her case.

"They might do that anyway," he said. "Don't you think the first person they're going to suspect is someone living in the house across the street?"

Lauren turned her head. Yes it had entered her mind, but she didn't have a say in the matter. She'd been given the opportunity to pass up the duty—but not to quit in the middle of it. Now that she'd committed, she was bound to stay until the bitter end. She would not be given the option to leave before it was done, and leaving right after would be impossible.

"Living across the street, right under their noses, is probably the safest place I can be. They'd never expect it." Lauren tried to relieve Rad's concerns by sounding indifferent about the matter. "Anyway, I don't pick and choose what duties I perform based on the danger level, and obviously neither do you, so don't lecture me on it."

"I'm not lecturing you on it, but what would I have to do to get you to not go back?" His demeanor made him appear stalwart and vigorous, like a man not accustomed to hearing the word 'no,' yet his expression revealed deep concern and a touching reluctance to let her go.

"If you knew what I've already been through, you wouldn't ask that."

"I know you've been through a lot. I admire that. But it's not your responsibility to get this guy by yourself."

"I'm not exactly doing it by myself." She crossed her arms. "If I'm not mistaken, you and your men will have something to do with the end result."

When he didn't respond, Lauren's gaze drifted over his shoulder to the distant sky. "I guess the chopper is running behind." She continued to stare at the wide-open landscape that seemed to repose in a hazy, comforting peace, but she knew that was not the case at all. Her heart thumped at the thought that her intelligence was sending the man beside her into one of the most dangerous missions of the war thus far. His detachment had to get into Pakistan, a sovereign country, without being picked up by radar, conduct a highly specialized mission, and get out. The secrecy, the brevity, and the danger of the operation dictated everything had to go right.

Lauren's attention drifted back to Rad as she continued to contemplate the complexities of the undertaking. Absolutely *everything* had to go right—in a hostile village whose inhabitants would fight until the end, and in a country that would scramble air support if they discovered the intrusion. The weight of the responsibility of all those lives lay heavily on her shoulders.

"I know you're used to this type of thing, but these guys aren't the type to surrender. Be ready to fight."

"We're prepared." Rad's eyes sparked, showing the flint and grit of the man.

"Yeah, well, last time I checked, *prepared* doesn't make you bullet proof." Lauren swallowed hard to clear the lump in her throat and blinked back moisture that appeared without warning.

He smiled out of the corner of his mouth. "Worried about me, baby?"

She turned her back on him and glanced up at the sky. "Don't do this."

"Do what?"

Lauren bit her lip to keep from saying what she was thinking. *Make me fall even more in love with you.*

"Just be careful," she said without turning around.

"Same to you." His tone softened.

Lauren turned around and forced a smile. "By the way, the phone number you have isn't good anymore." She was embarrassed when he studied her closely, knowing that long hours, high stress, and inadequate sleep had left dark circles under her eyes. "I'll be going completely dark now."

"Okay. Well, can you memorize mine?"

She nodded.

"Not sure how long I'll be in country with no phone access," he said after giving her the number and listening to her repeat it. "You know how it goes." They were both silent for a moment. "But I'll be waiting to hear from you after this. *Soon.*"

"Okay, but just so you know, I'm not in the habit of thinking too much about the future."

"What's that supposed to mean?" He stared down at her, a hint of anger—or at least uneasiness, on his face. "You make it sound like you're not looking forward to the future."

"No. It's not that." She shook her head but couldn't bring herself to meet his gaze. "I've just never been one to get my hopes up, that's all."

"Do me a favor and start thinking about it."

Lauren blinked at the possessive authority in his voice and the lethal intensity of his expression.

"Like it or not, you'll be seeing me again," he said. "I can promise you that."

"Sir?"

Lauren and Rad turned toward the voice. Neither had heard the approaching soldier.

"What is it?" Rad asked.

"Sir, there's a reporter from CNN here to talk to you."

Rad scowled. "Send him to McDunna. I don't talk to the media."

"Yes, sir, but she asked specifically for you. Said she was an old friend."

Lauren watched Rad as he took the card the man handed him and scanned the name. He swallowed hard as he stuffed the card in his pocket. Other than that, his face was unreadable. "I'll be right there."

The clunking reverberation of a chopper could be heard, and Lauren knew in another minute they would not be able to hear each other. As the soldier scampered away, she held out her hand. "Take care, Rad."

His face met the message from her eyes, and seemed to return it. He clasped her hand and leaned closer, obviously making a point to appear completely professional to anyone watching. "If we were any place but here, you know you'd be in my arms, right?"

Lauren looked up and studied his eyes. Instead of hearing his words, she was thinking about the conversation on the beach with Heather. Her heart pulsed at a fluttering tempo, caused partly by the regret that she had to leave and partly by a streak of jealousy she didn't even know she had within her.

The noise of the chopper thundered above them. "Be safe, Lauren."

She nodded and mouthed the words. "I have the easy part."

It appeared he wanted to disagree, but they both had to turn their backs from the sand and debris kicked up from the chopper. As soon as it touched down, Lauren threw her bag on the floor and climbed inside, giving the pilot a thumb's up when she was ready. She stared out the window as they rose and saw the dust from the rotor wash enveloping Rad in a misty, sinister-looking fog.

Dressed in cargo pants and a long-sleeved shirt, with a modified M-4 rifle slung across his chest, he walked with his head down against the flying sand and debris. His broad shoulders and above-average height, together with the way he carried himself with deft professionalism, gave the impression of great power and control. He was a warrior and a leader. Lauren knew things were in good hands with him leading the raid.

Lauren kept her eyes glued to his form, hoping he would turn around and watch her until she was out of sight. She wanted to see him smile and wave and let her know he was still thinking about her. But he continued to walk with that strong, purposeful stride back toward the hanger with a demeanor that told her his mind was already focused elsewhere.

As the chopper banked hard and turned away from the base, Lauren struggled to keep down the wave of fear that threatened to overwhelm her just when she most needed strength. It wasn't the fear of dying, and it wasn't the fear that Rad didn't love her. It was simply the dread—or the painfully uncomfortable feeling—she might never see him again.

EIGHTEEN

Rad took the stairs two at a time and burst through the door of the room where he'd been told the reporter was waiting, almost as violently as if he were on a raid. Once inside, he slammed it closed behind him. "What are you doing here?"

The woman, who stood with her back to him staring out the window, didn't turn around until the last trace of the exiting helicopter disappeared over the mountaintop. "That's not exactly the greeting I was expecting, Rad."

"That doesn't exactly answer my question." Rad ran his gaze over the woman he hadn't laid eyes on in person for nearly three years. Her blonde hair was pulled back and there wasn't a strand of it out of place. She wore khaki pants that clung tightly and boots with at least a two-inch heel—hardly war-zone attire.

"You look well." Angela Powers ignored his curtness as she moved toward him. "It's good to see you." She threw her arms around his neck even though he did nothing to return the embrace. "Is this any way to treat an old friend?" she whispered before kissing him on the cheek.

Rad wiped the red lipstick off his face with his hand as he took a step back. "Old *friend*? You mean ex-fiancée don't you?"

She let her arms fall to her sides. "Really, Rad? You're still jealous after all this time?"

"Jealous?" Rad laughed. "Of what?"

"Oh, come on." She gave him a pitying look. "I married someone wealthier and more powerful than you could ever be. I'm sure it has to hurt."

"I'll admit it hurt when I came home to find my apartment cleaned out and a note on the table." Rad stood with his hands on his hips, staring at her. "But do you want to know what hurt the most?"

She shook her head, looking up at him with wide open eyes as if expecting him to tell her he'd been left with a big hole in his heart.

"What hurt the most is that you never gave me the opportunity to thank you for saving me from the biggest mistake of my life."

Angela's mouth dropped open at the insult, and then slammed shut just before she turned her back on him to stare absently out the window. "Who was that woman?"

The hair on the back of Rad's neck rose. "What woman?"

She smirked and glanced over her shoulder at him. "*That* woman." She nodded toward the landing zone that was now empty. "The one you just said goodbye to."

For the first time, Rad's gaze fell upon the long camera lens sticking out of an expensive-looking tote bag on the table by the window. "None of your business, Angie."

She whipped around. "It's An-gel-a. Angela Powers."

Rad rolled his eyes. "Yeah, I forgot. So, for the third time, what are you doing here An-gel-a?"

"What do you think? I'm a reporter. I'm here for a story."

Rad looked at her incredulously. "Really? CNN sent *you* to cover a story in a war zone?"

Angela glared at him. "For your information, I volunteered. I happened to hear something big was getting ready to go down over here, and I wanted to get the story myself."

"Oh, I see." Rad's heart thudded at the thought there was a leak about the mission already. "I don't suppose you just happened to *hear* something from your husband, chairman of the Intelligence Committee."

"He's not like that. He won't tell me anything." She crossed her arms and turned away. "He's got the disease of moral integrity."

"Aw. That's too bad," Rad said sarcastically. He walked to the window and gazed absently at the landscape outside, trying to envision what Angie had seen and what she could infer from it. "So to make a name for yourself, you had to come and get the story firsthand."

"Something like that," she said. "Luckily, I have old friends who are sources in the field."

"You do?" Rad turned around. "Who?"

Angela snorted. "*You.*"

Rad laughed out loud. "Not on your life, Angie." He turned to leave.

"They wouldn't have called you in to lead this mission unless it was big," she said. "I'm not going home without a story."

He stopped and whirled around. "Who said I was leading it?"

She smiled deviously. "Like I said, I have sources."

Rad studied her a moment. "Well, sorry you wasted your time on this one. Win some. Lose some." Again he turned to leave.

"Let's put it this way." Angela no longer tried to sound agreeable. "I have enough sources to find out who that woman is."

The statement was made in such a threatening tone that Rad stopped with his hand on the doorknob. He didn't say anything and he didn't move.

"I know people. Men who will talk."

Rad tried to sound calm and indifferent as he turned his head. "I know you missed the class on journalism ethics, but do you know anything about national security?"

"You seem awfully defensive of her." Angela took a cigarette out of a silver holder and put it up to her lips. "And the way you two were acting out there," she nodded toward the window, "well, it has made me curious."

Rad stood perfectly still, trying to calm his pounding heart and decide the best way to proceed. *Is she bluffing or does she suspect something?* With Angie it was hard to tell.

"Anyway, Rad, I have a favor to ask." Angela touched a lighter to the cigarette and took a deep drag as if her threat was now forgotten. When he remained silent, she looked up as if to make sure she still had his attention, and then continued the conversation.

"I need an introduction."

Rad just stared at her.

"To your CO. McDunna."

He laughed. "And you think I'm going to do that for you?"

"You are," she said, casually, "if you don't want the focus of my story to be on her.

"You don't even know who she is." Rad hoped that was the case anyway. Angela Powers was good-looking, manipulative, and with a senator for a husband, powerful. There was always the possibility she did have sources that would talk. Not likely here—but definitely in D.C. The enemy he faced on the battlefield was not the only, or even his most formidable foe. The bureaucrats, politicians, and liberal media had the ability to bring this mission to an end before it even began.

"I have a pretty good idea of *what* she is," Angela said when he did not respond. "That's enough to get me started."

Rad blinked his eyes in disbelief. "So you would do a story based on your assumptions, not facts, possibly jeopardizing the lives of people serving their country?"

She shrugged. "Sure. I'm a journalist."

"So I can either protect the life of one of my fellow Americans by giving you the introduction, or decline and possibly ruin her career at best... or conceivably, get her killed."

"You needn't put it so bluntly," Angela said curtly. "I'm only asking you to make an introduction for heaven's sake, not enter a torture chamber."

Rad took a moment to contemplate the options and the risk. She could be lying about doing a story based on mere speculation—or she could be just malicious enough to be telling the truth. Was it worth the chance? He found it distasteful to introduce someone he loathed and did not trust to someone he respected, but the alternative could mean that an embedded American's identity would be revealed. Just as significant, and possibly more dangerous, was that Pakistan and the entire international community could be alerted that something was about to happen. There were so many ways this thing could unravel. Having Angela Powers in country just quadrupled all of them.

On the other hand, there was no one in the world he trusted to handle the likes of Angela Powers more than McDunna. He would not fall for her seduction tricks or her power threats. In fact, he would be insulted by both.

Rad took a deep breath and studied her. She wanted a story, and it appeared she was willing to do anything to get it. He was dealing with a woman who was calculating, cunning, and controlling—and just spiteful and vindictive enough to get someone killed.

"You know damn well I'm not going to jeopardize the life of a fellow American."

"Of course I do." She turned to pick up her leather tote bag, then looked over her shoulder and winked. "Let's go."

NINETEEN

After finding McDunna and reluctantly making the introduction, Rad returned to the empty briefing room and sat down. He could see the men were gathered around the picnic table outside again and assumed they were discussing the upcoming mission. He didn't want to join them just yet. He knew there would be questions from Wynn, and he wasn't ready to answer them. Hell, he didn't even know if he had the answers.

Sitting down on the couch, with his head leaned back and his eyes closed, he thought about his conversation with Angie. Had he said too much? Acted too concerned? Had he and Lauren been too sociable out on the landing zone? Or was Angela just grasping for straws?

He groaned and sat up straight. Here he was worrying about Angie's next move when his thoughts should be on Lauren. Had she landed yet? Even though McDunna had made light of her getting out of Pakistan to do the briefing, he knew she had a long ordeal to get back in. She would probably be dropped miles away from the village where she lived and would have to trek over dangerous terrain to either reach a pre-arranged ride or wait for cover of darkness and hike in herself. He knew she had the training, the background, and the smarts to do it—but it was still risky, and he hated the thought she would put herself in that type of danger. He hated even more that he had no way to contact her now, and no timetable as to when she would contact him.

Rad raised his hands to his head and rubbed his temples. Like Lauren said, he had to keep his focus on the mission. That's what she wanted him to do. That was his job. He leaned back again and closed his eyes. The voices outside the window created a soothing hum that lulled him into a half sleep.

"You okay, man?"

Rad looked up to see Wynn standing in the doorway. "Yeah. I'm great."

Wynn closed the door behind him and stared at Rad a moment. "Nothing personal, but you don't look like it."

Rad shrugged. He didn't even know where to begin.

"So I take it you just found out with the rest of us." Wynn sat down beside Rad. "That's some tough shit to handle, dude. Especially at a time like this."

"I'll get over it." Rad leaned forward with his elbows on his knees. "Anyone else say anything?"

Wynn nodded. "They figured it out. Be impossible not to."

"Okay." Rad stood. "I'll come clean at the next meeting. I don't want them to think I'm hiding anything."

To synchronize their preparations for war, he had called team meetings where he handed out to-do lists like taking inventory, requesting gear, and prepping weapons and radios.

"You sure you're good to go? To lead this thing?"

Rad looked over him. "Why wouldn't I be? Same shit, different day."

"'Cause you got a no-count love affair going on brother, that's why."

Although he was one of the most sensitive and emotional men Rad had ever met, Wynn was also a sparkplug for jokes and pranks. "I'm al-

most afraid to ask." Rad gazed at him inquisitively. "What in the hell is a
no-count love affair?"

Wynn leaned back and crossed his arms. "There ain't no countin'
what you'll do for it."

Rad rolled his eyes. "Don't worry. I got my head in the game, man.
Not on her."

And I've never wanted anything more than to get this guy. Rad gave his friend
a smile and squeezed his shoulder. He was excited about this mission and
felt honored to lead it. The man they were targeting had killed Americans
and continued to organize fighters to ambush U.S. troops.

He wanted nothing more than to show the terrorists they had un-
derestimated their enemy—in fact, picked a fight with the wrong one.
This group of men had the skill and the courage to prove just that. They
feared no one, and held back nothing, because they knew their enemy
only understood one thing—brute force.

Rad glanced out the window at the sound of voices and watched a
cluster of men hurry toward a vehicle parked outside. "Mail's here."

Wynn jumped off the couch. "Awesome!"

Mail was as close to a holiday as you could get on a military base. Rad
walked out and leaned his shoulder against the doorway as the men ran
around waving envelopes, acting like kids at Christmas.

"Radcliff, Michael."

"Here you go, boss." Pops took the stack of three letters and walked
it over to Rad.

"Looks like you're a pretty popular guy."

Rad joined the other men, sitting on the ground with his back propped
against the building. The first one he opened was from his mother in
Texas. It was long and detailed and made him smile. She talked about
everything from the weather to family matters, relatives, and general news
about home. The next one, from his sister, was shorter, but it was filled

with news from the states and an update on how Tara was doing. He hadn't heard from her in more than two weeks and was relieved to finally get word.

When he got to the last piece of mail, Rad paused and turned it over. He didn't recognize the handwriting, which was scrawled as if it had been written during a roller coaster ride. There was no address, just his name printed on a dirty, crinkled piece of paper that looked like it had been dug out of the trash.

Unfolding the letter slowly, he swallowed hard when he read the words:

Hey, Dude — Don't worry about me. Just kick some ass. I got it on this side. — L.C.

"You okay?" Pops sat down beside him.

Rad folded the piece of paper back up and stuck it in his pocket. "Yeah, I'm fine."

"Not bad news from home, I hope."

"No." Rad forced a smile. "It's all good." He stared into the horizon a moment as he visualized Lauren jotting down those words while heading back to Pakistan in the chopper. No wonder the writing was barely legible. She must have given the note to the pilot, who passed it on to someone else to put with the mail. They were words of comfort to him, yet written in such a way as to be inconspicuous if read by someone else.

"Looks like everyone's about done." Pops stood. "Ready to get this thing rolling? You're the lead guy, you know."

Rad nodded, although all he wanted to do was go back to his bunk and re-read the note. "Yeah, let's go," he said. "I got this."

TWENTY

U ntil they were given a "go," Rad and his team had to continue to plan and prepare and think about the mission. The men fine-tuned things they didn't like, but overall, they saw the true tactical genius behind it.

The first thing they examined was the infil. Tactics kept changing as the war had changed, and special operations were constantly being re-fined. The preference was to find a landing zone nearby and hike quietly to their target, taking the terrorists by surprise. In this particular situation, none of the routes worked. The location of the house and the mountain-ous terrain would require the team to walk up the streets, right through the center of town. The risk of getting compromised and the chance Ahmed would be alerted to the danger were too great with that avenue of approach. Flying in and roping down was the lesser of two evils. It would be loud, but it would be fast.

In addition to the assault teams clearing the buildings inside the com-pound, another team would rope in to act as external security. Two as-saulters and a combat assault dog would patrol the perimeter to track down squirters—anyone who tried to escape. Two others, along with an interpreter, would deal with onlookers or local police.

Besides its location in a sovereign country and the fact that it was a Tier One target, there was nothing unique or difficult about the operation itself. In fact it probably wouldn't be nearly as complicated or dangerous as the last mission this team had completed deep in the mountains of Afghanistan...

For that one, three assault teams had hiked in after making their chosen point of entry by a landing zone a few clicks away. Following the point man, they'd moved in staggered formation down a narrow, rutted dirt road, following the contour of the mountain. They carried an arsenal of weapons—from pistols to machine guns—because once they hit the ground, there was a chance they'd need every extra bullet and grenade they could carry to get back out.

Their target was three separate houses, located pretty much side-by-side, and owned by brothers who were all arms dealers and violent criminals. The fact the houses were clustered together was helpful, but the fact they were located in the middle of an al-Qaida hotbed was not. Every military age man—or MAM—was considered an enemy combatant in this part of the world.

After hiking over dangerous mountain terrain, they passed into the town and advanced through a maze of narrow alleyways. Threading their way between houses, they needed no verbal communication to complete this well-orchestrated maneuver they had all done hundreds of times. Stepping over trash and avoiding sewer pits were the most difficult parts of the operation as they moved noiselessly in the dark toward their target.

When they neared the houses, everyone moved to their positions and checked in. "Alpha is set," came over the radio.

"Bravo is set."

"Charlie is set."

Rad's team moved forward wordlessly, creeping through the shadows to get a good vantage point of the building they would assault.

Rad heard Reese's voice come over the radio. "Two sleepers on the front porch."

Acknowledging the call, Rad continued moving. When he was about thirty feet away, one of the men on the porch sat up, stared straight at him, and picked up his gun. Rad froze but was not that concerned. As dark as it was, there was no way the target could actually *see* anything without night vision goggles like Rad was wearing. But when the man's finger moved to the trigger, Rad tapped him with a suppressed shot no louder than a staple gun.

Although the shot was practically noiseless, the man falling back onto the porch was not. The soldier who had been sleeping beside him sat up and sprayed the area with his AK. He only got off a short burst before he fell onto the porch as well. A third man started out the door and was dropped by Reese before he even made it across the threshold.

"Probably woke up the neighbors," Rad said into the mic. "Let's move."

Ten seconds into the attack and already three were dead. The smell of gunpowder filled the air, and adrenalin pulsed through every warrior. By this time the enemy was starting to wake up and mobilize. Rad heard ineffectual AK fire coming from a smaller building to his right and knew the precariousness of the situation was escalating by the minute.

Making his way past the three dead men on the porch, Rad heard a blast just as the window frame near his head splintered from a shot to his right. Not even flinching, he shouldered his rifle, turned in the direction of the shot, and watched one of his men eliminate the problem.

The amount of incoming fire began building steadily but was not unexpected or cause yet for alarm. If need be, more shooters could be moved to the roof to bolster the snipers and light machine gun already in place. At the moment it was a target-rich environment made up of battle-hardened soldiers who were mortal enemies of the United States. Rad's only concern was that it probably wasn't going to take too long for the fanatics to come up with a better strategy that might involve bigger guns and rocket-propelled grenades.

Rad's internal radio link crackled to life in his ear. "Rad, it's Bipp. You need to come take a look at something."

Rad poked his head around the door frame and glanced down the street again through his night sight. At the bottom of hill, about a block away, he saw an enemy combatant taking up position to fire an RPG. "Hold on a second, Bipp."

Rad moved reflexively. With his laser, he painted the man's chest with a bright red dot and squeezed the trigger. The target crumpled to the ground, and Rad ducked back into the house.

"What's up Bipp?"

"We think we found something here."

Before responding, Rad edged his way to a broken window and sighted two men dart between two of the small outbuildings in the compound, about forty yards away. One of them made it. The other one didn't.

"Can it wait?"

Before Bipp could answer, the thunderous reports of a heavy-caliber machine gun boomed above the din of regular rifle fire, and a large hole appeared in the wall a few feet away from Rad. He hit the floor as chunks of dry mud rained down on him. Crawling back to the door, swearing under his breath, he pushed the switch on his radio for the command net. "Nighthawk Four this is Rattler One, where is my air support?"

"Just sit tight. It's on the way."

Sit tight? Seriously? Do you think I'm just lounging around in a freaking rocking chair down here?

It was the smugness of the tone more so than the words that irritated Rad. He looked skyward as if he could see those who were orchestrating the operation from a far-away place of safety. He primed his mic and remained calm. "I've got heavy-caliber machine gun firing on my position to the north."

"I see it, Rattler One. You have support inbound."

Rad didn't have time to ask for an ETA. He heard the "whoosh" of aerial rockets passing overhead, swiftly followed by a series of thunderous explosions.

As Rad headed for Bipp's location, he called for a situation report from his team and waited as one by one each man checked in. Things were proceeding as planned, but these engagements had a way of changing from calm to chaos in the blink of an eye. Especially here.

The people in the village and their ancestors had used the mountains to hide from invaders for thousands of years, making them masters at guerrilla warfare. They could hit the enemy and then disappear into the wild terrain, which made conventional forces useless against them.

Now the radio began to heat up. "Contact left."

"Contact rear."

Rad found Bipp in the back of the house on the first floor, stuffing computer discs and folders into a bag with one of the other men in a room that looked like a modern day office.

"Got the motherload here, dude."

Rad nodded and gave him a thumb's up. "Get as much as you can."

Now barely ten minutes into the op, it was apparent from the sounds outside that the whole town had awakened. The quarter moon shining in a clear sky provided relatively clear pictures through night-vision, revealing hostiles moving toward them in pretty much every direction. The numbers weren't alarming yet, but it was still early. What would probably appear as utter chaos to some, was really just another night of work for Rad and the other men. But there could never be certainty in how events would unfold five minutes from now or what would happen next.

Within moments of Rad's team taking out their target and securing their building, drive-by shooters began firing small arms onto the roofs and parapets around the sniper positions. Seconds later, an RPG streaked in and exploded against the roof, casting a cloud of dust over them.

The radio crackled as the teams reported the other two houses were secure. Their job here was done. Now all they had to do was get out.

"Let's move." The radio crackled. "I don't want to see what this place looks like in daylight."

Air support provided cover as they made their way back to the designated landing zone for pick-up, but the situation was still dicey even after everyone had been loaded on the choppers. There was always a chance of getting shot out of the sky by an RPG, or possibly even a surface-to-air missile, until they were well on their way.

Rad inhaled deeply as he thought about all the things that had gone right that night. The upcoming mission into Pakistan wasn't going to be nearly as complicated as that one had been—except for one unknown—Lauren.

TWENTY-ONE

Four days later

After months of training and weeks of planning and anticipation, the night was finally upon them. Rad sat on his bunk, staring into space, trying to visualize the coming mission he both dreaded and desired. Even though he had no appetite he forced down an MRE, not knowing when he would be able to eat again.

Leaving just enough time to get to the rally point at the fire pit, Rad went through his usual ritual before a mission. First, he re-checked everything he carried in the lower pockets of his cargo pants, making sure assault gloves, leather mitts for fast-roping, and extra batteries were easily accessible. After checking his ankle pocket, where he kept an extra tourniquet, he moved to the pockets on his shoulder. On the left, he kept a couple hundred dollars—American cash—in case he was compromised and needed to buy a ride or bribe someone. On the opposite side he carried his camera, and in the back of his belt, a fixed blade knife.

Satisfied with that part of his routine, Rad picked up his kit for inspection. Two radios were mounted on either side of the front plate with three magazines for his assault rifle and a frag hand-grenade mounted between them. He also carried a breaching charge in the back, as well as several chemical lights in the front of his vest. Visible only to those wearing night vision goggles (NVGs), the lights were used to mark rooms or buildings that had been cleared and were considered secure.

Rad picked up his helmet and switched on the light to make sure it worked and checked the NVGs. He then picked up his rifle and tested the red laser, visible to the naked eye, on a wall by his bunk, then flipped down the NVGs and did the same with the infrared laser. Pulling the bolt back, he chambered a round, and then double-checked to make sure it had seated. He confirmed the safety was on and rested the weapon back against the wall.

The final step was to pull the small laminated booklet—his cheat sheet—out of a small pouch in the front of his vest. Flipping past the first two pages, which contained an aerial view of the compound and radio frequencies, he continued to the page that displayed the names and photos of everyone expected to be in the target house. He studied the images as well as the height, weight, and known descriptions again, trying to commit each to memory.

With his camouflage uniform on and gear ready to go, Rad grabbed his boots and laced them. His mind now began to focus on the significance of this mission and the work that needed to be done. He pushed all thoughts of Lauren from his mind as he carefully double-wrapped the laces and tucked them into his boots.

Finally, Rad hoisted his sixty-pound vest over his head, tightened the straps, and touched everything again to make sure he could reach it. He then connected the antennas to the radio and put his earbuds in position. In his right ear would be the troop net, where teammates would communicate with each other during the mission. His left ear would monitor the command net, allowing him to communicate with other team leaders and officials.

Rad checked his watch. He could hear guys moving around, packing their bags and slamming the door as they headed to the fire pit, but he had one more ritual to complete. Dropping to one knee and bowing his head, he said a prayer for the success of the mission and the safety of his men, ending with "And protect Lauren with your merciful hand. Thy will be done. Amen."

"You ready for this?" Wynn patted him on the back when he got to the fire pit, his spirits obviously high.

"Can't wait." Rad gave him the thumbs up.

McDunna soon arrived and without fanfare, they loaded onto a bus for transportation to their waiting Black Hawks. With the engines running and rotors spinning while the pilots went through final checks, the choppers made conversation impossible—but that did not stop communication. As he stood in line waiting to load, Rad noticed a few hand gestures between teammates loading on the other chopper. These men would be all business in a few minutes, but now they were more like children on a playground, talking smack using only hand—or finger—signals, and smiling as if this was nothing more than an exciting fieldtrip.

Since he would be the first one down the rope, Rad was the last to board and barely had enough room to wedge his large body into the helicopter. Predictably, no one asked whether or not he was comfortable. The door clicked shut, the bird lifted, and they headed for the border.

Rad tried to scrunch around to make more room, which only caused someone's knees to gouge into his back more intensely. He closed his eyes, trying to convince himself he was comfortable, and tried to relax and snooze. It seemed like only moments later the radio crackled to life with the first transmission of the night. "Crossing the border."

Damn. We're really going to do this.

After closing his eyes again, he let his thoughts drift until he heard the radio come to live again with the call, "Ten minutes."

Those words were enough to shake him from his groggy sleep. He wiped his eyes and wiggled his toes to start working the circulation back.

"Five minutes."

All other thoughts disappeared and it became just another night of work. Rad pulled on his helmet and snapped the chinstrap. Pulling his NVGs down, he made sure everything was in focus by turning his head side to side. Then he pulled his gun in tighter to his chest, so it wouldn't hang up on the rope, and checked his safety one last time.

The cabin was now full of movement, yet quiet, as everyone performed the same checks.

"One minute."

The crew chief slid the door open and Rad slid the fast rope system into place, checking the pin and then giving a tug to make sure it was secure. The crew chief repeated the last steps to double-check him before Rad slid his legs out over the edge of the helicopter.

It was pitch black down below. Rolling blackouts were common, but it hit Rad as uncommonly good fortune that one would hit this area at exactly this time.

Rad glanced over his shoulder. Ten of the most highly trained and seasoned soldiers the world had ever known sat calmly behind him, their well-worn boots ready to touch the ground. They were on the verge of launching a raid in a foreign land that was among the most desolate and inhospitable places on earth, yet he knew every last one of them looked forward with great anticipation to what lay ahead.

Hearing the engine noise change as the helicopter hovered, Rad waited for the "go" as they hit their predetermined fast-rope point. Finally, he saw the outline of the target's house. About the same size as other compounds, it lay nestled on its own terrace and was surrounded by eight-foot walls on three sides that jutted out and overlooked the valley. The side nestled against the mountain had no wall, the mountain itself providing the defensive barrier.

As he got the "go," Rad threw the rope and dropped out of the chopper. Hurrying to get out of the way of the remaining men coming down the rope, he turned his head back and forth as he ran, swinging his gun from nine to three at the ready. All appeared clear.

We're in the hornet's nest, Rad thought to himself as he made his way to his first target. As others headed to the main gate, he approached a small detached building that was presumably a guest prayer room. As he checked the room and found it clear, he heard, "Breaching charge ready" in his ear and knew Bipp was getting ready to blow the main gate. Rad threw an infrared chemlight by the door as he left the building to notify anyone wearing NVGs the room was secure.

Moving back to the gate, Rad noticed the compound where Lauren lived to his left. It appeared dark and sinister, and he wondered for a moment if Lauren was hiding within, watching the assault unfold. He hoped not. Too much could go wrong.

Rad listened as Bipp announced the charge getting ready to blow. In anticipation of the blast, everyone dipped their heads to protect their eyes. There was a quick flash, followed by an explosion and a shock wave that blew a hole in the gate. Wynn was the first one up to it, kicking and pulling the metal wider so everyone could fit. Guys piled through and peeled off toward their planned objectives.

Arriving at their next target, a building to the right of the main house, Wynn took a position to the left of the door while Rad tried the knob. Finding it locked, he took a position on the other side of the door, covering Wynn who pulled out a sledgehammer. A couple of good whacks resulted only in a battered handle. Wynn turned to the window and tried to smash the glass, but the bars were too narrow to get the hammer through.

With the element of surprise gone and time slipping by, Rad decided to use an explosive. He pulled the breaching charge off his kit and moved in low to affix it to the door.

From across the compound came an explosion as another team attempted to gain entry by blowing a side gate of the compound. "Failed breach," came over the radio. "Moving to Delta gate."

Geez. They should be inside by now, and they are still trying to gain entry on the west side.

Rad did the calculations. It had been about five minutes since they'd hit the ground and twenty guys were swarming the compound. Taking into account the noise of the helicopters and the sound of at least two charges blowing, there was no way everyone in the compound was not awake.

Pushing these thoughts away, Rad took a knee to the right of the door and peeled the adhesive backing off the breaching charge before setting it across the mangled knob and lock.

Without warning an AK-47 round tore through the door to the right of his head. Rad rolled away as bullets cracked just inches away. Pieces of wood and shards of glass from the window beside the door hit his shoulder and tore into his skin.

Whoever was inside didn't stop, but continued firing blindly, now aiming chest high. Intelligence data gathered on this building had revealed this door as the only entry and exit point. The occupant apparently knew he was trapped, and was not going to go down without a fight.

Wynn, covering the door from the left, fired back as Rad opened fire from the ground. He felt a searing burn from the shrapnel in his left shoulder but didn't stop to think about it.

Rolling clear of the dangerous area in front of the door, Rad jumped back to his feet and ordered the man inside to come out in what little Arabic he knew. When the response was more gunfire, he stuck the barrel of his gun between the bars on the window and fired toward the terrorist's likely position in the house.

Everything went silent.

With no time to spare, Rad went back to the explosive charge to blow the door. He was about to attach the detonator when he heard the latch on the door unlock. He looked around to see if Wynn heard it too and saw he was backing away. Neither one of them had anywhere to move for cover, and no way of knowing if they were going to get sprayed with an AK or hit with a grenade. Backing up seemed like a good idea.

After they had taken only a few steps, the door opened a little wider, and a woman's form appeared. Rad breathed slowly and concentrated on her every move. If she was wearing a suicide vest both he and Wynn were dead. But trying to figure out whether she was or not was like predicting if and when lightning was going to strike.

Through the sweat running down his face and the grit that remained in his eyes from the rotor wash on the landing, Rad could barely distinguish that the woman had something in her arms. His finger slowly applied pressure to his trigger as lasers from both him and Wynn danced around her head. It would only take a split second to dispatch her.

Then he saw the bundle was a baby. Behind her, three more kids came out.

As Wynn moved the woman and kids away to another team member who did a pat down, Rad stood to the left, pushed the door open with his rifle barrel, and spotted a pair of feet lying in a puddle of blood with toes pointed toward the ceiling.

From behind him, Wynn squeezed his shoulder to let him know he was ready. Moving forward, Rad stepped over the body and kicked the terrorist's AK away. It was obvious he was dead. The entire room was shredded from the gunfire, and the floor was slippery from dripping water pipes and blood. After checking the rest of the building, Rad found it clear.

"Shots fired. Building is secure," Rad reported over the troop net as he tossed another chemlight at the front door. Then he moved toward the main building to backfill other teams.

Rad heard the boom from another breaching charge somewhere else in the compound as he made his way around the west side of the main house. His heart picked up its pace with anticipation as he thought about what they might find inside. Lauren had said the target and his father most likely resided on the third floor. If she was right, they would soon have their man.

Once inside the main door, the hurry and rushing turned into a slow, deliberate waiting game as Rad became stacked behind other men methodically clearing rooms. It was the impatient rhythm of battle—violent motion reduced to perfect stillness.

Listening to another door or gate being breached in front of him made the situation feel strangely surreal, like he was waiting to enter the house for Close Quarters Battle training. He'd done this hundreds of times, but this one was somehow different.

Rad heard a *bop, bop* coming from down a hallway ahead of him, and then the call over the radio. "First floor, secure."

The house was dark and eerily still as the team made their way to the stairwell to check the next floor. They did their best to be quiet, but Rad knew whoever was hiding up there had had plenty of time to get a weapon and prepare a defense. On some raids his men would use a flash grenade to clear their objective, but this one was all about throttle control. Everyone in the compound had certainly heard the helicopters, the shots fired, and the explosive breaches. The fact that everything had grown quiet again would keep the occupants upstairs guessing about what was coming next.

When Rad made it to the second floor, he saw it had four doors, two right and two further down on the left. His teammates crept down the hall, backing each other up on doors before expeditiously clearing each one.

It appeared this floor was made up mostly of women and children because no shots were fired. At the "all clear" call, Rad turned toward the next flight of stairs. Wynn was already on the landing, holding security between the floors. Rad squeezed his shoulder to let him know he was ready. "Take it," he whispered.

Everything was bathed in an eerie green hue as they moved up the stairs to the next floor. This was it. The culmination of Lauren's work and the hours of training and planning that had gone into this mission were going to be decided in the next few minutes. They had to be ready for anything now. This terrorist was not going to go down without a fight. There was no margin for error.

As he slowly walked up the stairs, Rad continued to scan the top landing. Every sense was on overdrive and strained to its limit, but he didn't know if he was breathing hard or not breathing at all. He was on autopilot.

Wynn stood outside the door of the first room and waited for Rad to signal he was in position. When he got the nod, he pushed the door open and immediately swept the room to the left as Rad followed and swept it to the right. Finding nothing but storage boxes, they exited and continued to the next room. After taking only a step, a man appeared at the next door and let go an un-aimed burst from his weapon. Rad hit him with two rounds and kept moving as two of his men went in to clear the room.

A quick movement from the end of the hall caught Rad's attention. He let go a burst and stepped back into the doorway, waiting for return fire, but none came.

Assured he was covered from behind, he ran down the hallway and swung his weapon into the room where the man had disappeared. Rad found the man sprawled in the doorway reaching for his weapon and put another round in him to keep him down. Then he did a quick sweep of the room with his muzzle and settled on an old man lying in bed.

The man raised one hand as if surrendering, but then without warning drew an AK from beneath the covers with his other, and fired a round while letting out a banshee-like scream. Something clipped Rad's arm, stinging him with a bolt of fire, but it didn't stop him from discharging a burst that sent the man sprawling back into the bed in a spray of red mist.

"You okay?" Wynn nodded toward his arm after they had made sure the room was secure.

"Yeah, just a stinger."

Wielding the rifle against his shoulder again, he took a deep breath and swung back into the hall to the last remaining door. Blood began to drip off the tips of his fingers, making him think that perhaps his wound was a little more serious than he thought. But he felt no pain.

With sweat dripping into his eyes, Rad moved forward as quietly as he could. His senses were hyper-alert, attuned for any sudden movement or noise. They had not yet found their target, and time was running out. The success of this operation depended on getting in and out in a set amount of time. Thirty minutes, with an extra ten minutes of flextime, was the deadline based on the volume of fuel held by the waiting helicopters and the length of time it might take Pakistan to assemble and launch their military. If Lauren's information was correct—and he believed it was—their man had to be behind this last door.

Rad stood in the hallway and strained his ears. No sound. Standing with his back against the wall, he quietly reached over and tried the doorknob. It was locked. Wynn, in the same position on the other side of the door said quietly into his mic, "Going explosive?"

Rad made a split second decision that ran counter to his better judgment and training. Time was running out. He was so close to the terrorist, he could almost feel him.

Fuck the explosives.

Taking deep breaths, he counted to three, turned toward the barrier and let his foot fly. The moment his boot connected with the door, he heard a roaring barrage of gunfire.

TWENTY-TWO

Rad returned fire while lying on his back and watched Wynn blasting away from the side as well. Scrambling to his feet, he followed Wynn into the room to find two shooters sprawled out on the floor, killed in the gunfight.

The two assaulters had apparently been standing to the side of the door, waiting to shoot whoever came through. The angle of their shots actually came closer to hitting Wynn, even though Rad had been the one directly in front of the door.

"What the hell do you think you're wearing?" Wynn said once they had made sure the room was secure. "Bulletproof everything?"

Rad bent over the men, studying their faces and physical characteristics. "Dammit. Not him."

He raised his gaze to meet Wynn's, and then stood, searching the room for any signs their target had been there. This had to be his room. Located at the end of the hallway, it seemed like everyone had been moving toward this position to defend it. It was the room beside the father's room just as the intelligence had noted. It was the only locked door, and there were files and a laptop in a small enclave off to the side.

Rad listened to the others check in and give updates. After hearing the third floor was secure they had already begun the SSE (Sensitive Site Exploitation) phase of the operation, gathering files, computer disks and hard drives into their mesh evidence bags.

He stared absently around at his surroundings. Whoever's room this was, he was a neat freak. Unlike most of the other rubbish-filled living areas they had seen, this one was organized and tidy, everything neat as a pin and in its place.

He looked back over his shoulder. Except for one thing. A large floor to ceiling bureau sat a little cockeyed from the wall as if it had been moved and not placed back in its original position.

Pulling on some of the drawers, Rad found everything folded and neatly arranged by color and size.

"Is this some OCD or what?" Wynn rummaged through the drawers. "Who folds their stuff like that?"

Rad shook his head, stood back, and studied the bureau again.

"What's wrong, dude?"

"Something's not right. Why is this thing out of place when everything else is so neat?"

Wynn continued searching through drawers to see if he could find anything of interest. "Maybe one of those guys fell into it during the fight."

Rad studied the distance from the door where the two bodies were located to the bureau in the back of the room. "I don't think so." Acting on impulse, he put his shoulder into the bureau and moved it out of the way.

"Holy shit." Wynn took a quick step back and positioned his rifle to his shoulder, pointing it at the plain white curtain that hung behind the bureau.

Placing his back against the wall, Rad waited for Wynn to nod, then tore down the piece of cloth with one hand, revealing another door.

Rad's heart twisted a little. The choppers were probably already on their way back for the pick-up. This operation had been planned and choreographed down to the minute. There would be no leniency on time and no second chance.

As if on cue Rad heard the call, "Fifteen until exfil."

"Third floor not secure." Rad spoke calmly into his mic, even though his heart was racing. They had less than fifteen minutes to find out who or what was behind this door.

"I hope it's not a freaking tunnel into the mountain." Wynn voiced exactly what Rad was thinking. The way the house was built into the hillside, the third floor in the front was actually ground level in the back.

Fearing it was booby-trapped, but pressed for time, Rad pushed the latch, held his breath, and opened the door. He was greeted by the scent of musty air, the kind that hits you when you descend into a dirt cellar. He glanced at Wynn and knew by his expression he smelled it too. Definitely a tunnel.

Swinging through the door with his gun at the ready, Rad almost hit his head on the low ceiling. He felt Wynn give his shoulder a squeeze and continued walking slowly and quietly. It was so pitch black that even with NVGs, the images before them were murky.

After taking a few dozen steps, they both paused and listened, every nerve strained to its limit. Hearing nothing but their own steady breathing, they continued forward, guns moving back and forth as they probed the darkness in front of them.

Just as they started to round a sharp turn in the tunnel they heard the *pop, pop, pop* from a gun and saw the flash from its muzzle not thirty yards ahead of them. They both took an instant step back for cover and waited for the shooting to stop. When it did, Rad pointed his gun around the corner and sprayed that direction with gunfire. Even with their ears ringing from the close quarters, they both heard the body drop, and the *whoof* sound that escaped from the man's lungs when he hit the ground.

Walking cautiously toward the prostate form, Rad could see from the size of the puddle of blood he was dead.

"Looks like the tunnel's not quite finished." Wynn nodded toward the equipment that lined the walls. The terrorist had gone as far as he could go and had been cornered. Although he probably couldn't see them, he had heard them start to make the turn.

Rad and Wynn both looked over their shoulders at the same time, obviously thinking the same thing. If the shooter had waited until they had completely rounded that corner before firing, just another split second, there was a good chance he would have gotten one of them—if not both.

"Looks like we almost got an acute case of lead poisoning," Wynn murmured.

Rad went down on one knee and rolled the man over, breathing a sigh of relief. He switched on his helmet light to examine his face and saw the birthmark on his cheek. "It's him."

"Good job, dude."

"Ten minutes to ex-fil."

"Third floor secure. We need an extra five."

"Ten minutes to ex-fil," the voice repeated calmly.

Rad quickly shot photos of the body while Wynn worked on DNA samples. He dabbed a cotton swab in blood, and then took another and jammed it in the dead man's mouth for saliva. Finally, Wynn stuck a spring-loaded syringe into the terrorist's thigh for a blood marrow sample, just to be on the safe side.

From the transmission he was hearing on the radio, Rad knew a group of curious villagers had heard the noise and were gathering at the gate. The interpreter was busy trying to get them to disperse by telling them there was a security operation under way.

"Post assault, five minutes," came over the troop net.

As Rad and Wynn made it down the stairs, other men on the team appeared like a bunch of elves carrying their mesh bags full of computer disks, hard-drives, and documents over their shoulders.

The sound of the choppers coming in greeted Rad's ears as soon as he made it outside. Grabbing an extra bag from one of the men he began sprinting toward the waiting helicopter, stumbling and almost falling like everyone else over the uneven terrain. When he got to the chopper he flung his bag onto the deck and climbed aboard, his chest heaving.

Glancing at his watch, he saw they were six minutes past planned drop-dead time. Law enforcement, and possibly even Pakistani military, were likely inbound by now.

Only when they lifted off and banked hard toward the Afghanistan border did his heart begin to beat at a regular pace. After about five minutes of flight, Rad began to relax even more. Leaning his head back and taking a deep breath, he noticed something out of the corner of his eye and turned for a better view. The interior of the chopper was pitch black except for a series of dim lights on the cockpit control board. The one that caught his eye was the big one in the center, flashing red.

That doesn't look good.

Rad turned away and closed his eyes so he wouldn't see it. He wasn't a pilot. For all he knew blinking red lights were good things—like at Christmas or something. Damn, he hated this part of the mission. No longer in control, there was nothing he could do but trust the pilots to get them safely back to base.

When the chopper changed speeds, circled and began to descend, Rad knew they were taking care of that blinking red light. The delay of a few minutes had cost them vital fuel, and they wouldn't make it back into Afghanistan without replenishing their tanks.

Once the crew chief opened the door, Rad could make out the faint image of a CH-47 and guys moving toward them with a hose. It was a necessary stop that would cost more time. Rad checked his watch, and then closed his eyes, wishing he hadn't. With the noise they had made between the landing, the raid, and the takeoff, Pakistan must have received reports about something happening and scrambled F-16's by now. Hopefully they were heading toward the village where the commotion had emanated from—not the airspace near the Afghan border. Getting shot out of the sky over Pakistan was not how he envisioned his otherwise successful night coming to an end.

Once they were back on their way, Rad took off his helmet for the first time and ran his hand through his matted, wet hair, his thoughts turning to Lauren. Did she know the raid had been successful? He wished he could see her face when she found out all her hard work and sacrifice had paid off. Even though she would never receive any credit for a dangerous terrorist's elimination, he knew the end result would be enough to satisfy her. It would mean she could leave this dirthole she'd resided in for the past five years.

Exhausted as he was, his heart picked up its pace at the thought. She'd said she didn't have a home in the United States. He intended to change that.

The radio squawked in his ear, interrupting his thoughts. "Welcome back to Afghanistan, gentlemen."

Wynn tapped him on the shoulder to get his attention. "Never thought I'd be glad to hear those words. How about you?"

Rad smiled and gave him a thumbs up sign, then laid his head back and closed his eyes.

When the helicopter touched down, the men loaded their gear into trucks and headed to a large hanger where CIA specialists waited to go through their bags. There were tables with food and coffee in the hangar, but the men were still all business as they dumped their contents on the appropriate tables and wrote down where they had found whatever they were unloading.

As Rad started to pull off his kit, he felt a stabbing pain in his shoulder.

"You caught some major frag, man." Wynn touched the wound. "Hurt?"

"Feels more like an axe blade than frag."

"Yeah, well you better get that arm looked at too, dude. You definitely got winged there."

Rad glanced down at his bloody shirt sleeve from when he'd gotten hit in the house. He'd forgotten all about it. "I'll get Crock. Just needs to be cleaned and wrapped."

"Radcliff, what the hell'd you do?" McDunna examined the bloody shirt sleeve. "Get your ass down to the infirmary."

"Not done here yet, sir." Rad continued to unload his gear.

"That *was* an order."

Rad's head jerked up to see if he was joking. He'd been taught to take care of team gear, then department gear, and then personal gear—always and in that order. It went without saying he considered his arm as personal gear. Just as he was getting ready to explain that, Wynn interrupted.

"I got this, Rad. Go get cleaned up."

"Good grief, dude." He shook his head. "It's just a scratch."

"Which one? The ding in your arm or the frag in your shoulder?" Wynn took him and turned him toward the door. "Tell them Mommy was worried and sent you. Go."

The sun was starting to come up by the time Rad had his arm cleaned up and a couple of pieces of glass removed from his shoulder. Just as he thought, the bullet had only nicked his arm, causing more blood than pain or damage—but the nurse in charge didn't see it that way. She'd insisted on IV fluids to get him rehydrated and wrapped his arm as if it had been detached and needed to be taped back on.

As it turned out, the timing was perfect. It had taken the guys more than an hour to unload and categorize all their intel, so they were just starting to gather around the fire pit and unwind. After a normal mission they probably would have hit the rack, but they were too keyed up for that.

"Here comes da man!" Bipp handed Rad a celebratory cigar. "Dude, you were the heat."

"Ah, my favorite. Romeo y Julieta No. 3." Rad took the cigar and inhaled deeply as he held it under his nose. "You guys rock."

"Glad to see they were able to save your arm, man." Wynn laughed at the size of the bandage.

"Yeah, got there just in time or I would have lost it for sure." Rad lowered himself onto the picnic table and pulled a soda out of a tub of ice. "Thanks, Mommy."

"Did you need mouth-to-mouth from Nurse Nancy?" Wink sat down beside him.

"She the blonde? With the big—"

"Umm hmm." Wink nodded. "Hands off."

"Sorry to break it to you, son, but you're probably a little young for her taste." Rad looked at him with a serious expression. "She was *all over* me."

That sent the entire group into peals of laughter.

"Seriously, dude, you kicked some ass back there." Bipp sat down on a lawn chair and lit his cigar. "But what the hell were you thinking going into that tunnel?"

"I was thinking we were running out of time to get that guy." Rad took Bipp's burning stogie and held it to his. After a few tokes it finally glowed red. "But frankly, if any of you guys would have done that on my watch, I would have kicked your ass."

"It was fucking crazy is what it was." Crockett opened a bag of chips and held them up. "Eat up, boys. Breakfast of champions."

"Any pushback from Pakistan yet?" Rad walked over to a chair and sat down, stretching his legs out in front of him as he enjoyed his cigar.

"I'm sure the shit is hitting the fan in Washington," Pops said. "The Pakis got wind of something going on and scrambled two F-16 Fighters—"

"With 30mm cannons and air-to-air missiles," Wink interrupted.

Rad's head jerked up. "No shit?" He gazed around the group and read the look in each man's eyes. Not one of them would hesitate to give his life for his country, but all were glad to have their feet on the ground. Getting blown out of the sky was not the way they wanted or expected to go.

"It's apparently all over the news back home." Pops took the bag of chips and grabbed a handful. "Annie asked me what was going on. Said the media's going wild."

Rad's brow tightened and he tilted his head. "The White House isn't releasing details I hope."

"Not yet," Wynn said. "We're taking bets on how long it will take the president—or vice president—to leak it."

It was common knowledge military troops were just tools in the president's publicity box. When things went well, he'd promote the success and greatly inflate his own role. Whether or not he would do it at the expense of the safety of others was yet to be seen.

Rad's thoughts turned to Lauren as the others continued their conversation about the mission. She would be starting her day, pretending she knew nothing about what happened across the street. But would they believe her?

"Yo, Rad. You still with us?"

Rad looked up at Wynn who was staring at him. "Crock wants to know if you carry a good luck charm."

"If I did, do you think I would tell you losers and risk getting all the luck rubbed off?" Rad smiled, but he was thinking about the gift from Lauren he always carried. He only wished it really was time in a bottle— that he could open it up right now and be transported to that day on the beach. He knew one thing for sure. He was never going on another mission without it.

TWENTY-THREE

Angela Powers heard the doorbell ring, and then the sound of the door opening and closing. "I'm out by the pool," she yelled. She assumed it was Jackie, who knew it was the housekeeper's day off.

A few moments later Jackie opened the sliding screen door and stepped out on the patio. "Nice office, Cuz."

Angela laughed but barely looked up from her computer. "Yeah, nice view, huh. Gerry re-did everything for my birthday."

Jackie stood with her hands on her hips taking in the scene of the small pool surrounded by a professionally designed garden. The patio was lined with lush potted plants and extravagant furniture, designed to feel like a room in the outdoors. "Not bad." She turned back to Angela. "What are you working on?"

When Angela didn't answer, Jackie glanced at the computer screen and leaned down for a closer look. "That's the girl from the beach."

Angela's head popped up and turned around in one movement. "Wait a minute. What?"

Jackie grabbed a grape from the center of the table, and then pulled out a chair as she put it in her mouth. "The girl from the beach I was telling you about. What's she doing in your picture?"

"Are you sure?" Angela turned the computer screen toward her so she could see.

"That's her. Don't tell me she traveled all the way to Afgannyland to see Rad."

"I think she was there in connection to whatever is going on." Angela leaned in closer. "If I can figure out what she's doing, maybe I can break this story after all."

"Oh, so you're an investigative journalist now?" Jackie snorted as if she found that amusing.

Angela shot her an angry glance. "I'll do what I have to do to break a story no one else has. Wait and see." She sat back and took a long sip of wine. "What'd you say her name was?"

Jackie closed her eyes. "Laura, maybe? No, Lauren."

"Lauren, what?"

"Heck if I know. I never heard anyone say her last name." Jackie looked around. "What does a person have to do to get a drink around here anyway?"

Angela waved her hand toward the bar. "Help yourself. I don't have wait staff."

"Really? You have to make your own drink?" Jackie laughed as she stood and poured some of Angela's husband's expensive scotch into a glass. "How are you and the senator getting along these days, anyway?"

"Who?"

"Your *husband*, the senator."

"Oh, fine." Angela leaned back over her computer, her mind obviously still on the images.

With a drink in her hand, Jackie walked back over to the table and glanced again at the photos Angela was skipping through. "This for a legitimate story, or are you practicing your bitchcraft again?"

"Bitchcraft?" Angela turned. "What's that supposed to mean?"

"You should know what it means, since you're the queen of it." Jackie chuckled good-naturedly. "I figured you would take it as a compliment."

Angela stood and poured another glass of wine at the bar. "People have the right to know what their military is doing."

"While they're doing it?" Jackie took a sip of scotch and grimaced. "Seems like it might be better to wait and do a story after the fact."

"You don't know much about the journalism profession." Angela sat back down. "It's all about being first."

"I stand corrected." Jackie gazed at her sideways. "And here I thought it was about being fair and objective."

"Like I said, you don't know much about the business." Angela leaned back over her computer, focused once again on the photos. "These shots make it appear fairly businesslike to me." She clicked through a couple of pictures, and then turned the computer toward Jackie. "Except maybe for this one."

The photo captured the moment when the helicopter was descending and the two subjects were shaking hands. The body language was professional and detached, but the expressions on their faces were not.

"Hmmm." Jackie continued to stare at the photo. "Rad's looking damn good. Can't believe you gave that up."

Angela's eyes narrowed angrily. "If I hadn't given *that* up, you'd be drinking Bud Light from a can instead of expensive scotch from a lead crystal glass."

Jackie rolled her eyes in such a way, she made it obvious she'd rather have Rad in her bed every night than an expensive house and a glass of scotch.

"Now that I have a name," Angela said, rubbing her hands together, "I should be able to get somewhere. This is going to be fun."

"Seriously, Angela." Jackie leaned forward with a hint of concern in her eyes. "Is this a real story or are you doing it because of Rad?"

Angela's smile disappeared. "What do you mean?"

"You're acting like you're jealous."

The glass of wine Angela held hit the table with a loud *clank*. "Jealous? *Me?*"

Jackie leaned back and crossed her arms. "Okay, maybe you're not jealous. Maybe it's more like, you can't have Rad anymore so you don't want anyone else to have him."

That elicited a loud round of laughter from Angela. "Believe me honey, if I wanted Rad, I could have him."

"Really? You didn't stay very long on your trip to Afghanistan, and as far as I know, you don't have anything more for a story than you did before you left."

Angela shot her a look of disapproval. "I didn't stay because military people are fanatical patriots who won't tell me anything. All my contacts are here." She put her hand on her glass but never picked it up. "And besides, you wouldn't believe the god-awful accommodations. No civilized person could last long there."

"Well, it doesn't sound like Rad was much help either."

"Then I gave you the wrong impression." Angela's eyes narrowed to mere slits. "Sure he was busy doing whatever it is he does, but he found the time to introduce me to his commanding officer."

"I don't suppose you threatened him with anything—like doing a story on what's going on over there."

"Maybe." She finally picked up her drink. "So?"

"So-o-o the subjects of your story are in a war zone." Jackie leaned forward and put her arms on the table. "Someone could get hurt."

"I can't be a babysitter and a journalist at the same time." Angela snorted. "Something big is getting ready to happen over there, and I need to report on it. It's not my job to worry about things like that."

"It's not your job to destroy lives either," Jackie said under her breath.

"What did you say?"

"Look, Angela." Jackie took a deep breath as if trying to choose her words carefully. "Why don't you pick another topic to make a name for yourself and leave Rad alone?"

"First of all, this isn't about Rad—it's about getting the biggest story of my career," Angela replied, her eyes flashing with anger. "And second of all, I'm beginning to think you have something for Rad."

Jackie laughed out loud. "I guess I'd have to be blind or dead not to. Why should you care? You're a married woman."

Angela merely shrugged as if she had no interest in the conversation.

"He's unattached, isn't he?" Jackie did not let her off the hook.

"I'm not sure." Angela leaned forward and stared at the photo she had cropped and enlarged to just the two faces gazing into each other's eyes. "I'm beginning to think maybe he's not."

TWENTY-FOUR

R ad sat in the operations center finishing up details from the after action review, grumbling over the amount of paperwork his job involved.

"Hey, Radcliff. Just the man I wanted to see." McDunna walked into the room and sat down at the table opposite him. "You guys are heading home tomorrow, I hear."

"Yeah, gotta get this shit done." Rad kept working, but when McDunna didn't say anything else, he looked up. "Anything wrong?"

"No, not really."

Rad slid the papers into a folder and pushed it to the side. Despite his CO's words, he could tell something most definitely *was* wrong.

"I don't know how much you keep up with what's going on back home." McDunna pulled a pack of cigarettes out of his pocket. "You know, with politics, I mean."

"Not much." Rad looked at him quizzically. "Politics are the least of my concerns."

"Well it's an election year."

"I do happen to know *that* much." Rad leaned his chair back on two legs, glad now for the break. "This got something to do with me?"

"Well, the White House is bragging about the mission." McDunna lit a cigarette and took a long drag. "You know, how the president ordered it and everything."

Rad could feel his blood pressure rise. "Ordered it? The idiot delayed it every step of the way. He couldn't have done more harm if he'd tried!"

"Yeah, well, you know how politicians are." McDunna stared at the ceiling and repeated the words he'd apparently read in a paper. "With the commander-in-chief's authority and under his direct command, a classic mission was conducted and brilliantly executed. This surgical operation, which showed precision, courage, and skill, could not have taken place without decisive decision-making from the White House."

"Wow. What a bunch of PR bullshit." Rad laughed. "Is that what you came to tell me?"

McDunna's face turned slightly red, and he moved restlessly in his seat as if he didn't know exactly what to say. "No, actually there's more."

Rad let his chair fall forward with a loud thump, his heart seeming to do the same. From the look on McDunna's face, this wasn't going to be good news..

"They ah, I mean, they didn't just leak a story that the president authorized and commanded the raid." He paused and stared at the smoke rising in the air for a moment as if trying to decide how to proceed. "I guess they wanted to give out some really juicy stuff for the news because they leaked that they authorized a spy in Pakistan who was responsible for identifying the target and the ultimate success of the raid."

Rad leaned forward and spoke in a low, grave voice. "But they got her out first."

McDunna stared at the folder on the table and shook his head.

"She's still in there?" The whooshing in Rad's ears made it almost impossible to concentrate or think. "Where?"

"That's the problem." McDunna tapped his fingers nervously on the desk. "No one knows."

Rad slammed his fist on the table and stood in one movement. "What do you mean no one knows?"

"They've lost communication." McDunna took a deep breath. "Look, calm down. You know it happens. It might not mean anything. I just wanted to tell you before you heard it somewhere else."

"Like on the news?"

McDunna stared silently out the window. "Yeah, like on the news."

"How many check-ins has she missed?"

"Three."

Rad started pacing. Missing one check wasn't too out of the ordinary. Things sometimes happened that made it better to lie low than communicate. Sometimes missing two was necessary. But three? With pulse-pounding certainty he knew. She was in trouble.

"I get the feeling you're in a little deeper with her than you let on to me."

Rad sat back down and leaned his forehead into his hands. "You asked me how long I knew her, and I told you I'd just met her once. That's the truth."

"Okay. Good," McDunna said.

"You didn't ask me if I planned to spend the rest of my life with her—but I do."

McDunna gazed at him intently with his head tilted. "You fell in love after one meeting?"

"I know, it's crazy. I can't explain it." Rad stood again. "Twist of fate. Grand design. Whatever. It happened. She's my heartbeat."

When he paused and noticed McDunna's face had turned a shade paler, he felt his heart flutter with something akin to panic. He took a deep steadying breath. "There's more, isn't there?"

McDunna sucked air into his lungs as if he wished he were anywhere but in this room. "Yeah, there's one more thing. Something that didn't make it into the debriefing on the mission."

Rad forced himself to breathe and pushed away the uncomfortable sensation of an icy hand closing around his throat. The elated sense he'd felt at being part of a successful mission seeped from his heart, replaced by a feeling of shock and fear. He tried to concentrate on the disastrous news he knew was coming, but his thoughts were moving so fast, everything started to blur.

"You okay?"

He looked up at McDunna, blinking his eyes to clear his head. "Yeah. Go ahead."

"Apparently a Paki military patrol saw or heard your choppers. Follow-up reports say a dozen fully loaded trucks were heading your way— enough to have kept you guys busy for a while and throw everything out of whack." He took a few long moments to crush out his cigarette in an ashtray. "Cantrell flagged them down. Told 'em she'd seen choppers landing and directed them down the wrong road."

Rad put his head in his hands again. "Geez-uz."

"You're familiar with the layout of that town. The road she sent them down was narrow and had a dead end, so by the time they got their trucks untangled, turned around, and straightened out, you guys were long gone."

Rad sat silently, assessing the international catastrophe that would have resulted if his men had gotten into a gun battle with Pakistani military. He had led an invasion into a sovereign country in order to eliminate one person. If any civilians or military personnel had been killed in carrying out the mission, if shots had even been fired, it would have become a crisis of monumental proportions.

He pictured Lauren standing perfectly calm in the midst of the enemy, while being aware of the choppers, the gunfire, and the chaos of battle simultaneously occurring down the street. Instinctively his hand went to his chest where he kept her hand scrawled note close to his heart. *Hey, Dude—Don't worry about me. Just kick some ass. I got it on this side. – L.C.*

He bit his lip and closed his eyes. *Lauren, why didn't you just stay where it was safe?"*

But he knew the answer to that. Her instinct to shield his men, to protect her country, was stronger than her own self-preservation. That kind of devotion to duty required more than simple resolve, more than just courage and rash audacity. She had literally placed her life on the line.

His mind drifted back to the piece of Berlin Wall at Ripley's museum. *Don't Go With The Flow.* He'd felt the power of those words as he gazed at them that day, and remembered feeling an inexplicable connection to Lauren when he'd seen the look of wonder and admiration the sentiment had evoked in her as well.

The sound of McDunna's voice brought him back from his thoughts.

"Yeah, so without the leak, it probably seemed like an innocent mistake. But now…"

"Then what are they waiting for? We need to do an extraction."

"That's impossible."

"Come on. We can have a spin-up team together in fifteen minutes." Rad leaped out of his chair and headed for the door.

"Slow down." McDunna's voice was severe. "Not in this political climate. Pakistan already has its hackles up over the kill and the way it was carried out."

"Fuck the politics!" Rad turned around, incredulous that McDunna could just sit there. "We're talking about an American life!"

McDunna winced when Rad swore, probably because he knew he didn't do it very often. He slid a file across the table. "Okay, fuck the politics. But she was under non-official cover. The United States has already officially denied any knowledge of her."

"But they sent her in there." Rad's heart jolted at the realization this administration would have no problem writing off a faceless operative who had given them the greatest victory of their lifetime.

"They sent her in there and told her there would be no help coming. She understood the consequences."

"But she—"

"She knew. Read the first page."

Rad opened the file, and his eyes flicked over the handwritten note clipped inside the front cover:

At the verbal request of Lauren Cantrell, no lives are to be put in danger with a rescue or extraction if kidnapped, captured, or otherwise endangered in Pakistan.

Rad's eyes blurred as he studied the date the missive was signed. He stood, threw his chair across the room, and then banged the table with his fist. "*Damn* her!"

"I'm sorry, but there's nothing we can do."

Rad nodded his head, thinking back to that day on the beach. He looked back over his shoulder at McDunna. "I was with her the day she had that put in her file. She took a phone call, made a decision like that— and then told me it was her fucking travel agent."

His commander took a deep breath. "Well, you of all people know what it's like to risk your life for your country. You do it every day."

Rad ran his hand through his hair and growled. "It's *not* the same. If I die, it will be with a bullet hole or two in me." He put his hands on the table and leaned toward McDunna. "They're going to kill her by inches, slow and deliberate."

McDunna closed his eyes and nodded but didn't bother to reply.

Rad's thoughts went back to the briefing and his snarky remark about having to do an extraction. No wonder she'd been so offended. She had gone out of her way to make sure no other lives would be put into danger. She'd been keenly aware of the difficult international situation the operation would entail and had not wanted any action taken that would jeopardize American lives or its standing.

Images of Lauren as he had last seen her arose unbidden before him. Her dark eyes had been full of fortitude, shining with steadfast and deliberate resolve when she'd climbed into the chopper. Had she known what was coming? Suspected it?

God has a plan for me, she'd told him at the landing zone in Afghanistan when they were waiting for the chopper. *It can't be changed. Only completed.*

The recollection of those chilling words practically made him shiver. She possessed an inexhaustible spirit of dauntless determination and surprising strength of will. The combination, he feared, could be a dangerous one.

Rad closed his eyes and winced when he thought of her reaction to the torture room at the Ripley museum and where she might be now. Courage and resilience were a part of her very being, but would they be enough to sustain her?

To face this danger and her greatest fears alone and without help was far more impressive than heroism on the battlefield where soldiers could depend on each other and their weaponry. She sacrificed all for her convictions and her country, her only consideration being the importance and magnitude of the mission.

"Fortitude and strength are powerful weapons." McDunna interrupted his thoughts with a tone that conveyed awe and respect. "Don't give up hope."

Rad headed to the door for some fresh air to clear his head. *Give up?* He would not rest until she was safely back in his arms. Reaching for the knob, he turned to McDunna with a look of fierce determination in his eyes.

"I promised her I'd see her again," is all he said before slamming shut the door.

TWENTY-FIVE

Half a world away, Angela Powers sat on the back veranda staring absently at the gardens and the pool in between sips of two hundred dollar-a-bottle wine. She thought she heard the sound of a car pull in but didn't bother getting up. The housekeeper was in today. If the bell rang, she would get it.

But the doorbell never rang. Instead, the front door slammed shut with enough force to cause the wine in her glass to tremble. She was about to get up and investigate when she heard the familiar sound of her husband's expensive shoes echoing through the hall and into the kitchen.

"What are you doing home so early, honey?" she asked innocently when he appeared in the doorway. "Sit down. I'll get you a drink."

"I guess you're proud of yourself."

Angela jerked her head back toward him when she heard his tone.

"Overall, yes." She could tell something was terribly wrong but didn't want to let on. Anyway, she wasn't really worried. She knew how to handle this man. "If you're talking about something in particular though, you'll have to share."

Senator Powers walked over to the outdoor bar and poured some scotch into a glass. "I guess you're proud you've single-handedly gotten a

U.S. spy captured by terrorists." He downed the entire glass in one gulp.

Angela blinked innocently. "What are you talking about?"

"You know damn well what I'm talking about, Angie." Powers poured himself another drink. "You ran with that story, knowing full well you were outing a spy, and now she's gone missing."

Angela set her glass down and exhaled with exasperation. "I simply did that story to give the girl the credit she was due. If she's gone missing, it's because of the career she chose—not anything I did. She knew the danger."

"She knew the danger of operating in a foreign country. She surely didn't know the danger of an insanely jealous woman who happens to be in the journalism field."

Angela pushed out her chair and stood. "How dare you make such an accusation!"

Senator Powers spoke calmly now. "It's not an accusation. It's the truth."

"You don't know what you're talking about, Gerry. I wouldn't have been able to get that story without the help of the White House." Angela lowered her voice. "You know that."

"Just because the White House leaks bits and pieces of a story to you doesn't mean you have to run with it and make up the other half."

Powers became so angry his voice quaked, making Angela feel a twinge of apprehension for the first time.

"Honey, I didn't make it up." She tried to calm him down. "I did the groundwork in Afghanistan and put two and two together."

When he didn't respond she walked up to him and put her hand on his arm. "Why can't you be proud of me for breaking the biggest story of the year?"

Powers growled in response and stamped back into the house. Angela gulped a few swallows of wine as she listened to him rummaging through his briefcase. When he returned, he dropped a file on the table without saying a word.

Her gaze dropped down to the folder, and then snapped back to meet his. "You can't be serious."

"If you would have had the decency to show some remorse, I might have reconsidered."

"Remorse?" Her voice rose in anger as she lowered her glass onto the table. "For doing my job?"

Powers shook his head and sighed. "You technically have thirty days to sign." He reached down and turned the page. "And you will see I've been very generous. But for every twenty-four hours you delay, the offer goes down substantially."

Angela took a step backward. "Do you think I'm a tramp who's going to walk quietly out of your life with a little payoff?"

Powers said nothing, but his silence spoke volumes.

Grabbing her wine glass, Angela hurled it at him. "Did you ever think of the scandal this will cause? What this will do to your career?"

"The scandal of divorcing you can't be half as bad as the one I created by being married to you." The senator picked up his coat, turned, and walked away.

"Where do you think you are going?" She ran after him.

"A hotel." He stopped. "Surely you don't think I'm going to stay here until this is legally over."

"You'll be sorry for this," she yelled after him. "I'll make you regret the way you've treated me."

"Take anything you want, Angie." He waved his hands in the air toward the paintings, the china, the furniture. "Just sign the papers and get out."

Angie heard the front door bang closed with thundering finality and contemplated her options. She wasn't that upset her marriage was breaking up. She'd never been in love with the man whose name she took. But the impact it would have on her career gave her pause. Being the senator's wife had opened doors, and now they were all closing with a bang.

But what could she do about it? He had the money and the power to fight her and could close all avenues to future employment if she pushed him. He knew it. And he knew she knew it. The quieter they both kept this, the better off both of them would be.

Angela's mind drifted back to Rad. She would be a free woman. And he was an unattached man. Very unattached if what her husband just told her was true.

She smiled to herself, walked over to the bar, and poured herself another drink.

TWENTY-SIX

Lauren thought she heard Rad's voice, and then watched him come into view, calm and unruffled, as if daring anyone to halt or delay him. Dressed in camo and armed to the teeth, he was all manhood and muscle, the very picture of a soldier. When his eyes met hers it was with an intensity that made her blush and a fearlessness that left her enthralled.

He held out his hand. "I told you I'd come." His voice was smooth and measured and deep—the voice of authority. She took his hand and suddenly he was no longer a soldier and they were no longer in Pakistan. They were walking along a lonely stretch of beach with water tugging at their ankles, talking and laughing and embracing life.

Running her tongue across her dry, cracked lips, Lauren swallowed the iron-tasting glob in her throat and awoke from the dream that had seemed so vivid and real. Breathing was difficult—and painful—so she tried to focus her thoughts on a part of her body that didn't hurt. But if there was an inch of bone or muscle that didn't involve a pulsing nerve screaming with pain, she couldn't find it today.

Despite the hurt, she lifted her hand to touch her eye, wanting to see if it was open or closed. The cell she lay in was dark and her face numb, making it impossible to tell. When her hand was almost there, it was forced to a jolting halt by a chain attached to her wrist and the floor. The pain that flashed through her when she got to the end of its length was excruciating, causing her to groan out loud.

She lowered her hand to her cheek, which felt swollen and pulpy beneath her touch. It struck her as funny that she wished no one would see her like this—hair dirty and stringy and caked in blood. She accepted that her death would be messy, but had hoped it wouldn't be public. The fact that her interrogations had been in English with a video camera running had pretty much dashed that hope.

Lauren sat up with great effort and leaned her back against the wall. The floor of the place where she sat must have been concrete once, but now only a few broken patches remained. For the most part, she felt only dirt and grime beneath her hands. The stench that emanated from the filth suggested this was not the first time it had been used as a prison cell.

But the nauseating aroma did not stop Lauren from attempting to take deep, slow breaths. *Mind over matter* she kept telling herself. The fact her cell was practically devoid of light provided some relief—no walls could be distinguished. For all she knew, the room was huge... perhaps even opulent and luxurious. She envisioned it as she wished it to be until at last the claustrophobic panic subsided.

Lauren tried to count the number of days she had been here. Two? Three? More? Time was lost to her now. But what did it matter? She had won. The man who had been responsible for planning the deaths of countless Americans had been eliminated. Her goal had been accomplished. Knowing no American lives had been lost in the effort and future lives would be saved, made her feel fortunate, not sorry, for her current circumstances. When she added up the lives avenged, the future lives that would never be lost, and the terror network reeling from the removal of their leader, she felt the tradeoff a fair one.

Added to that positive outcome was the intelligence likely gained by Rad and his men when they seized computers and communications from the house of a most-wanted terrorist.

At the thought of Rad, a tear unexpectedly squeezed through her eyelid to slide down Lauren's cheek. She remembered the briefing for the mission when her eyes had first fallen upon Pops. *Why is he here?* she remembered thinking. As realization set in, her eyes had sought Rad's and found them waiting. They were not carefree and relaxed as she had remembered them at the beach, but strong—so strong. Even from across the room she felt the intensity, the concern, the solemnity of his gaze.

Lauren laid her head against the wall and closed her eyes as the recollections rocked her. Despite her circumstances, she recalled the sensation of being held against his strong body; of his kiss, so slow and thoughtful—and surprisingly gentle. It was his ruggedness and vibrant power that had first attracted her to him, but his tenderness and calm authority had kept her entranced.

Drawing a deep breath, Lauren felt an agonizing twinge in her lungs. It wouldn't be long now. It couldn't be long—for the simple reason she couldn't take much more. With her vitality failing, a new pain ripped through her with an intensity that closed out all else.

Not willing to succumb to the pain, Lauren concentrated instead on the memory of Rad's shirt on her shoulders, the smell of it, and clung to that thought as she would a life preserver in a stormy sea. It would be a sweet consolation if she could have something of his to hold and feel—to die with—but she knew memories would have to sustain her now. Anyway, she could feel him with her. Feel him to the very marrow of her bones.

A sudden peace washed over Lauren, filling her heart with gratitude that God had shown her the path of duty and given her the strength to follow it. All the vitality and courage she would need for what was yet to come flowed from that Source. She'd asked to serve and she'd served. She felt the pride of it—and the weight of it.

Lauren drifted off while listening to the wind whine through the crevices of the walls. But as her thoughts returned to that distant beach, she recalled eyes full of expression and a gaze that felt like a caress. The roar of pain in her ears became the gentle roll of waves, her unconscious moans of agony, the gentle call of sea gulls.

Yet when she heard the voices of her captors approaching from outside, her body involuntarily shook despite her mental composure. She did not fear what was to come, but she wished it were over. No matter what happened in the hours or the days ahead, she held onto her one consolation.

One life in exchange for the hundreds saved.

I won.

"Our greatest glory is not in never falling, but in rising every time we fall."
— Confucius

PART III

NO PLACE
LIKE HOME

TWENTY-SEVEN

R ad heard his phone ring and blinked until he could make out the time—0200.

He closed his eyes before reaching for it. *This can't be good.*

"Radcliff here."

"It's McDunna, Rad. Get dressed and get down to HQ. We've got a meeting in twenty minutes.

Rad looked again at the time and tried to clear the sleep from his brain. "With who?"

"All kinds of high-ups… CIA mostly."

Rad sat straight up in bed. "They got something?"

"Apparently." McDunna was quiet for a moment. "I don't know if it's good or bad, Rad. You need to be prepared for the worst."

Again there was silence.

"You still there?"

"Yeah, I'm still here. I'll be there in fifteen."

Rad was already sliding into a pair of pants before he even hung up the phone and was in his truck and on the highway shortly after that. The crystal clear vibrancy of the sky drew his gaze heavenward, and he couldn't help but notice all the stars shimmering against the velvety blackness.

Please don't be up there, Lauren, he thought to himself as he remembered her words about angel eyes. *You can't be up there.*

No one introduced Rad when he entered the conference room or even seemed to notice he was there. There were ten men, most of them whispering in groups until one of them cleared his throat and told everyone to take a seat.

"Gentlemen, as you know, we are in a precarious situation here with an asset in a sovereign country and a fucked up mess for a press."

No one said anything or even cracked a smile.

"The pressure on Pakistan seems to be working. Of course, publicly they refuse to cooperate, which they have to do to appease the fanatics. But secretly they know they stand to lose a whole lot of money from the United States if they don't cooperate."

He stopped and took a drink of water from a bottle before continuing. "The Pakistani police raided a house along the border last evening and found the video I'm going to play for you. The CIA has a copy in Langley and is going over every image to see if they recognize anything. I ask that you do the same."

With that he picked up a remote control and hit the play button before walking over and dimming the lights. All eyes went to the small projection screen at the head of the table.

Rad's heart thumped once in his throat as he saw Lauren, sitting calmly at a table in a small, dimly-lit room. She wore a brown and tan headscarf, which accented her dark eyes and long lashes. Her arms were lying casually on the table before her.

From off camera a voice could be heard. Lauren answered the questions addressed to her in an indifferent tone and appeared relaxed and confident, seeming to be free of all knowledge or suspicion that any evil or danger confronted her.

Name. Aminah Umar.

"What do you do in Pakistan, Aminah?"

Before she could answer, the camera zoomed out so now both Lauren and the interviewer were in the picture. The man had a long, scraggly beard and dark, angry eyes. Rad gazed around to see if anyone at the table appeared to recognize him, but their faces were blank as they concentrated on the screen.

"I'm the Lady Health Visitor for this region."

"I see." The man's voice changed and sounded strangely cold now. "And how long have you been in this position?"

"A little over a year." Lauren sat back in her chair. Her relaxed posture spoke of boredom, but Rad knew the casualness on the surface masked something far more complex. "I volunteered at first because I—"

The man held up his hand and cut her off. "I see." He chuckled and began pacing in front of her. "Well, Aminah. I apologize for the inconvenience, but we cannot be too careful... you know?"

"Perfectly understandable," she said as she began to stand. "I assume I may return to my home now."

He studied her with slant-eyed hatred that he did not try to hide. "Not so fast. First my men must process your belongings."

The video flickered and went black before coming back to life. Rad's eyes narrowed as he stared at the image. There was a different interviewer standing in range of the camera now. It was impossible to tell how much time had elapsed, but Lauren's clothes appeared wrinkled and stained as if she had slept in them. Her hair was disheveled, and lines of fatigue marked her face. Never had he seen anything so frail and indomitable.

"Aminah Umar."

"Yes." Her voice cracked with exhaustion.

"What are you doing in my country?"

"I'm the Lady Health Visitor for this region." The words sounded mechanical, as if she had already repeated them a hundred times.

"And you take pictures?"

"Yes, sometimes I take pictures."

"Why is it Aminah Umar, you have pictures of these buildings?" The man threw a stack of photos in front of her.

She did not waver or hesitate. "I like the architecture." Her eyes went down to the table as if looking at what he had thrown there. "I take pictures of unique…"

He cut her off angrily. "Why is it Aminah Umar that this one—" He threw a photo on the table in front of her. "And this one—were attacked by your government's forces?"

"General Mohammad, I have attempted to explain to you that I…"

His voice rose with fury. "Do not say my name on video! Do you hear me? No more say my name on video!"

"I'm sorry," she replied, looking down. "I forgot."

There was no doubt she had overheard his name and said it on purpose, and that she did not think she was getting out of Pakistan to tell it to anyone in person. She was meeting her fate as Rad knew she would, demonstrating utter coolness in her hour of deadliest peril. Her emotional resilience was admirable… but it terrified him.

Lauren appeared to gaze down again at the photos before her. "But this one, sir… this hospital we are in, was not attacked." She held it as if to show him, but as she handed it to him she tilted it toward the camera. He grabbed it and ripped it to shreds.

"No more of your stupid tricks!"

The officer seated at the head of the table stopped the video and went back to the photo.

"We have a team working on this now. Anyone recognize the building she said is a hospital?"

It was blurry. No one did. But Rad was not looking at the building.

He was staring at her face, at her eyes, completely devoid of fear. Yet he could see in them the knowledge of impending doom as he stared at her face frozen in time.

Before the general restarted the video he gazed concernedly around the table. "This next segment... it is the last... and I must warn you it is graphic."

Rad saw McDunna glance sideways at him, but he kept his eyes on the screen.

When the video started again, Lauren was sitting in a chair at the same table, but her hands were now tied behind her back, and her face was bent down to her chest. She no longer wore civilian clothes, but the plain clothes of a prisoner, and these appeared torn and bloodied.

"Aminah Umar."

There was no answer.

"Aminah Umar."

"Yes," came the weak reply.

"I apologize if my men have been a little rough with you. They are not like American men, eh?"

He laughed when she failed to respond, but it sounded more sinister than humorous. Rad closed his eyes and clenched his fists on the table.

"I understand you are quite a fighter... but those tranquilizers quieted you down, eh?"

No one failed to notice that the target of his jests began to shiver. There was no sound for a few moments except the heavy breathing of the prisoner and the sickening sound of her teeth chattering with pain or repugnance.

"Would you be surprised to learn, Aminah Umar, that I watch CNN?"

It sounded like the interviewer was standing now and pacing back and forth in front of the table, but he could not be seen on camera. His voice seemed to be getting louder and angrier as he talked.

"And on CNN they talk about this spy who helped American forces kill my friend, Ahmed Hasan Arif." His voice sounded almost jovial now.

Rad felt all the blood in his body surge and throb in his head.

"And I think, no, it cannot be. Too much a coincidence that I have this innocent Aminah Umar who takes such nice picture." He laughed. "But then I see your picture... on the TV." He leaned across the table and pushed her head back violently so she was looking at him. "And I think, good news! *I have American spy!*"

Lauren's eyes were watchful and guarded now, as if depending on senses rather than thought. Yet the spark in them spoke of defiance without saying a word.

Her silence seemed to infuriate the man even more. "American woman," he spat, letting go of her head. "You wish now you stay home and be a good wife, eh? Act like a woman should? What you say to this?"

Lauren's forehead lowered again as if she were too tired to keep it up, but the words were easily understandable. "I knew the risks."

The man pounded his fist on the table.

"Yes, and you have encountered your risk... your *nightmare*." He appeared to think of something funny and began to laugh. "Do you know what Aminah means in my culture?"

Again she did not respond, but Rad entertained little doubt she had picked the name herself and knew well its meaning.

"Trustworthy. Faithful." The interrogator's voice grew loud again. "I believe you will wish you did not serve your country to ruin mine, my *faithful* friend."

Lauren lifted her head. "My country... will avenge any wrong." She talked painfully as blood dripped from a split lip.

So steadfast was her gaze, so calm and defiant her tone, it seemed to Rad she was speaking to each man in the room, acknowledging her probable demise and challenging them to action and vengeance on her behalf.

"Oh, no, no, no. You are wrong." The interviewer's voice sounded gleeful now. "We have contacted the American authorities. They will not admit even knowing you. Your people will not negotiate for your life."

"Didn't say... *negotiate*." She struggled to speak, yet her eyes showed no fear. "*Get even*."

The tape went to black as if the camera was turned off but soon flickered back to life. It appeared to be the same interview, but Lauren's forehead now rested on the table, not on her chest, and she was breathing hard as if she'd just run a race. Her hands remained tied behind her back.

"This is last time Aminah... *Last chance*. Understand?"

The loud, gasping sound of her panting breath was all that could be heard as she nodded weakly. Without warning, a man standing behind her wearing a dark mask jerked her head up by her hair. When the camera zoomed in, it took a strong man not to groan.

The left side of her face was so swollen the eye could not be seen. Her lips and mouth were bleeding and puffy as if she'd been punched. The right side of her face was purplish black and blue. There was little to recognize, save the spirit of that which was Lauren that flickered, albeit dimly, in her remaining eye.

"You understand?"

Her eye focused on the camera for a moment as if pondering how to respond. Then she turned her head slightly to the side and bent down to spit bright red fluid out of her mouth so she could speak.

"Yes." Her response was calm, but she began to cough violently as if trying to clear blood from her windpipe. When she was done, she rested her forehead on the table again as if too weak to lift it up.

"Listen to me now, spy. You answer me like this when I ask question. You read this." He stabbed a piece of paper with his finger. "You say 'I apologize for helping American soldiers kill innocent Pakistani people.' You say, 'I am sorry the infidel Americans make war with sovereign country.'"

He paused a moment as if watching her try to breathe. "Then, Aminah Umar, you say this, and we let you go home."

The sound of rustling paper could be heard as if they were placing the paper so Lauren could read it for the camera, without it being seen. Rad held his breath as he watched Lauren nod with her head still resting on the table.

When the man pulled her head back up with a jerk, her eye drifted away from the camera, apparently toward the script she was being commanded to read. Again, she showed no sign of fear. Yet neither did she show any sign of hope.

Rad found himself leaning forward, breathless, a low roar building in his ears. *Do it Lauren. For the love of God, just to do it.*

But deep inside he knew this was not a woman who would consent to being used as propaganda by the enemy as long as breath remained. His heart beat frantically for what was about to come on a piece of recorded video that he knew was now part of the past. Something inside him tried to prepare his mind for the possibility he was watching her last moments on earth.

"Lauren Cantrell of the USA, I ask you to tell the world—" The interrogator's voice was so angry and loud it cracked. *"What are you doing in MY COUNTRY?"*

The man behind Lauren pulled her head back further, which caused her to jerk with a painful, reflexive wince. Otherwise, her face appeared completely unemotional as she stared at the piece of paper.

You could have heard a pin drop in the conference room as every man leaned forward and drew a collective breath. No one expected the loud, clear voice that came out of the battered prisoner as she shifted her gaze away from the paper she was supposed to read and instead looked calmly into the camera with an expression so impassioned, it both comforted and alarmed everyone watching.

"PROUDLY… DYING… for MINE!"

She had just enough time to spit a mouthful of bloody saliva in the direction of the interrogator before her head was slammed into the table from behind with such violent force that it lifted her out of the chair and sent a spray of fresh blood running in crimson droplets down the glass of the camera lens. Her body went instantly limp, as if it were suddenly filled with nothing but sand, and slid lifelessly to the cement below.

There were a few excited and angry voices in the background as the camera jerked and then panned down to the unmoving figure lying in an unnatural position on the dirty floor. A pool of dark blood had already formed beside her parted lips and under her nose, and was running in tiny rivulets to coagulate in her hair.

Rad leaned forward to see if she was breathing, but the tape came to an abrupt end and the screen went black as if a piece of light had left the world.

Not a man in the room moved. No one it seemed even breathed. Many had closed their eyes in shock and disbelief. Veteran military men who had witnessed the destruction and ravishes of the battlefield were sickened beyond words and appeared incapable of speaking.

Rad stood abruptly and walked outside where he vomited off the side of the porch. Everyone within knew it wasn't what he had just seen that had made him physically ill. It was the fact there wasn't a damn thing he could do about it.

TWENTY-EIGHT

One week later

R ad picked up his vibrating phone and saw it was McDunna. "What's up?"

"We may have something. Get up here."

Click.

Rad jumped in his truck and drove faster than he should have, bursting through the office door in less than ten minutes. McDunna appeared mildly surprised but didn't wait for formalities.

"They picked up some communication with Afghanistan."

"What does that mean?" Rad asked impatiently.

McDunna paused a moment to light a cigarette. "The CIA thinks the White House has put enough pressure on Pakistan that they don't want the liability anymore. They likely sold Cantrell to the Taliban and are going to be moving her.

Rad's heart sank and rose all at the same time. She was still alive. And if she made it to Afghanistan they had a chance of getting to her. But what the Taliban would do to her was unthinkable.

"When do I leave?"

McDunna took a deep breath and blew smoke out slowly. "The in-country team will be handling this one. I'm not sure you should be involved, attached as you are."

Rad could not have felt more pain or raw torment if someone had just stabbed him in the heart with a dull blade. "You can't be serious."

McDunna lifted his gaze and stared at him with slit-eyed scrutiny, seeming to rethink his decision. "Jenkins is the lead on this. If I let you go and he says pull out and you don't have her, you sure as hell better follow his orders."

Rad swallowed hard. He did not even allow himself to contemplate the possibility they would not have her. "Yes, sir. I will."

Rad was in the air that same day while a plan was being prepared with a rushed special operations tempo. The adrenaline surge and anxiety he felt for this mission was stronger than usual, making the plane ride feel like days.

Once on the ground and back in familiar territory he felt a little more in control, even though in reality he was in limbo. All action and orders were out of his hands now. Being acquainted with Jenkins from a previous mission, Rad had no trouble assimilating into his command, but Jenkins made it clear Rad's job was to ID the prisoner and otherwise lie low.

There was nothing he could do but wait…and try to force down the dull ache of foreboding that threatened to overtake him. The old saying, "so close, yet so far away," had never so accurately reflected his circumstances. Missions like this had a way of stalling or even dissolving before they made it off the ground. And even if everything did move as planned, there would be no do-overs. As usual, everything had to go perfectly

After a few more days of intercepted phone calls, it appeared the operation was going to be a go. The kidnappers would be taking their "package" through the Khyber Pass, mixing in with a wagon train of farmers transporting their produce. When the line of farmers made it completely out of Pakistan, a unit of Marines would temporarily close up the pass behind them while Jenkins' men would search the wagons for the special cargo they were seeking.

Once the wheels of the operation started turning, everything began to unfold at lightning speed. Rad and the team were dropped in the area under cover of darkness and watched the caravan proceed through the valley. When the word came to move, they used trucks and all-terrain vehicles to stop and surround the procession of wagons, carts, and donkeys loaded down with produce. Half of the men formed a security perimeter while the rest began to round up the farmers and go through the wagons.

After about forty-five minutes Rad started to worry, and fifteen minutes later, he was practically distraught.

"We got nothing here," Jenkins said over the mic. "False alarm. Let's go."

Rad stood firm, his gaze moving up and down the line. She had to be here. These guys were too jumpy to just be transporting vegetables over the mountains. He noticed two men standing nervously beside one wagon, their eyes shifting and darting from the ground to the wagon.

"Let's go. Move out!" Jenkins said again. "That means you too Radcliff."

Rad kept walking toward the wagon. He put his hand inside and moved some of the produce around, but like the others who had searched it before, found nothing.

"Move out Radcliff, or I'm reporting you. Now!"

Rad bent down and examined the bottom of the wagon. Nothing out of the ordinary there either. He went to stand back up and noticed his hand was wet where he had laid it against the side for balance. When he studied his fingers, he saw they were sticky and pinkish. Leaning back down, he ran his hand over the corner. It came back red.

"I need a crowbar over here." Rad turned and motioned toward Jenkins, and held up his hand to show the blood. "This thing has a false bottom."

An operator ran over with a crow bar while others threw vegetables from the wagon right and left by the armful. Still others on the team moved forward to help corral the supposed-farmers who were now chattering angrily, as the creak and splintering of wood ripped through the air. "We got something!"

Jenkins leaned in, holding a photo. He stared at the form lying in the small cavity of the wagon, but then turned to Rad. "Can you tell it's her?"

The face of the person lying in the pool of blood was completely unrecognizable. The eyes were closed and swollen, the mouth bloody and shredded. Her cheeks were bulging, yet there did not seem to be any bones to support them. One tooth was cracked and two were missing.

Rad noticed her bare feet sticking out and picked up a foot. Seeing the crooked toe, and small patches of nail polish, he primed his mic for all to hear. "It's her. Positive ID."

The other men in the team quickly herded up the farmers, while others spread out in a defensive position. The roar of a helicopter landing about one hundred yards away seemed to occur simultaneously.

Picking her up as gingerly has he could, Rad ran toward the chopper with his precious cargo, all the while thinking, *My God, she weighs less than my ruck pack. There's nothing left of her.*

In full kit and body armor, Rad ran across the uneven terrain, trying not to stumble and go down. He heard sporadic gunfire, but it sounded like it was from a distance or coming to him through water. *Guess the Taliban paid for their package and aren't going to let it go without a fight.*

Rad knew the men behind him were prepared for that situation. He kept churning his legs despite the bullets now kicking up dust at his feet. *Got to make it to the chopper*, he kept telling himself. *No matter what.*

Now the gunfire was unmistakable and growing louder. Rad fought the urge to look over his shoulder to see what was happening behind him. Instead, he put his head down and ran even faster until a sudden spurt of fire and pain in his thigh caused his knee to twist, buckle and hit the ground. Stumbling to his feet despite the pain, he tried to keep his legs moving, but that was no longer possible. His right leg crumpled beneath him at every step, so he had to sort of hop and drag it behind him.

Rocks and dirt continued to spray around Rad's boots as gunfire tore up the ground around him. Every step was agony. His lungs felt like they were about to burst, and yet it seemed like he was running in slow motion. He looked up and saw hands in the helicopter waving him on, and then felt their firm grasp as they pulled him inside just as the chopper lifted off the ground. The gunfire continued but was drowned out by the sound of the blades slicing the air as the chopper struggled to gain altitude in the thin mountain air.

"Holy shit," he heard someone say as they pulled Lauren out of his arms and onto a backboard. "This ain't good."

Rad lifted his head and watched three men on their knees working silently and quickly over her as another pushed Rad gently down and began cutting away what was left of his pants. He struggled to sit up, to see if she'd been hit by the gunfire, but the world tilted sideways as if the helicopter had suddenly become a ship rolling in thick ocean swells. He felt his head loll to the side and his stomach lurch. Pain flared and pulsed in his leg.

"Take it easy, soldier." The medic pushed him down. "You're losing a lot of blood."

"Is she okay?" Rad thought he asked the question out loud, but no one answered. Instead he heard the medic who was leaning over him say to his comrades in a loud but calm voice, "I need some help over here."

Rad wanted to argue, to tell them to keep working on Lauren, but a sudden surge of nausea and dizziness made it difficult to hold his eyes open. He heard a muffled roar in his ears and thought at first the helicopter was having engine trouble. The next moment he thought it was the sound of angry waves violently hitting the beach. At last, he realized it was the sound of his own panting, echoing and reverberating in his ears in a way that made him shake his head to rid himself of the confusion.

"Stay with me, soldier." The sound of the medic's voice came to him as if through a dense fog, followed by the slight sting of a needle as someone put an IV in his arm. Other voices seemed to be talking over him now, but they were indistinct, like listening to a conference call with a bad connection.

Why aren't they helping her? Rad curled his right hand into a fist as it lay on the floor of the chopper and felt something sticky and warm and wet. Lots of it.

"Once you get that one going, start another line." The voice broke through the distortion, but Rad didn't know what it meant. "I'll be damned if I'm going to have two DOA's on the same flight."

These words Rad somehow processed and he struggled to sit up. "Jesus, is she okay?" Again, he thought he asked the question out loud, but the voices hovering over him never replied. Their tones simply grew more anxious. "Stay with me, brother. Can you hear me? Stay with me."

Rad heard them but couldn't find the strength to respond. He was being sucked into a deep, black void and had to use all his energy to fight it. He tried to reach out and grab onto something, but his arms wouldn't move, and anyway, there was nothing to grab. He was being swept along in a sea of dark, swirling water that carried him closer and closer to a giant abyss. The medic's voice came to him again, this time more urgent. "Stay with me, man!"

Rad struggled to open his eyes, to stay conscious, to take another breath. *I don't think I can,* he thought just as a roiling wave swept over him, spinning and swirling him down, down, down, into the depthless hole.

TWENTY-NINE

R ad slowly became aware of light against his eyelids and the muffled sound of someone moving around the room. He moved his
fingers and felt sheets but could tell he was not in his own bed.

When he finally mustered the strength to open his eyes, a young woman stood over him, smiling.

"Are you awake?"

Rad blinked and tried to focus his vision on the speaker. He wanted to
speak but found an impenetrable wall between will and action.

"I'm Donna. You're at Walter Reed. Do you remember how you got
here?"

Rad stared over her shoulder blankly a moment without responding,
trying to clear his head from the hazy images that seemed caught in a
sticky web.

"Lauren," he finally said.

When there was no response from the nurse, his gaze drifted back to
her.

"Lauren," he repeated. "Where?"

"Is that your wife?" The nurse sounded confused. "I'm sure she's
been contacted."

Rad closed his eyes in order to summon the strength to talk. "On the chopper." He ran his tongue over his dry lips and swallowed. "Rescued. Where is she?"

"Radcliff, I see you've finally decided to rejoin the living."

Rad turned his head painfully and watched a good-looking blonde with a folder in her hand and a stethoscope hanging around her neck walk into the room.

"I'm Dr. Bradley. Lindsey Bradley. How ya feeling?"

Rad ignored the warm greeting. "Lauren. She okay?"

"Hello or nice to meet you might be a more appropriate way to greet someone who's been working night and day to save your life." The woman's tone was gentle even if her words were not. She reached for his wrist and proceeded to take his pulse.

Rad struggled to sit up. "Is she okay? Was she hit?"

"Whoa, cowboy." Dr. Bradley put a restraining hand on his shoulder and pushed him back down. Looking up over her glasses she asked the nurse, "Is he talking about his wife or what?"

The nurse shrugged. "I'm not sure."

Rad's hands curled into fists as he looked from one to the other. "What the hell is going on?"

Dr. Bradley kept her hand on his arm and sat down in the chair beside him. When she leaned in, he caught the faint scent of her perfume. "You're pretty heavily sedated Radcliff. Maybe you're a little mixed up."

Rad bristled at the insinuation as she bent over with a stethoscope and listened to his heart and lungs. "Why am I here?"

Dr. Bradley remained silent a moment as she finished checking his vitals. Then she leaned back in her chair. "You were hit in the thigh with a bullet that ripped you apart to the bone and ruptured your femoral artery. You subsequently almost bled to death on the hop."

Without thinking, Rad reached down to feel his leg, to make sure it was still there.

"Yes, we saved it," Dr. Bradley said. "But it was touch and go for a while."

"How long?"

"How long, what?"

"How long have I been here?"

"You spent a day in a field hospital getting stabilized, then went to Germany where you had your first surgery." She paused a moment, seeming to study his blank stare. "And you've been here about ten days."

Rad focused his attention on her. "Ten days?" He struggled to sit up again. "Where's Lauren?"

Dr. Bradley pushed him back down and sighed heavily. "Tell me who Lauren is."

Rad winched at the pain induced when he turned his head fully toward her, his brow wrinkled in confusion. "She was on the chopper with me."

He watched Dr. Bradley make eye contact with the nurse, then lower her gaze to the folder she carried.

"I'm sorry, but there's no record of any other injured combatants coming in with you."

Rad closed his eyes and tried again to clear his groggy mind. *Maybe it is a drug-induced dream. Maybe she hasn't been rescued at all. Maybe...*

But then he remembered holding her in his arms, running to the helicopter, the pain when he was hit. It had to be real.

Rad moved his attention to the doctor again and studied her intently. Was she lying? Was she afraid to tell him the truth? He reached out and touched her arm. "Level with me. Is she dead?"

The doctor still did not raise her gaze to meet his. "Here's something." She appeared to be reading from the file. "It says here you were injured in a routine live-fire training accident."

Rad's eyes widened. "*Training* accident?"

He took a deep breath as he grasped two reasons why that would be placed in his chart. Either Lauren Cantrell survived the ordeal and the government didn't want anyone to know the rescue had taken place—or she had not and they wanted to make it appear she had never existed. His pulse began pounding in his ears as he thought about the latter, and then a machine beside his bed started beeping with an alarm that surpassed the loudness and intensity of his throbbing heart.

"I need to talk to my CO," he said impatiently.

"You need to calm down is what you need to do." Dr. Bradley nodded to the nurse who pushed a button on the machine, silencing the alarm. "See what you're doing to yourself?"

"I need to talk to my CO," Rad repeated. When there was no response, he reached up and wrapped his fingers around the doctor's wrist. "Right away."

Dr. Bradley gave him a serious and sympathetic smile. "Okay. As soon as you wake up."

He blinked in confusion. "I *am* awake."

"You won't be in another few minutes." She nodded to the nurse who stood near his IV bag with a syringe.

"No! No! Don't!" The sound of his voice made his head pound like it was in a torture device and caused the machine to start beeping again.

"I'm sorry," Dr. Bradley said, "but you're scheduled for another surgery on your leg. In the meantime, I'll look into the missing Lauren."

Rad thought by the tone of her voice she knew more than she was admitting, but he had no time to dwell on it. He fought with every ounce of strength to combat the effect of the drug, but it was no use. He looked up pleadingly at the nurse, then at the empty syringe, and remembered nothing more.

Rad lay in his bed two days later staring at the ceiling when he heard someone enter the room.

"Did you have a nice talk with your CO?" Dr. Bradley said the words lightly as if the two of them were friends who had known each other for years.

Rad shrugged. "I guess."

"I take it he couldn't tell you anything."

"Nothing I didn't already know."

Dr. Bradley sighed and sat down. "I'm sorry about the other day. The surgery was scheduled. There was nothing I could do."

Rad didn't respond.

"Well, look what I brought you." She stood and pushed the wheelchair a little closer to the bed. "I thought a nice spin in the courtyard would do you good."

"A wheelchair?" Rad stared at it for a moment, and then raised his gaze to meet hers. "No thank you."

Dr. Bradley shook her head. "Look, superman. Your leg was blown apart and you basically bled out on the way here, so no need to feel like a weakling for sitting in a wheelchair for a few weeks."

Rad just turned away. He was tired of arguing with her. All he wanted to do was get out of the hospital so he could start looking for Lauren. McDunna had promised him he was doing everything in his power to find her, but Rad wanted to do more.

"Your chart says you're not eating much."

Rad didn't know if she was trying to make conversation or actually wanted to discuss his eating habits. "Maybe it should tell you I'm not hungry."

When he looked up at her silence, she was biting her lip.

"I'm trying to make you better so you can get out of here."

"Here's an idea." He turned his head away and stared at the ceiling as he talked. "If I could get out of here, I would probably eat—and then I would feel better."

"Radcliff, if you think I'm going to partake in your pity party, you are grossly mistaken. The only way you are going to get out of here is if your health improves. And the only way your health is going to improve is if you eat."

The phone on the stand beside Rad rang, and Dr. Bradley reached down and answered it. "Hello?" She looked at Rad sternly. "Yes, he's here. Hold on."

She handed him the phone. "It's someone named Wynn."

Rad took the phone. "Hey, brother. When you coming to break me out of this joint?"

He watched Dr. Bradley roll her eyes, and then proceeded to talk to Wynn as if she were no longer in the room.

"Yeah, that was my doctor." He cocked his head to the side and squinted as he stared her. "Yeah, I guess so. She's kind of tall, blonde… What's she wearing?" Again he studied the doctor, who was wearing navy blue scrubs. "Right now she's got on this little short skirt and heels. Yes, high heels. Red. They match her lipstick."

Not pausing in his conversation, Rad said, "Hold on, I'll ask." He smiled and moved the phone away from his mouth. "He wants to know if you give sponge baths."

Dr. Bradley grabbed the phone. "When can you come get him?"

She handed the phone back to Rad and turned to leave. "I'm going to see about getting your discharge papers together. You'll be moving to a rehab building. I'll make a call to warn the staff."

THIRTY

Wynn sat at a table in the exclusive Georgetown pub, squeezed in between Heather on one side and Rad on the other. Joining them in the celebration of Rad's release from Walter Reed were Pops and Annie, Reese, Crockett, Bipp and Holly. They had all decided to splurge for a night of good food and good company over drinks in Washington, DC.

A fireplace blazed along the far wall, giving off a warm glow that danced and shimmered in concert with the soft light of the candles at their table and in every window. The mantel was draped with boughs of pine decorated with red ribbons, and a large Christmas tree dominated one corner. It was homey and festive and warm.

Wynn lifted his nearly empty glass into the air. "To brothers," he said as glasses clinked together. "To friendship," Heather added as the clinking continued.

"I'll drink to that." Rad lifted his glass unsteadily, killed it in one swallow, and then set it down with a resounding *clank*.

Heather touched Wynn's arm. "I need a refill. Let's go to the bar."

"I'll just grab a—" Wynn turned to wave down a waitress but felt Heather kick him under the table. "Yeah, you're right," he said, giving her a questioning look. "Let's go the bar. It's probably quicker."

Guiding his fiancée through the crowd with his hand on the small of her back, he leaned down and whispered, "What's up?"

"I don't think Rad is his old self. I'm worried about him."

Wynn laughed as he leaned on the bar and hailed a bartender from the other end. "He almost lost his leg—and his life—a month ago. He's not one hundred percent yet."

"It's not his leg," Heather said as he ordered the drinks. "It's Lauren. Isn't there anything you guys can do?"

"Believe me, we've been trying to move heaven and earth but it's not easy dealing with that type of bureaucracy." He paid for the drinks and turned to head back to the table. "I know what you mean though. It's like the spark has gone out of his eyes."

"It's worse than that." Heather took her drink from his hand. "I'm worried about him. His heart is so big and it's breaking. You can see the pain on his face. I'm afraid he'll do something crazy."

"I'll have a talk with him." Wynn paused a moment to let someone squeeze by and had walked only a few steps more before he froze in place, causing Heather to almost collide with him. "Holy *shit.*"

When Heather followed his gaze to the doorway, her reaction was even stronger. "Fu-u-ck."

Wynn stared down at her and smiled. "Damn, Heather. I've never heard you say that word before. Ever."

"I've never had reason to use it." Heather put her hand on her stomach. "I think I'm going to be sick."

Standing in the doorway, looking like an actress arriving on stage, was none other than Angela Powers with her cousin Jackie at her side. Dressed to the nines in a tight red dress with matching shoes, she looked like she had just stepped out of a fashion catalog.

Wynn didn't know whether to be angry or amused, but decided on the latter. Angie might be able to manipulate and coerce Washington insiders, but the guys at the table in the corner were not going to fall for her sweet talk and flattery. If she wanted to try playing with the big boys, it might be fun to watch her getting taught a lesson she would never forget.

"Oh, come on. Play along." Wynn nudged Heather with his elbow. "This should be good."

Angela's eyes roam the room as if seeking someone. When she spotted the table, she moved through the crowd slowly and regally as if she were a celebrity walking down the red carpet. The only things missing to complete that picture were flashing cameras and an adoring crowd.

"Poor, Rad," Heather whispered as Angela went straight to his chair, leaned down, and kissed him on the cheek.

By the time Wynn and Heather made their way back to the table through the crowd, Angela and Jackie had helped themselves to their two empty chairs.

"Oh, look," Angela said when she saw them, "the whole gang is here." Even though it was obvious she had taken the couple's seats, she made no effort to move. Instead, she waved down a waitress and ordered two drinks as if she were simply a late-arriving guest.

"I hear you guys really kicked some ass over there." She kind of leaned into Rad. "I'm sorry about your injuries during that rescue. I hope you're recovery is going smoothly."

Wynn watched Rad's hand tighten around his glass, but he made no comment. Neither did anyone else. In fact, if the people sitting around the table had been the only ones in the room, you could have heard a pin drop.

"What *rescue* is that?" Since no one else seemed capable of speaking, Wynn decided to see how much she knew. He casually pulled a chair from another table for Heather, and then found one for himself.

Angela didn't blink as she gazed around the table at the serious faces.

"Oh," she said, putting her hand across her mouth dramatically, "maybe I'm not supposed to know that."

Just then the waitress brought the new arrivals' drinks and the table grew silent again. Wynn studied Angela as he tried to figure out her motive in divulging highly classified information to this group of men. He knew her well enough to comprehend she hadn't dropped that bombshell by accident. The question was, did she know more? Like where Lauren was? Or was she bluffing because she wanted something? Like, Rad. The news of her sudden divorce from Senator Powers had just started to hit the news.

"Hey, brother," Wynn said, looking at Rad and playing dumb, "I thought your records said it was a training accident."

Rad's chest was rising and falling as if he'd just run a sprint. His gaze drifted from the wall he'd been staring at to Wynn. "Yeah, that's what the official record says."

Angela cackled with laughter. "When will you boys learn that *classified* information doesn't mean anything as long as you have sources in high places?" She took a long, leisurely sip of her drink. "Doctors, lawyers, politicians—it's all in who you know."

"Things are classified for a reason," Heather said icily. "Like to protect innocent people from those who would intentionally do them harm simply to get ahead in their career."

This time it was Wynn who kicked Heather under the table.

Angela's eyes slanted into mere slits as she stared at Heather. "I don't know what you're trying to insinuate, but I don't like your tone."

"Calm down, Angela." Wynn leaned forward. "She's not insinuating anything—"

"That's right. She's not *insinuating* anything." Pops didn't let Wynn finish. "She's merely stating the fact that if it weren't for you, nobody would have been taken captive and Rad wouldn't have been injured rescuing them. That's all."

Angela's drink hit the table with a loud bang. "How dare you!" She looked at Rad as if he should do something, and do something he did.

"Back off, guys," he said. "Leave Angie alone."

Wynn had to work hard to suppress a smile. He knew Angie was one smart cookie, but she was sitting with a tableful of seasoned interrogators. They all wanted to find out what she was hiding, but understood she wasn't the type who could be threatened or intimidated. That would just make her dig in. No. She needed to be coddled and massaged, made to believe she was the one in charge.

Pops had taken the first step to reel her in using the "bad cop" ruse, and Rad was going in for the kill as the "good cop."

"This is a celebration, and I propose a toast." Rad held his glass in the air. "Here's to getting the job done." He clinked his glass against Angie's. "No matter one's occupation."

All the guys at the table smiled and raised their glasses, understanding the scheme, while the wives and girlfriends appeared bewildered and confused, refusing to take part in the toast.

Rad waved at the waitress. "A round for the table, on me." She nodded, but he grabbed her arm before she walked away. "Make mine a double this time."

Drinks continued to flow, and although the conversation was more stilted since Angie's arrival, there were plenty of stories about the good 'ole days and exploits that grew more daring and dangerous each time they were told.

Rad leaned back and grimaced when his leg hit the table.

"You poor thing." Angie put her hand on his thigh. "I hope it's not too painful."

Rad actually winced when her hand made contact, and Wynn knew it wasn't from the pain of the injury—it was from the amount of self-control it took not to forcefully remove her hand from his leg and her body from the room.

"It's not bad," he croaked.

"Well, you helped save a life. At least it wasn't in vain." Angie turned to say something to Jackie, but it felt like everyone else at the table sucked in a deep breath. Rad's head turned slowly toward Wynn, and the expression on his face showed new hope mixed with heightened desperation. It was heartrending.

Wynn closed his eyes. *So help me God, Angie, if you are pretending to know something or are lying, I will kill you with my own two hands.*

"I went to school with a doctor who works at Walter Reed, so I know they took good care of you." Angie went on talking, changing the subject from doctors to stories of her college years, apparently taking great delight in seeing how engrossed everyone was in what she was saying.

After knocking off the last of his drink and setting his empty glass down unsteadily again, Rad leaned back in his chair and put his arm carelessly around the back of Angela's chair.

"So you going to do a follow-up story or anything?"

"On what, honey?"

Wynn put his hands under the table as they curled into fists. He had never hit a woman before, but Angela was testing him. Severely.

"Oh, that spy." She picked up her glass and took a sip. "I haven't thought about it, but that's a good idea."

She set her glass down. "On second thought, it's probably impossible."

Everybody's gaze zeroed in on her.

"Why?" A flicker of tortured agony crossed Rad's gaze and then vanished.

"She's got a new identity now. A new life. Don't you think? That's what they do with people like her, right?" She turned to Jackie and winked. "I mean, she could be just down the street right now and who would know?"

Rad leaned back in his chair and laughed. It was superb acting because everyone knew how much he was hurting.

"We need to get going." Wynn stood and pulled out Heather's chair. He knew the longer the night went on, the more anxious Rad would become, but they had to go slow. One wrong move, and Angie would clam up. The interrogation could continue another day when minds were clearer and they had a plan in place.

"Already?" Angie looked at her watch.

"Come on, Rad, I'll give you a lift." Wynn helped Rad out of his chair, and then handed him his cane. "You okay to walk? I don't want you falling and breaking that."

"I'm fine."

"I can give you a lift to the hotel if Wynn's car is full," Angie said. "I practically go right by it to get home."

The hustle and bustle of everyone grabbing their belongings and pushing in chairs stopped as they waited for Rad to answer. They all knew he was pretty well plowed. Getting information out of Angie was one thing. Going to bed with her to get it, another.

"Wynn will take me."

Rad never had a problem sleeping on a rattling, old C-130, or in a hard bunk bed in a barracks, or even on the cold, hard ground in the middle of winter. But try as he might, he couldn't seem to fall asleep in the five-star hotel room in Washington, D.C., that Wynn and Heather had booked for him.

He tossed and turned, trying to quiet the voices in his head and to stop the images that appeared from the deepest recesses of his mind. It felt like he was watching a television set that kept changing the channels and wouldn't turn off.

It probably didn't help that he had consumed too much alcohol at the restaurant, and the room was still spinning. But the whiskey had been the only thing stopping him from picking Angie up and throwing her out on the sidewalk. The fact she felt no remorse for her actions just added to his anger. In *her* mind, jeopardizing an American life was an indirect consequence of breaking a big story. The ends justified the means.

But now he had to figure out if she knew anything or was just playing him. It didn't take any great knowledge of her character to know she'd string someone along if it meant getting what she wanted—and she'd made it pretty clear tonight she wanted *him*.

He reached for the remote control and turned on the TV, hoping the background noise would help him sleep. How much more of this could he take? He'd pursued every lead and called in every favor from friends he had in the DOD, CIA, and DHS ever since he'd awakened at Walter Reed. Now that he'd been released he planned to bang on doors—or knock *down* doors—of politicians who wouldn't give him the time of day on the phone. He even intended to make an unannounced visit to Senator Gerald Powers.

But maybe none of that would be necessary. Maybe the one who had caused the whole tragedy, would be the one to help him find Lauren. He continued going over everything Angie had said, wondering if she had dropped a clue they all had missed.

Rad closed his eyes and tried again to relax. One of the sequences that kept replaying in his mind was the time he'd gone for a spin in the wheelchair at the hospital. Deciding to explore, he'd taken the elevator to the upper floor and run into Dr. Bradley in the hall. She'd seemed flustered to discover him there and had even escorted him back down. It hadn't seemed like a big deal at the time, and even now, he couldn't figure out why his mind kept rewinding over that event.

After getting up and doing a couple of shots from the room's private bar, Rad finally decided it wasn't the hotel room or the bed. His brain was trying to work something out, something that didn't fit. He may as well accept it and let it do its thing.

At about at 0700 he sat straight up, breathing heavily. Getting dressed, he slipped out of the hotel and took a taxi to Walter Reed.

THIRTY-ONE

D r. Bradley juggled the cup of coffee in her hand as she rummaged through her purse for her key card. As soon as she found it and swiped her office door, she felt a presence over her left shoulder.

"Here, let me get that for you."

Michael Radcliff pushed the door open with his left hand, and with his right hand, the one holding his cane, he gently but firmly pushed her through the door.

"Radcliff." She said his name as calmly as she could because he appeared like a mountain to her. She could sense his power and vitality and knew better than to challenge or question him. Instead, she kept her voice light, even though she was scared to death. "I could have sworn you were discharged."

"I was."

Putting her purse on the desk, she shrugged off her jacket. "So you miss us that much? I'm flattered."

"I learned something interesting last night."

The way he said the words made Dr. Bradley's heart pick up its pace. "Really?"

"I ran into my ex at a restaurant."

Dr. Bradley could feel his eyes probing her, so she tried to keep her face expressionless. "Is that right?"

"She mentioned she knew you."

Dr. Bradley considered pretending she didn't know who he was talking about, but one look at his face told her that would be a mistake. "You mean Angela? Yes, we've met, but we—"

"Actually it sounded to me like you went to school together." Rad corrected her.

"Oh, well. That's a big school so—"

"And that you were sorority sisters."

The room fell silent for a moment as Dr. Bradley tried to decide how she could call security without Rad knowing. She bit her lip and looked away.

"Funny, you never mentioned it." He crossed his arms and stared at her with slanted eyes.

"To be honest with you, I didn't know my college years would be of any interest to you." Dr. Bradley forced a laugh but could not bring herself to meet his gaze.

"If we're being honest then I have to admit she didn't actually tell me that." Rad leaned down and looked her in the eye. "I was just guessing."

Dr. Bradley's head jerked up. "Okay, you can stop with the games." She took a deep breath to calm her nerves. "What do you want?"

"Who's in room 313?"

Trying to catch the breath his question knocked out of her, Dr. Bradley walked over to her desk. "A lot of patients come and go here, Radcliff. I don't have the rooms memorized."

Rad grabbed her by the arm and led her back out the door. "It's right down that hall, to the left, at the end."

"Oh, that one," she said weakly as she turned back to her office.

"Yeah. That one." His voice was low and serious. "I couldn't sleep last night and remembered the day you gave me the wheelchair and I went exploring on my own. Remember that?"

"Vaguely."

"Only vaguely? Because you seemed pretty nervous when you saw me on this floor."

"I was surprised, that's all." She laughed nervously. "I mean, really, I just didn't expect to see you up here."

"Okay, let's cut to the chase." He stood in front of her and hit the floor with his cane as if agitated. "Why is there a guard in front of the door?"

"I don't know. She's not my patient."

The doctor couldn't help but notice the expression on Rad's face at the use of the word 'she' and realized he had come here only on a hunch. Angela must have said something last night that had gotten his wheels turning and Dr. Bradley had just confirmed his entire theory.

"But you've seen her."

Dr. Bradley bit her lip. "Yes. We have rounds. I've seen the patient in that room."

"I want to see her."

She looked him straight in the eye. "No. You probably don't."

"I'm a big boy, Dr. Bradley. I can take it."

"It doesn't matter if you can or can't." She went back to the desk, sat down, and fingered through some files. "I don't have the authority to get you in there. Those guards weren't placed there by me."

Rad put one hand on the back of her chair and one on the desk, and bent down with apparent effort. "Was she shot?"

The look in his eyes and the tone of his voice startled her.

"No. Why?"

He pulled himself back up and dropped into a nearby chair with a loud sigh, as if a tremendous weight had been lifted from his shoulders. "When I was shot…" He paused, apparently trying to keep his voice from quivering. "I thought maybe she was hit too… that I had gotten her killed by running through the gunfire." He choked up again and paused. "But I was just trying to save her."

Putting his head in his hands, he sat breathing heavily, rubbing his temples as if trying to clear the images from his mind. "They worked on me on the helicopter—not her. I thought she was dead."

Dr. Bradley stood and put her hand on Rad's shoulder. "I'm sorry you thought that. They were working on you because you were bleeding to death. She had critical injuries, but not the type that could be treated on a helicopter. All they could do was try to get her stabilized."

She sat back down and stared at the mountain of a man who had appeared so frightening a few minutes ago. Now he seemed on the verge of tears, an emotional wreck caused by the anguish he'd been living with without telling a soul. She leaned toward him and lowered her voice. "She's got a traumatic brain injury. She's been in a drug induced coma to help her heal."

Rad stared straight ahead. "She doesn't have any family. No one to visit."

"Yes, I noticed that." Dr. Bradley leaned back in her chair with a pencil in her hand, tapping it on the desk. Then she stood. "There is nothing I can do that won't jeopardize my license. I've already disclosed more than HIPPA rules allow. I'm sorry."

Rad continued to stare at the wall on the opposite side of the room and nodded, but his mind seemed elsewhere.

"But sometimes the guard goes outside with me for a smoke." She glanced at her watch. "Right around now."

Rad's gaze slowly returned to hers, and the look on his face made her want to wrap her arms around him and comfort him. They burned with want and need and a yearning she had never before seen in a man's eyes.

She pulled out a piece of paper and wrote #1833 on the page, underlining it twice even though she knew he understood it was the keypad code to get through the door. Then she grabbed a cigarette and a lighter from her purse. "I hope the hell you're out of this hospital by the time I get back in about ten minutes."

Rad waited for the sound of the two voices to disappear down the hall. He'd grabbed a white lab coat from Dr. Bradley's office, and although it was snug, hoped it helped him fit in. Walking to the door, he took a deep breath and tried to prepare himself for what he was going to see.

The click of the door lock unlatching after he'd punched in the numbers sounded like a gun blast to his tightly strung nerves. As soon as he stepped inside, the sound of machines greeted his ears, some beeping rhythmically, others humming, still another making a sickening sucking noise. He walked toward the bed and noticed how small and fragile she appeared as she lay amidst a maze of blinking modern technology.

"Lauren." Rad tried to fight the inclination to run from the room as he saw the number of tubes sticking out of her nose and mouth and even her head. He inched closer and saw her face was still swollen, but the black and blue patches now had a yellowish cast. Her head was shaved on one side, and a tube disappeared into a hole above her ear. Even though her eyes appeared to be slightly open, he could tell they were not seeing.

There was barely an inch of her he could touch that was not hooked up to some sort of life-giving or life-monitoring machine, but he found a finger and grasped it firmly.

"Hey, baby," he said, choking back tears. "I promised I'd see you again. Remember?"

Within moments, the timer on Rad's watch beeped, and he knew he had to leave. Bending down, he kissed her cheek tenderly. "I'll be back," he said. "Don't worry about anything but getting better. I got your back now."

As he exited the room, he almost ran into a nurse coming in. He gave her a nod and continued walking, stripping off the lab coat in the elevator.

Once outside the hospital, he sat down on a bench and called Wynn.

"Hey, man. I need a ride."

Before he could tell Wynn where he was, he heard Heather's voice come on the phone. "Michael Radcliff where are you? Why haven't you answered your phone? Tell me you didn't sleep with Angie last night. I'll kill you if you did."

The phone line became scratchy and muffled as if there was a tug of war going on, and then Wynn came back on. "Sorry about that. She grabbed the phone out of my hand. Where you at?"

"No, I didn't sleep with Angie. And sorry, I had my phone turned off. I'm at Walter Reed."

He heard Heather yell something in the background but couldn't make it out.

"Why? Your leg bothering you? You sick?"

"No." Rad paused a moment, wondering how much to tell over the phone. "Remember the comment Angie made last night that for all we know someone could be right down the street?"

Wynn paused as if he were thinking. "Yeah."

"And remember that story you told me about a no-count love?"

For a moment, Wynn was silent. "What did you do, Rad?"

"I found someone I was looking for."

The line grew quiet, and then Wynn whispered as if he'd moved to a room where Heather could not hear the conversation. "You kidding me?"

"No, brother. I'll be waiting out front. We have some work to do."

When Wynn and Heather pulled up, Wynn had to grab Heather's arm to keep her from bounding out of the car to give Rad a hug. Instead, they waited for him to climb into the back seat.

"How'd she look, brother?" is all Wynn said.

"Alive."

Wynn glanced back at the mixture of relief and pain on Rad's face. "You wanna talk about it?"

"Not right now." Rad turned and stared out the window, overcome with a mixture of emotions. The relief that came with knowing Lauren had successfully made the transition from survival to recovery was tempered with the knowledge that she was still beyond his reach. "We have a lot of work to do."

After a few minutes of going over his plan in his head, Rad pulled out his phone. Before he dialed, he leaned forward and put his hand on Wynn's shoulder. "Think we can keep those rooms another night?"

Wynn looked over at Heather, who nodded. "Sure."

"Then let's head back to the hotel."

As soon as they got back to the room, Rad laid out his plan. He would call McDunna, tell him he'd found her, and ask for authorization to get past the guard to visit. The circumstances, in *his* mind, outweighed normal protocol, and he assumed the higher-ups would agree.

But he soon learned this was not the case. Even with McDunna going to bat for him, the officials continued to deny her existence, and even threatened Rad with discipline for saying he had seen her.

After a few hours of trying, Wynn put his phone down. "I'm sorry, man. I don't know who else to call."

Rad leaned back in his chair, his lips pursed, his jaw set, and nodded. "Thanks for trying."

"Guess it's time to move to Plan B."

Rad gazed at Wynn curiously.

"I'll take out the guard, tie him up and stick him in a closet while you go in for another visit."

Heather leaned in from the balcony. "No you won't."

Rad smiled. "Sorry, bro. I gotta go with Heather on this one. I don't think that will work."

"Well, let's go back and check it out anyway." Wynn stood and squeezed Rad's shoulder. "You're good at bluffing. Maybe you can just talk your way past the guard."

Rad nodded and shrugged. "It's worth a try."

When they got back to the hospital, Rad told Wynn and Heather to stay in the waiting room while he tried his luck at getting past the guard.

He squared his shoulders when he stepped off the elevator and walked confidently toward the room. He knew the guard at the door would only be following orders, but maybe he could get him to see his side of things and bend the rules just a little.

When he turned the corner, his heart jumped and dropped all at the same time. There was no guard. Maybe Wynn had been right with his theory the guard took more than one smoking break a day.

As he got closer, his pulse quickened at the thought of getting to see her again. But when he pushed the door open, his heartbeat came to a thudding halt. There was no buzzing or beeping or blinking lights. The bed was empty, but the room was not. A nurse turned and jumped in surprise.

"Can I help you?"

Rad tried to act calm, even though his mind was racing. Had something happened? Had they rushed her to surgery? Where was she?"

"I, ah, just came to see this patient."

The nurse smiled and turned back to a piece of equipment she was wiping down. "Oh, sorry. She's gone."

"Gone?" Rad swallowed hard.

She glanced at him over her shoulder. "Yeah. Been moved, I guess."

"Oh. Moved." He breathed again. "You know where?"

"No." She gazed up at him curiously. "I'm new to this floor."

"But you're sure she's just been moved. She didn't... she didn't..."

The nurse paused a moment as if just understanding what he was saying. "Oh, no. No." She shrugged. "Pretty sure, anyway. I heard them talking about a chopper for transport, but there's no record to check."

Rad stood silently in the doorway another moment as his eyes swept the room. "Thanks for your help."

When he made it down to the waiting room, the expression on his face must have told Wynn and Heather things had not gone as planned. Neither asked any questions or even said a word. And when they got to the car, Wynn turned up the music loud enough that Rad's choking sounds of disappointment and despair could barely be heard.

THIRTY-TWO

Six weeks later

Rad threw the pillow across his head, trying to blot out an irritating ringing sound. After a few moments, his weary brain began to function enough to realize it was the phone lying beside the bed. As he reached for it, he noticed the time—0500.

"Radcliff here."

"It's Pops."

Rad glanced at the time again and struggled to catch his breath. Knowing that Pops and the whole team were deployed caused the blood to rush out of his heart before he even heard another word.

"We have an Eagle down."

Rad heard a slight tremor in Pops' usually calm voice even through the bad connection. He waited for him to continue.

"It's Wynn."

Rad sat straight up. "How bad?"

"Don't know anything yet." The line went silent for a moment, except for the sound of heavy breathing. "Dude, it's bad."

"Heather know yet?"

"Negative."

"On my way. Keep me posted."

The line went dead.

Rad groaned as he threw his legs over the side of the bed. Getting his joints moving in the morning was the hardest part of the day. After letting Tara out for a few minutes, he threw on a pair of jeans and a tee shirt, and splashed some water on his unshaven face.

It would only take about thirty minutes to drive to Heather's. He hated the thought of getting her out of a warm bed and had no idea what he was going to say once he did it.

Even though he had plenty of time to think about it on the ride over, Rad mostly thought about Wynn and the guys. What had gone wrong? Had he let his brothers down by not being there? Could he have done something to prevent it?

His hands tightened on the steering wheel as he continued to wrestle with the idea of retiring from active duty. With his reenlistment date approaching in less than a year, he had to make a decision. Most of the time he leaned toward going back for one more, rationalizing that what he needed most was to do what he did best.

After sitting the last few months out for his recuperation, Rad was straining at the leash to get back into the action. He knew it would probably sound strange to most people, but the acrid scent of gunpowder to him was like the smell of freshly brewed coffee to most people. A sunset filtered through the smoke of a burning building or bomb drop was captivating. Even the constant need for caution and carefulness was a vital part of his being. Everything harsh and unnerving about being in a war zone energized and excited him.

Anyway, what would he do if he got off this fast-moving train and tried to assimilate into civilian life? After moving at an "all in, all the time" pace for all these years, he wasn't sure a slower lifestyle would appeal to him. Plus, he felt it was his duty to defend his country as long as his body was able to do it.

But was he able to do it? Could he keep up with the new guys? Rad had spent the last fourteen years of his life trying to be the best soldier he could be, but he was not getting any younger. Even though he was close to being fully recovered from his injury, he still had more than the average aches and pains for a man his age. His mind drifted to Lauren. If she were by his side, things would be different. Clearer. *Right.*

But she wasn't. Since losing her again he'd started his search all over, leaving no stone unturned in trying to discover her whereabouts. He pleaded, questioned, implored—and sometimes threatened—in an effort to get someone to give him a lead. But those who had known she was in the hospital had apparently been kept in the dark as to where she was now.

Was she being cared for somewhere close to him? Or on the other side of the country? He had no way of knowing. It felt like he was trapped in a nightmare or stuck in the middle of the Twilight Zone.

Not knowing her whereabouts or where to even look, tormented Rad during the day and haunted his dreams at night. He'd not slept more than a few hours straight since the last time he'd seen her, and knew it probably showed. Night after night she came to him in his sleep, calling his name and crying for help. And night after night, he'd run toward the sound of her voice, searching blindly for her in the darkness. When he'd finally see her and reach for her hand, he'd wake up sweating, exhausted, and gasping for breath.

She was always just beyond his grasp.

Rad pushed those thoughts away and focused on Heather. This was going to be hard on her. No matter the ultimate outcome, the next few hours—possibly days and weeks—were going to be difficult. Not knowing when, or if, you would ever see the person you loved again was a feeling comparable to no other—like having your heart squeezed by a giant fisted hand. Being told your loved one was injured, alone, and thousands of miles away, would only add to the awful torment.

As he turned onto Wynn's road and drove by the large, dark houses, Rad pictured the occupants snug in their beds with no knowledge of what was occurring half a world—and half a block—away. Their idea of stress and suffering was seeing their electric bill double or enduring the loss of a game by their favorite sports team. They had no idea what was happening outside of their doorsteps or beyond their own little world.

Rad entertained little doubt these people supported their country and their troops, but to them that meant flying the flag or celebrating the Fourth of July. Maybe they knew the guy down street was in the military and was gone for long periods of time, but they didn't pause to think about the long hours he spent suffering in the cold mountains of Afghanistan or about his fiancée sleeping alone, worrying about his safety night after night. The war on terror wasn't on their radar. It was someplace else and someone else's job to fight. The discrepancy between those who put their lives on the line every day and those who enjoyed a life of freedom because of it, was strikingly clear.

When he finally pulled into the driveway, Rad felt like his chest was going to explode. He turned off the engine and took a deep breath to control his pounding heart. He'd rather be out on the battlefield taking enemy fire than do the job that lay before him. Heather was a sensible woman, strong. But she was devoted to Wynn. Rad wasn't sure how she would handle his news—if she could handle it. To be counting down the days until your wedding one moment, and then praying you'd just get to see your loved one again the next, was a lot to ask of a twenty-eight-year-old. How would she recover if she lost him before she could even claim him as her husband?

Rad sat in his truck, staring at the small rancher a moment. Wynn's house—and pretty much his second home—was a cozy, inviting little place, right down to the white picket fence that ran around the yard. Rad smiled. *Dilapidated white picket fence that is.* Heather had been after Wynn to repair and paint it for months.

He had to give Heather credit. She'd done a lot of work sprucing up the interior since moving in a few months ago, insisting it would take the better part of a year to get the man cave, as she called it, up to her standards before officially moving in as Wynn's wife.

Rad's heart kicked again. *Let's get this done.*

Walking to the door, Rad noticed the kitchen light was on. Good. Maybe she was already up. That would make things a little easier.

After ringing the doorbell, he saw the curtains move, and the door opened almost immediately. Heather stood there in sweatpants and an oversized sweatshirt that had to be Wynn's.

"Rad? What the heck are you doing up and around so early?" She ran her eyes across his unshaven face and smiled. "Or maybe you just haven't gone to bed yet."

If Rad had figured out what he was going to say beforehand, the words completely left him now. Heather stood in front of him casually braiding her hair to the side, smiling with such a carefree, innocent expression, he found it difficult to breathe, let alone talk.

The awkward silence that ensued apparently alarmed her, and the smile disappeared.

Rad cleared his throat. "Can I come in?"

The expression on Heather's face changed from warm and welcoming to one of fear—and then anger—before returning to fear again. For a moment he thought she was actually going to refuse him and close the door as if that would make whatever he was going to tell her go away. But at last she lifted her chin and opened the door for him.

Once he was inside, she took a deep breath and turned to face him.

She still didn't say anything. Just waited for him to speak.

"I don't know any details, Heather."

She nodded, her chin and lips trembling. "He's still alive?"

Rad nodded, even though he was thinking, *God, I hope so.*

"I wanted to be here when you got the official word."

"Because you know it's bad." The words were stated as a fact, not a question as she looked up at him with fawn-like brown eyes that glistened unnaturally.

"That's what they think in the field." He knew it was best to be honest with her. "But it always seems that way when a brother is down."

He took a step toward her and wrapped his arms around her. "You don't have to handle this alone. I want you to know that."

She cried softly in his arms a moment as she absorbed the news and comprehended what it would mean. Then she began to cry harder.

"Heather, we don't know anything yet." Rad rubbed her back, trying to comfort her. "Don't let your mind make it worse than it is."

She shook her head against him. "You d-d-don't understand." Choking sobs left her almost unable to speak. "I'm pregnant."

Rad's heart jumped into his throat in jubilation for the length of a heartbeat, and then landed hard in his gut. He closed his eyes tightly as he thought about Wynn's love of children and how desperately he looked forward to being a father.

"Wynn doesn't know?" His voice cracked despite his best attempt to sound calm and in control.

"I didn't want him to worry about me while he was deployed."

Rad pulled her out to arm's length and shook her gently. "Listen. You're going to have to take care of yourself through this, do you hear me?"

She nodded, but her eyes were slightly glazed as if not completely comprehending what was happening.

"Do you see these shoulders?" Rad shook her again.

She lifted her eyes to his broad shoulders and nodded again.

"They're here to hold you up, to carry you if necessary. Got it?"

"I got it," she murmured. "I'm okay."

But Rad could tell she was not okay. Her entire body was trembling, and he wasn't sure how much longer she was going to remain standing. Guiding her over the couch, he made her sit down. "Look Heather. We'll get through this. Just take some deep breaths."

Heather nodded with her face in her hands, but her shoulders shook as she sobbed. "This has to be a bad dream." She glanced at Rad as if to see if he was really there, and then started crying again. "It can't be real."

"I'm sorry, Heather." Rad tried to keep his own voice from quivering. "We need to stay positive. We might be making this worse than it is."

She wiped her face with an oversized sleeve. I-I couldn't sleep last night. It's like I knew something was wrong. I even put his sweatshirt on to feel closer to him."

"He knows you're pulling for him, honey." Rad squeezed her shoulder. "That will help him get through this."

"But how will *I* get through it?" she whimpered. "He's the strong one, the one I lean on. I need *him*."

Rad pulled her back into his arms. "You'll find out how strong you are. Wynn knows he can count on you."

Heather sniffled for a few more minutes before turning to a table behind the couch for a tissue. "I was getting ready to make some coffee." She dabbed her eyes. "I'm sure you could use some."

"I'll get it. You take it easy."

Rad strode into the kitchen and filled the container with water. As he dumped it into the coffeemaker, his hand shook.

"You're as worried as I am." Heather's voice came from just behind him.

Rad forced a laugh as he measured out the coffee, but he didn't turn around. He didn't want Heather to see his face. "I guess we'll have to fight over him when he gets back."

He hoped his tone sounded more convincing than he felt. Pops had not sounded very optimistic, and as he thought back on the conversation, he wondered if he had actually been preparing him for the worst.

"I hope the phone rings soon." Heather walked back and forth beside the kitchen table, her oversized slippers making a scuffing sound on the hardwood floor.

Rad nodded. She was a military wife—almost anyway—and knew a phone call would mean he was still alive. The last thing either one of them wanted to hear was the sound of the doorbell.

"How long will we have to wait do you think?" Heather took two mugs out of the cupboard and set them on the counter. Her voice sounded calm, but her hands shook and her eyes were brimming again.

"It's hard to say. Waiting is going to be the hardest part." Rad didn't want to say it, but he wasn't sure Pops was even out of harm's way when he had called. The connection was bad, but he could have sworn he'd heard sporadic gunfire. It would be just like Pops to send word so Rad could have a head start in protecting Heather from the media.

Rad glanced at the small television sitting on top of the refrigerator. His jaw clenched when he saw it was on and turned to a news channel. Instead of following his first instinct of ripping it out of the wall and throwing it out the door, he turned to take Heather's arm and lead her from the room. But something on the screen caught his eye and he stopped.

"What's *that* about?" He nodded toward the TV just as the reporter covering the story mentioned the name "the former Angela Powers."

Heather looked at the television and her expression turned to one of disdain. "Haven't you heard? It's going to be the biggest society event of the year."

Rad shook his head as he stared at the picture of Angie walking out of a nightclub holding hands with Joey Stanton, the lead singer for one of the hottest rock bands in the country. "She's *marrying* him?"

"Umm-hmm." Heather nodded. "She's been divorced for more than a month now. I'm surprised it took her so long."

For the first time, Rad saw the trace of a smile on Heather's face. He led her back toward the living room, pleased that her thoughts had been diverted from Wynn, even if it was only for a few minutes. "I wonder if we're invited," he mused.

That made Heather laugh. "Don't hold your breath. I get the feeling you're no longer on her 'A' list."

"Well, I wish her future husband luck anyway."

"No you don't."

Yes, I do." There was no humor in his tone now. "Seriously, he'll need it."

Heather smiled pensively, but the amusement soon drained from her expression as her thoughts returned to Wynn. When she raised her gaze, rekindled pain flickered there despite obvious efforts to stay strong. "Thanks for being here, Rad."

He ignored the comment. "What did you have planned for today?"

"I'm supposed to go into the office at nine."

"What's the number?" Rad walked over to the phone. "I'll tell them you won't be in."

Heather wiped tears from her eyes as quickly as they formed. "Maybe I should go. Maybe it will keep my mind off things."

"You really think you'll be able to get any work done?"

Heather shook her head while biting a fingernail. "No. You're right." She rubbed her temples. "I can't think straight."

Rad wrote down the number and glanced at his watch. It was too early to get hold of anyone now. He'd wait another hour.

"Really, Rad. I don't know how to thank you for this."

Before he could say anything, the phone rang. They both froze.

"Do you want me to get it?" Rad put his hand on her shoulder to calm her.

"N-no. I'll get it."

"Hello? Yes, this is Heather Kane." Her voice shook only slightly. "Yes."

Rad watched her swallow hard, and then her chin began to tremble.

"No, I don't understand. Hold on." She handed Rad the phone and walked away with her hands covering her face, her shoulders heaving with the sobs she tried to suppress.

"This is Michael Radcliff." His voice sounded calm and commanding, even though it was not what he was feeling. "I'm here on behalf of Miss Kane."

After a few questions about his relationship, the voice on the phone explained what they had already told Heather.

Matthew Wynn had been hit with shrapnel from an RPG close to his spine. He was in a drug-induced coma and on life support.

"Is he going to make it?" Rad suddenly felt like Heather. Unable to hear. Unable to comprehend.

The person on the other end of the line ignored the question. "He's being flown to Landstuhl this afternoon. You'll probably get an update from there."

Then the line went dead.

Rad stood unmoving, still holding the phone in his hand.

"What am I going to do, Rad?" Heather's voice beside him made him realize he was not the only one in the room. She laid her head on his chest and wrapped her arms around him. He could feel her whole body tremble. "I don't know what to do."

"Be strong, Heather." Rad put the phone down and wrapped his arms around her. "He'd want you to be strong."

Rad thought back to that night in the car when he'd discovered he'd lost Lauren again. He wondered how he would have made it through without Wynn and Heather holding him up. Now she was the one who was inconsolable, sobbing hysterically at the thought she might lose Wynn, and he didn't know what to do or say.

"I can't live without him. I don't even want to try."

The facts had finally hit her. Hard as she'd tried to stay strong, the truth of the matter was Wynn might not be coming home, and even if he did, things were going to be different. He helped her over to the sofa to sit down again, afraid her trembling legs would give out.

"What would Wynn do if he knew you were this upset?" He wiped a tear from her cheek with his thumb.

"He'd say, 'Heather, get a grip. Time to cowboy up.'" She smiled at Rad through her tears. "That's what you're thinking too, right?"

Rad shook his head. "I'm not saying this is going to be easy, Heather. But worrying—"

"Won't solve anything," she finished for him.

"I'll call Annie if you want."

Heather nodded, and then stood. "No. Maybe not. Not yet. It will just make her worry about Pops."

She began wandering around the living room, fluffing pillows and rearranging knickknacks as she talked, as if that somehow helped her think. "Let's wait until we get some real news. And that the rest of them are safe."

Rad nodded, amazed at her strength. Wynn had always said the ones at home had the tougher job. He was right.

Heather moved toward the small room off the living room. "When he gets home, he might have to sleep in your room if he can't make it up the stairs. Maybe we should start getting it ready."

Rad strode to the doorway of the room he always used when he was unfit to drive home. It was really Wynn's exercise room and Heather's sewing room, all mixed up with some spare boxes of books and a fairly comfortable sofa. He'd spent more nights than he cared to remember—or could remember—in this room.

"Might as well wait until we know what's going on." Rad glanced around the room, assessing what would need to be done. "I'll be sleeping here the next few nights, so don't plan on kicking me out yet."

Heather walked up and threw her arms around him again. "I don't want you to feel like you have to stay."

"No arguments. I'm staying." He put one arm around her waist. "You don't know what time of the day or night you might hear something."

She nodded against him. "You're right. I can't do this without you."

"How about some breakfast?" Rad let her go and headed toward the kitchen. "I make a mean omelet."

Heather smiled through her tears again. "Really? You cook?"

"Don't tell me Wynn never told you of my prowess in the kitchen."

Heather followed him and showed him where the pans were. "No. He might have mentioned your prowess elsewhere, but definitely not in the kitchen."

Rad chuckled. "That's logical, I suppose." He grabbed the eggs out of the refrigerator. "He was probably afraid if you knew I could find my way around a kitchen, you'd make him learn."

"I don't care if he can't cook." Heather's chin began to tremble again. "I just want him back."

Rad put the eggs down and wrapped his arms around her again. "We'll get him back, honey. And someday we'll laugh about how scared we were for him."

Heather pulled away and searched his face with a panicked expression. "*You're* scared too?"

Rad closed his eyes and pursed his lips. *Damn, why can't I find the right words?*

"I just wish it were me, Heather." He put a hand on each shoulder. "I'd give anything to switch places with him so neither one of you had to go through this."

"You're a good friend. Thanks for being here." She paused a moment. "He really looks up to you, you know? Like an older brother."

"I'm not *that* much older." Rad turned and put the pan on the stove. "Anyway, seriously," he said, glancing back at her. "He's one hell of a man—and a soldier. He's going to make a great husband too."

She smiled and bit her lip, blinking back a fresh set of tears. "*And father.*"

"Yeah." Rad nodded and smiled. "And father."

Heather took a deep breath and changed the subject. "How's your leg doing anyway? Are you sure you don't need any help?"

"I got it. Just relax."

"You still in a lot of pain?"

"No, it's not bad." Rad turned and glanced at her over his shoulder. "Except during PT. Those women thrive on torture."

Heather sat down at the table. "Wynn said you got an award or something for... what you did. He didn't tell me much about it, except that it's a pretty big deal."

Rad noticed she didn't mention the rescue or Lauren's name, and he was grateful. He'd gladly give up every medal and commendation he'd ever received to have her back in his arms. He decided to change the subject.

"I talked to McDunna. If things keep going the way they are, I should be ready for the next deployment."

"Why would you want to go risk your life for those people?" Heather's voice was loud and angry. She put her head down on the table and sobbed. "I'm sorry. I shouldn't talk like that."

"I don't do it for them, Heather." Rad walked over and put his hand on her shoulder. "I do it for you and your future kids."

"I know. You guys are so good at what you do." She took a deep breath. "The country is lucky to have you."

Rad turned back to the stove. "Wynn is like a brother to me. You know that."

"Yeah, I know."

"It's going to be hard the next few days, but don't let yourself think about the what-ifs. It doesn't do any good to worry about what we can't control."

"You're right." Heather nodded. "We'll deal with whatever hand God deals us."

THIRTY-THREE

Heather stood outside the door for a moment trying to calm her nerves and prepare herself for what she would see. She had been given advice on what to say and do, but now that the actual moment had arrived when she would see Wynn for the first time since his injury, she couldn't remember any of it. Earlier she had felt nervous, worried, and excited. Now she felt just plain terrified.

Taking a deep breath, she grimaced at the medicinal smell that greeted her, and then pushed the door open. The room she stepped into was not nearly as intimidating as she feared it would be. Wynn lay on a bed with his eyes closed, looking as if he might be asleep. The IV bag at the head of his bed dripped silently while a single small machine beside him made a gentle beeping noise that was almost comforting. Pretending a calmness she did not feel, Heather moved toward the bed and wrapped her fingers around his hand.

Wynn did not respond for a few long moments, but at last his eyes fluttered open and slowly focused on her.

"What are *you* doing here?" His voice was weak, but there was no denying the anger in it.

"I'm here to see you, Wynn."

"You've seen me. Now go." He turned his head away. "I don't want you to see me like this."

Heather knew he would be angry, that he would feel vulnerable and helpless. His vibrant, muscular body was not accustomed to being waited on and cared for. He detested weakness and could not accept that he would have to rely on others while his body healed.

To reassure him, she sat on the side of the bed, leaned down, and wrapped her arms around his neck. "I've been so worried about you. I'm not going anywhere."

Heather heard the door open behind her and knew it was Rad. They'd come to the hospital together, but he'd pretended he had someone to talk to down the hall to give her time to have a few moments alone.

Even though he now stared at the wall, Wynn must have heard someone enter the room too. He turned his head and glared up at Rad.

"Great. You're here for the pity party too?"

Rad gazed at Heather, now sitting up and staring at the wall, and apparently noticed the distraught look on her face.

"If there's a pity party, I'm thinking you're the only one in attendance, my man." Rad leaned toward the bed. "You need to cowboy up, bro."

"Easy for you to say." Wynn swallowed hard. "Standing on your own two feet."

Rad casually removed his jacket and laid it on a chair. "I seem to recall I was exactly where you are not so long ago."

"And you weren't a very good patient either," Heather chimed in.

"Thanks for the support." Rad glanced over at her before turning his attention back to Wynn. "You all messed up on pain medication or what? You're not making much sense."

Wynn removed his gaze from the ceiling for a moment to cast an angry glance at Rad before returning to impassive coldness.

Heather squeezed Wynn's hand again. "I know you're probably worried about the wedding, but don't. We'll just postpone it until you're ready."

Wynn turned slowly toward her. "No wedding." His voice was firm and final.

A sudden hush filled the room as if a hurricane wind had come through and sucked it clean of life. Even Rad appeared unable to find a way to break the silence or lighten the mood.

"I'm not making you go through with it, Heather." Wynn pulled his hand away and stared at the ceiling. "I'm letting you off the hook."

"Who says I want off the hook?" Heather bit her lip to keep from crying. She had known he was going to take his injuries hard. The doctor had warned her he would be angry and depressed. But this was worse than she expected. "I agreed to spend the rest of my life with you, and that's what I plan to do."

"That was before—" Wynn turned his head away and did not finish.

Rad stepped forward and put a hand on Wynn's shoulder. "I think Heather has pretty much made up her mind on this, dude. You might as well accept it. You're stuck with each other."

"No. She didn't bargain for this." Wynn remained defiant. "She didn't plan to spend the rest of her life taking care of a—"

"For better or worse." Heather interrupted him and squeezed his hand. "Remember?"

"We didn't say our vows yet," Wynn answered sullenly, his eyes dark with emotion. "And like I said, you're off the hook."

Heather raised her gaze to Rad and blinked away the tears as hopelessness consumed her.

"Man, I sure could use a cup of coffee," he said calmly.

Heather stared at him a moment, then jumped to her feet, taking his hint to leave the two of them alone. "Me too. I'll go get us some."

"How about you, Wynn?" Rad asked.

"None for him." Heather already had her purse slung over her shoulder. "Even if it's allowed, caffeine makes him irritable."

Rad waited for the door to close behind him, but when it didn't he glanced around to see Heather motioning to him from the doorway.

"Don't say anything about the… you know," she whispered when he walked over, pointing to her stomach.

Rad nodded, and then said in a loud voice. "That's right. Two creams. No sugar."

As soon as the door closed with a soft click, Wynn spoke. "Don't even bother, dude."

Rad pulled a chair closer to the bed. "Don't bother what?"

"Don't bother trying to change my mind." He opened his eyes and gave Rad a withering glance before closing them again. "I know how you two operate."

Rad sighed loudly and leaned back, crossing his arms. "Really? We were that obvious?"

"Let's just say you're better at being a soldier than an actor." Wynn's words were slightly slurred from the pain medication. "Making Heather leave was a waste of time."

"Not necessarily." Rad leaned forward again. "This might get ugly. I don't want her to see it."

Wynn opened his eyes and even turned his head this time to get a better view. "Oh yeah?"

"Yeah. I'm going to try to talk some sense into your head."

Wynn sighed loudly. "You can talk all you want—"

"And if that doesn't work," Rad continued, "I'm going to beat some sense into it."

That comment brought a slight smile. "I didn't think you were the type to hit a man when he was down."

"And I didn't think you were the type to throw in the towel and surrender so easily."

The reaction to this comment was stronger. Wynn tried to sit up but slumped back onto the pillow. "You have no right to say that, dammit. You have no idea—"

"I think Heather has an idea. And she should probably have some say in that decision." Rad gazed at him steadily. "It affects her life as much as yours."

"It affects her life *more*. That's why I'm not going to let her go through with it."

"Even if she wants to?"

"She's young. Smart. Gorgeous." Wynn talked to the ceiling. "She'll find someone else in no time."

Rad was fairly sure it was the pain and medication talking, and Wynn would eventually return to his old cheery self. But in the meantime, he wasn't going to stand by and watch him throw away the best thing that ever happened to him.

"But she's *here*. To be with *you*. She doesn't *want* someone else."

"She'll get over it. It's for her own good." Wynn's voice had a slight tremor in it, as if he was trying to convince himself rather than Rad.

"You think you have this all figured out, don't you?"

"I've had a lot of time to think about it."

"You mean sulk about it, don't you?"

Wynn's voice flared again and his hands tightened into fists. "You don't think losing the career you love is reason to sulk? I don't want to go out like this, man."

"No one does." Rad tried to comfort him. "But you're just fighting a different battle now."

"I wanna be back with the guys. On the battlefield. I don't want to live like this." Wynn took a deep breath and let it out slowly. "I *can't* live like this."

Rad nodded, knowing he had felt the same way. The close friendships forged in war created strong ties. Being away from that brotherhood, even for a short time, was a hard pill to swallow. Not knowing when—or even if—you would return, would be even harder to bear.

"Look at what you overcame to get where you are. This is just a bump in the road."

"Bump in the road, my ass." Wynn turned his head angrily toward the wall. "The best part of my life is over. I'm going to spend the rest of my life in a wheelchair."

"Who told you that?"

Wynn nearly choked his reply. "I can't feel my legs, man. I know the drill."

"From what I've been told, your spine was severely bruised." Rad's voice was low and serious. "Once the swelling goes down, there's a chance you'll recover feeling."

Wynn looked away again. "Yeah. There's a chance, I guess."

"Come on. I know how you feel. I felt helpless when I was down too."

"Not that your injuries weren't serious, but this is a little different." Wynn's hands tightened again. "In case no one informed you, I can't walk."

"Like I said. Just because you can't now, doesn't mean you never will."

"According to whom?"

Rad pointed toward the sky. "According to Him for one."

"Inspiration from the lips of Reverend Radcliff." Wynn shook his head. "I feel better already."

"And according to your doctor, too. I have no doubt you'll be up and driving the nurses crazy in no time."

Rad had hoped the remark would draw a comment, but it didn't even induce a smile.

"Okay. Here's the bottom line, dude." Rad leaned forward with his elbows on his thighs, his hands clasped together. "Don't push her away. For *her* sake, if not yours."

Wynn's eyes flew open. "What do you mean?"

"I mean, she's fragile right now, and—"

"What do you mean, she's fragile?"

"I mean you're breaking her heart."

Wynn turned away again. "Better now, than later—"

"Dammit, Wynn! Stop being an asshole." Rad threw his hands in the air and stood, his voice trembling with emotion. "Do you know what I'd give to have what you have?" He strode to the window, staring out at the landscape with his hands in his pockets, shaking his head as he choked out the words. "Do you have any idea how lucky you are to have the woman you love within your reach? To not have your heart feel like it's being pulled out of your chest by time and distance that you have no control over?"

When Wynn didn't respond, Rad turned and gazed at him with a look that demanded a reaction. "Don't you *dare* throw what you have with her away." He walked back over to the bed and stabbed his finger into Wynn's chest. "No matter how low you sink in your own self-pity. Don't. You. *Dare*."

Wynn blinked at the frank retort but made no comment. He appeared dazed and a little regretful as he contemplated Rad's words.

"Let her take care of you." Rad sat down again and put his hand on Wynn's arm, his voice softer now. "She wants to do it. She *needs* to do it.

"Why?" Wynn's voice had turned quiet and questioning. "It will only make it harder further down the road."

"Maybe it will make everything easier."

Wynn studied him intently, seemingly trying to read between the lines. "You know something I don't know?"

"I know she loves you. Is that something you don't know?"

Wynn let out his breath in exasperation. "What I know is I've had about enough of this bullshit. Do I need to buzz for the nurse to get you to leave?"

"Maybe." Rad raised his eyebrows. "Depends what she looks like."

"Nothing like the good-looking ones you had, believe me." Wynn lay staring vacantly at the ceiling again. "I think Heather called ahead and had all the hot nurses moved to another floor."

That made Rad laugh, causing Wynn to finally crack a smile, and then break into laughter too.

"I wouldn't put it past her," Rad said.

"Wouldn't put it past who?" Heather stood in the doorway with two cups of coffee, her head tilted as she observed the smiling face of Rad, and then the laughing Wynn.

When neither one answered, she shrugged her shoulders. "Well, it appears everyone's in a better mood than when I left." Her eyes shifted to Rad with a look of relief and appreciation. "Maybe I should leave again."

"No. Stay." Wynn gazed at her with welcoming and apologetic eyes. "Rad was just leaving, and we need to talk."

THIRTY-FOUR

Five months later

Rad strode into McDunna's office with a cup of hot coffee and sat down with a loud sigh. "Where's McDunna?"

"Out." An aide named Ace didn't even look up from his work. He was a brawny, barrel-chested man with tattoos on both meaty forearms and a closely shaved head, reminding Rad of a human version of Popeye.

"He told me to stop by... about my re-enlistment."

Ace continued writing, and then raised his head as if just realizing who he was talking to. "Oh, hey dude. McDunna said he'd be right back."

He started writing again, and then seemed to remember something else. "By the way, someone's been trying to get hold of you, bro."

"Oh yeah?" Rad assumed he was joking. "Not the police, I hope."

"No, seriously." Ace stopped writing and started paging through a stack of notes. "A woman."

Rad's breath caught in his throat and he leaned forward. "Who? What's her name?"

"Here it is." He grabbed a crumpled looking piece of paper and unfolded it, his meaty fingers fumbling at the job so terribly that Rad was practically on the edge of his seat by the time he said the name. "Elsie."

Rad took the scribbled note out of his extended hand and leaned back against the chair again, disappointment spreading through him like a fast-moving poison. He had told himself he was not going to get his hopes up again. The pain of the roller coaster ride was getting to be too much for him.

He stuck the note absently in his pocket. "What's her last name?"

"She didn't say."

"She leave a number?"

"No. Said you'd know where to find her."

Rad's brows narrowed. "What?"

"Yeah. She called last week and again this morning. Figured it was some chick you laid but didn't want to give your number to, so I didn't bother calling you. You know how that is."

Rad ignored the comment. "And her name was Elsie. You're sure?"

"It's right there on the paper, dude." Ace cocked his head. "You don't remember waking up with someone named Elsie?"

Rad frowned. "Not so much."

"Your loss. She sounded nice."

Ace went back to work and Rad leaned back in the chair. He took the note back out of his pocket and studied it. *Tell Radcliff — Elsie called.*

"I don't know any Elsie's," Rad said as if to himself, and then glanced up at Ace. "You're absolutely sure that was the name?"

Ace put down his pen and took a deep breath. "Dude. Read my lips. She said her name was, EL-SIE." He shook his head, picked his pen back up, and bent over his work again.

Rad stared out the window a minute, and then his heart banged against his chest again. He rose to his feet and walked over to the desk.

"Wait. Do you mean—L.C.?"

Ace closed his eyes and raised his head slowly before opening them again. "Are you fucking deaf? I *said*, Elsie."

"No. I know." Rad talked fast. "But did she say it like, E-l-l C-e-e."

"Read my fucking lips. That's what I've been fucking telling you. El–sie."

"Did she spell it for you?"

"Are you insinuating I don't know how to spell something so goddam simple as Elsie?"

"Okay. Okay." Rad held his hands up in the air to calm Ace down. "What did she say again?"

Ace angrily put his pen down again and stood. "Like I told you at least three mother-fucking times. All's she said was, you'd know where to find her."

Rad strode around the desk, grasped Ace in a big bear hug, and kissed him on the top of his shaved head. "Thank you, man. I love you." Then he turned and sprinted toward the door.

"Sorry, dude. I'm taken," he heard Ace yell just as he slammed the door shut.

Rad sat down on a bench with a hot cup of coffee while Tara lay at his feet. It was a foggy morning in Ocean City so no one was around except the older lady knitting next to him. There were any number of other benches available, but he had to sit on this one. Their bench. The bench he had found Lauren sitting on that sunny summer day.

"If you came to watch the sunrise, you didn't pick a very good mornin'," the woman said with a noticeable Irish accent, her needles clanking together.

Rad looked over at her and smiled. "Yeah, I noticed that."

"Don't see the need for it myself," the woman said. "If it weren't for that one wantin' to come out every mornin', I'd still be under the covers."

The woman nodded toward the beach, and Rad noticed two chairs sitting in the sand, barely discernible in the haze. One of them was occupied.

"Well, there's nothing like dawn at the beach—even if you can't see the sun," Rad responded, thinking back to the one sunrise he would never forget as long as he lived.

"That one says the same thing, though I don't share the feelin'."

Rad squinted his eyes toward the figure but still could not make much out through the haze and fog. He saw a walker leaning beside the chair that was occupied and an umbrella pole already in place behind it, apparently in anticipation of the sun making an appearance. The scene reminded him of his own grandfather, who loved going to the beach even when his advanced age made walking on the sand impractical. There was something about the sand and the surf—even on old bones. The memorial plaques on the backs of all the benches on the Boardwalk attested to the fact that beachgoers continued to be drawn to this place until the day they died.

Finishing his coffee, he stood to put the cup in a trash can. "Nice talking to you, ma'am."

She nodded, but the clicking of her needles never slowed.

Deciding to take a stroll down the Boardwalk, Rad let his mind wander. If Lauren were here, where should he even begin looking? It had seemed like it would be easy when he'd loaded Tara into his truck and headed north. Now he realized it was going to be like looking for a needle in a haystack.

Strolling as if in a daze, Rad found himself standing in front of Ripley's Museum, just staring at the sign as he replayed every minute of that memorable summer day. The museum was quiet and empty now, but that's not what he was seeing. He was seeing her smile, hearing her laugh, and feeling the sensation of her hand in his.

Feeling a nudge on his leg, he looked down at Tara, who stared up at him with her head cocked to the side as if wandering why they had stopped.

He stared in silence for a few more moments, allowing the memories to rekindle. It seemed only natural his thoughts should linger upon what had been such a remarkable experience. He lifted his gaze to the Ferris wheel towering behind and pictured the two of them at the top. He could almost hear the music and see the flashing lights as the scene unfolded before his eyes. His heart throbbed and swelled with the feelings the visions inspired.

Another nudge from Tara and a loud bark of impatience interrupted his musings.

"Okay, girl. I guess I did promise you a walk on the beach."

Unhooking her from the leash, he headed out toward the water. A gentle breeze had begun to wipe away the fog, but it was still too hazy to see very far in the distance. Tara ran ahead, disappearing into the mist, but Rad knew she wouldn't go too far ahead. After losing sight of her for a few minutes, he gave a quick whistle. She soon came loping back out of the fog, carrying something in her mouth.

"Tara, here." Rad patted his leg and called her over. "What do you have?"

He pulled the ball cap out of her mouth and took off at a dead run down the beach.

"Lauren?"

Rad slowed down as he approached the figure in the chair, not believing his eyes.

"Hey, stranger." Her words were slightly slurred from her serious injuries, but he could hear the relief in her tone. "What took you so long?"

Lauren pulled herself up out of the chair as he stepped closer, and then she was in his arms, laughing and sobbing, then laughing again. "Couldn't remember your number... and the base wouldn't tell me anything..."

"It doesn't matter." Rad buried his face in her hair. "I found you."

The woman he'd been talking to on the Boardwalk suddenly appeared, watching with her arms crossed as if she were both body guard and nurse, and was beginning to grasp what was happening. "So this is the one you've been pining for," she said, looking at Lauren before she turned an appraising eye to Rad. "And why didn't you tell me you were looking for a lass not the sunrise?"

Lauren pulled away from his arms. "You two know each other?"

"We talked on the bench earlier, lass."

Rad thought how close he had been to her and yet how close he had been to leaving without seeing her. Lauren must have been reading his mind.

"Fate has caused our paths to cross three times." She looked up at Rad. "What do you think that means?"

Rad pulled her back into his arms. "It means I'm not taking a chance relying on fate any more. I'm never letting you out of my sight again."

Lauren's nurse threw her hands in the air and mentioned she had some errands to run. Rad helped Lauren sit down, and then pulled the empty chair closer.

"I'm not that fragile," Lauren said, looking over at him. "I'll be racing you on the beach before you know it."

Rad smiled, but his brows were creased as he thought about all she had been through, and all that had happened since they'd last seen each other. Her once vigorous body appeared small and delicate. Her eyes were sunken, and her smile uneven.

"I guess I missed the wedding." Lauren interrupted his thoughts.

"What wedding?"

"Heather and Wynn's."

Rad paused a moment. "No, actually you didn't. It was postponed.

Wynn was wounded."

"Oh, that's terrible." Lauren reached out and touched his hand. "Is he okay?"

"Yeah. He is now." Rad gazed over her head a moment, thinking about the seriousness of his injuries. Though he still had months, maybe years, of rehab to do, Wynn could walk and would not need a wheelchair. "It was pretty dicey there for a while."

"Poor Heather."

"Poor Heather?"

"Yeah, she must have been through a lot."

Rad studied her with his head cocked to the side. "She's not the only one."

"I know." Lauren squeezed his arm. "You've been through a lot too."

"Not *me*, silly. *You*."

Lauren sat back and closed her eyes. "Oh, no. It wasn't bad on my side. I hit my head somewhere along the line and don't remember much of anything."

Rad contemplated her words for a moment, at the way she'd put it so lightly, and made the decision not to tell her he'd seen the video. There'd be time for that. Anyway, he could tell she was only saying that to make him feel better. She hadn't forgotten her time in captivity. She'd only chosen not to remember.

"I thought Heather and Wynn would be married with a baby by now," Lauren mused.

"Well, they did everything a little backwards."

Lauren looked over at him, her brows creased. "You mean? They have a baby?"

"A boy. Just a few weeks old."

"Oh my goodness." Lauren's eyes sparkled. "That's such wonderful news."

Rad moved his chair even closer. "So anyway, want to go to the wedding with me? It's next week."

"Do you think they'd mind?"

"Are you kidding me? They'd be ecstatic."

"Then I'd love to."

Rad was quiet for a moment. "Want to make it a double?"

Lauren looked at him questioningly, and then apparently understood he meant a double wedding. "No, I want my own." She kind of smiled and stared into the distance. "I mean, if anyone would ask or anything."

Rad got down on one knee beside her chair and held her hand. "Lauren Cantrell, will you marry me."

Lauren frowned, but her eyes were warm and tender. "That's not my name anymore. I had to change it and get a new identity."

"Okay, whatever-your-name-is, will you marry me?"

That made Lauren put her head back and gurgle with amusement. "Seriously? You're making the biggest commitment of your life to a girl whose name you don't even know?"

"I don't know the name." He smiled out of the corner of his mouth. "But I know the girl."

"Barely." Lauren's expression and her tone turned serious. "You may not know what you're getting into."

"I know what I'm getting into." He leaned forward and looked deep into her eyes. "And I know whatever-her-name-is well enough to want to spend the rest of my life with her."

When she still hesitated, he reached into his back pocket and pulled a well-worn piece of paper from his wallet. "Remember this?"

He watched her eyes grow wide as she read the words: *When you pull a card and draw a heart, you and your beloved will never part.*

She raised her gaze to meet his. "You kept that?"

"Of course. I kinda thought 'ol Zoltar might know something we didn't."

"I guess he kind of did," Lauren said as if to herself. "It's like it was all meant to be."

"Is that a yes?"

She wrapped her hands around his neck, and he pulled her to her feet. "That's a yes," she murmured. "That's an absolute yes."

When Rad at last released her, Lauren stood staring toward the ocean with a pained expression on her face, blinking repeatedly. Rad lifted a finger to her cheek and wiped away a tear. "Thinking about your parents?"

Lauren nodded, her chin trembling. "They'd be very happy."

"They'd be very proud, too."

At that moment the sun broke the fog and clouds, sending a shaft of dazzling light over the water. They both gazed at the spectacle in amazement and then at each other. No words were necessary to express the sparkling light in Lauren's eyes.

Rad took her hand in his as the sun dipped back behind a cloud. "I think I'm the happiest man in the world right now."

Lauren nodded and sighed as if she were now completely at peace with her past and could accept and embrace her future. "And I'm the happiest woman." She turned to face him. "...Unless you're going to be deployed soon."

Rad took a deep breath and let it out slowly. "Funny thing about that," he said, his voice grave. "I only have one more day."

She looked up at him, her eyes full of alarm. "*One* day?"

He smiled. "I mean one day to make a decision. I've been thinking about calling it quits on active duty. They want me to instruct."

Lauren leaned into him, resting her cheek on his chest. "You think you'll be happy? That's a big change."

"Before, I wasn't sure. Now, I'm thinking I will be." Rad paused a moment, listening to the sound of the waves hitting the sand and feeling her heart beat against his. He'd always told himself he was going to find her, but now, even with her in his arms, he couldn't believe it.

"What about you?" He finally relinquished his tight hold and held her at arm's length. "You're back in the States to stay?"

"I haven't thought that far ahead yet." Lauren's gaze drifted to somewhere over his shoulder. "I'm still getting used to this new pace." She glanced down at the walker beside the chair with an expression so agonizing Rad pulled her into him again. He could only imagine the pain that still coursed through her body. For the most part she showed no outward sign of it.

"You have me to lean on now." He tightened his grasp even more as he thought about how hard it had been for both him and Wynn to recover, even when surrounded by family and friends. What she must have gone through, alone, was unfathomable. "I'm so sorry I wasn't here for you sooner."

"I knew you'd come," she said, obviously making an effort to sound upbeat. "The worst is behind me."

She pulled away then, seeming not to want to think any more about the past. "When do we leave?"

Rad laughed. "We make a great team. I don't know you're name, and you don't know where we're going."

"I know it's in Virginia somewhere."

"Pretty much due south. Virginia Beach."

Lauren looked up at him. "Near the beach? The water?"

"Not too far away. It's small though. Made for a bachelor. Don't get your hopes up."

"But you'll be there every night, right?"

"Yeah. If I don't re-enlist."

"Then I love it already." She leaned over and patted Tara on the head. "Think she'll accept another woman in your life?"

"Appears she already has." Rad stared at his dog sitting dutifully on her left instead of his. "Looks like it was love at first sight."

"Funny how that works." Lauren wrapped her arms around his neck again, and they were both silent, enjoying the closeness of the moment.

"I feel like I'm dreaming," Lauren finally murmured. She wrapped her arms around Rad even tighter. "I'm afraid I'll wake up and you won't be here."

"I'm not going anywhere, baby. Except home. With you."

Lauren nodded against his chest. "Somehow it feels like we're already there."

The End

About The Author

Jessica James is an award-winning author of multiple fiction and non-fiction works ranging from the Revolutionary War era to modern day. She is the only two-time winner of the coveted John Esten Cooke Award for Southern Fiction, and was featured in "50 Authors You Should Be Reading," published in 2010. Her books have been used in schools to teach visualization techniques and can be found in more than one hundred libraries, including at Harvard and the U.S. Naval Academy.

Contact the Author

Interested in the "Story Behind The Story" of *Meant To Be?*

Email the author: Jessica@JessicaJamesBooks.com

www.JessicaJamesBooks.com
www.Facebook.com/romantichistoricalfiction
Twitter: @JessicaJames
Pinterest: www.pinterest.com/southernromance

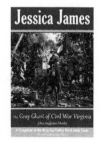

Military Charities

We are so fortunate to live in a country where volunteer troops place their lives on the line night and day in support of our cherished freedoms. Please help support these fantastic causes by either donating monetarily or with your time and talents.

Chris Kyle Frog (www.chriskylefrog.com)

The Red Circle Foundation (www.redcirclefoundation.org)

LZ-Grace Warriors Retreat (www.lz-graze.com)

K9s for Warriors (k9forwarriors.org)

Special Operations Warrior Foundation (www.specialops.org)

Operation Hawkeye (www.ophawkeye.com)

Navy Seals Fund (www.navysealsfund.org)

Wounded Warrior Project (www.woundedwarriorproject.org)

Thank you! I am honored that you took the time out of your busy schedule to read this book. If you enjoyed the journey, would you consider sharing the message with others?

- Write a review online at amazon.com, bn.com, or goodreads.com.

- Recommend this book to friends in your book club, church, school, workplace, or class.

- Go to facebook.com/romantichistoricalfiction and "like" the page. Post a comment about what you enjoyed most.

- Mention this book in a Facebook post, Twitter update, Pinterest pin, or blog post.

- Pick up a copy for someone you know who would be impacted by the story—or send a copy to a soldier serving our country.

- Visit the author's website at jesssicajamesbooks.com and sign up for the newsletter to keep up on giveaways, new releases and special events.

Discussion Guide

1. What is the significance of the title of *Meant To Be*?

2. List five words that describe the first half of the book.

3. Did the opening chapters elicit any summer beach memories for you?

4. List five words that describe the last half of the book.

5. Do you think Rad and Lauren would have wanted to meet and fall in love if they had known ahead of time what the other did for a living?

6. Were you surprised at the way Lauren responded during her interrogation? Do you think it was wise? Could you have done the same?

7. Do you believe in love at first sight?

8. Does this novel make you think about those who serve and the sacrifices they make for us?

9. What do you think the central theme of the novel is?

10. What passages strike you as insightful, even profound? Perhaps a bit of dialog that's funny or poignant or that encapsulates a character? Is there a particular comment that states the book's thematic concerns?

11. Is the ending satisfying? If so, why? If not, why not…and how would you change it?

12. If you could ask the author a question, what would you ask? Have you read other books by the same author? If so how does this book compare. If not, does this book inspire you to read others?

13. Has this novel changed you—broadened your perspective? Have you learned something new or been exposed to different ideas about people or a certain part of the world?

14. Is there anything in this book to which you personally can relate? Is there any advice or ideas you can take and apply to your own life?